Behind the **PINE** Curtain

GERRI HILL

Bella
BOOKS
2006

Bella Books
P.O. Box 10543
Tallahassee, Florida 32302

Printed in the United States of America on acid-free paper
First Edition
2nd Printing March 2008

Editor: Anna Chinappi
Cover designer: Sandy Knowles
Front Cover photo by: Deb Couvillon

ISBN10: 1-59493-057-0
ISBN 13: 978-1-59493-057-7

Dedicated to Diane . . . thanks for all your childhood stories about growing up in the pines. And you didn't think I was listening!

About the Author

Gerri lives in East Texas, deep in the pines, with her partner, Diane. They share their log cabin and adjoining five acres with two labs, Max and Zach, and four cats. A huge vegetable garden that overflows in the summer is her pride and joy. Besides giving in to her overactive green thumb, Gerri loves to "hike the woods" with the dogs, a pair of binoculars (bird watching) and at least one camera! For more, visit Gerri's Web site at www.gerrihill.com.

CHAPTER ONE

She ignored the persistently ringing phone, wondering once again why she didn't just get up and turn the damn thing off. She paused, staring at the words she'd written, unconsciously drumming the keyboard with her fingers. A moment later, her cell rang. She glanced at caller ID, then flipped it off.

"Christ, Ingrid, I'm trying to work here," she murmured.

But her concentration was broken. She leaned back in the chair, stretching her arms behind her neck before taking off her glasses and slowly rubbing her eyes. She had been at it since seven that morning, breaking only once to refill her coffee cup. She'd been on a roll, and she learned long ago to take advantage of that. Too many days—nights—she sat there, struggling to get her thoughts down coherently enough to form sentences.

She stood, tossing her tiny wire-framed glasses on the desk, and picked up her cell phone, dialing Ingrid's number as she opened the fridge.

"It's me."

She sniffed the orange juice. It was four days past expiration, but she filled a glass anyway.

"Where the hell have you been?" Ingrid demanded.

"Here. Working. As you informed me two days ago, I have a freakin' deadline," Jacqueline mimicked.

"I've been calling for hours."

"Yes, I know. I've been ignoring you." The orange juice was indeed sour, and she poured it out, eyeing the coffee instead.

"Some man has been trying to reach you. He said it's a family emergency."

Jacqueline paused, putting the coffee pot back on the warmer without looking. "Family? Whose family?"

"I gathered yours. But I wasn't aware you had a family."

"I don't," she murmured. She hated the nervousness, the adrenaline that coursed through her, making her heart pound faster. She took a deep breath. "What was the man's name?" She waited, hearing papers rustling on her agent's desk.

"John Lawrence."

Jacqueline leaned against the counter as her eyes slid shut.

"Daddy?"

"In here, little darlin'."

Jackie stood in the doorway of her daddy's study, staring at the stranger sitting in one of the large leather chairs across from her daddy.

"And just where are your shoes, young lady?"

Jackie looked down at her dirty bare feet and grinned. "Been out playing, Daddy."

"You better make sure you're cleaned up before your mother gets home," he warned. "Or we'll both have heck to pay."

"I will. But can I take my bike into town first? It's still early. I wanna go to Kay's."

"Sure. Just be careful."

Jackie looked again at the stranger. "Who's he?"

"This is my new attorney, Jacqueline. Meet Mr. Lawrence."

"Do you know him?" Ingrid asked, bringing Jacqueline back to the present.

"I know him, yes." Jacqueline walked to her desk. "Give me his number."

After a mumbled good-bye to Ingrid, Jacqueline paced in her living room, pausing occasionally to stare out her windows at Monterey Bay. The earlier fog had dissipated, giving way to sunshine as it tried to chase away the cold. It did nothing to warm her, however.

She wouldn't call him. Whatever news he had—and it most definitely involved her parents—was of no interest to her. In fact, she couldn't believe that John Lawrence had tried to track her down at all. After all, it's been . . . *fifteen years*.

Fifteen years. She slowly shook her head. A lifetime ago. In fact, honestly, she couldn't remember the last time they'd even crossed her mind. And Kay. God, it had been so long since she'd thought of Kay, but she had little trouble recalling the smiling face of her childhood friend. Her best friend. Of course, her friendship with Kay was another casualty of the war inflicted upon her by her parents. But, it had been a short war.

And they had won.

She walked quickly into the kitchen and slid a wineglass off the rack. It was only two, but her writing was done for the day. John Lawrence had seen to that. From the fridge, she retrieved the bottle of chardonnay she'd opened just last night. Beside it was the dinner she hadn't bothered to eat. After her first sip of wine, her stomach reminded her that she hadn't remembered breakfast, either.

Her deadline was fast approaching, but that wasn't the reason she worked right through meals. She was simply on a roll. For the last two days, the words had come easily, filling page after page. Her first draft was due in three weeks, and even though she hadn't told Ingrid, she was already finished with the draft. But when she beat her deadlines, her publisher had a habit of shortening them. So, she'd wait until the last day to send it to Ingrid. No, what she was working on now was a completely new novel, one Ingrid knew nothing about. She didn't like to share outlines until she was at least three-quarters done with it. Too many times, she'd written half a story, only to find it fell apart, and she ended up trashing it. Then she'd have Ingrid on her ass, urging her to finish a book she'd lost desire for.

She went back to her desk and stared at the paper where she'd scribbled John Lawrence's phone number. Maybe it wouldn't hurt to call him and find out what was going on.

She walked out onto her spacious deck overlooking Monterey Bay. The cold, biting wind of earlier had subsided somewhat, but the early spring day was still cool. In the distance, she stared at the Santa Cruz Mountains, a sight the fog usually kept hidden. She was relaxed, calm, when the phone was answered.

"John Lawrence. May I help you?"

She swallowed once. "This is Jacqueline Keys, Mr. Lawrence. I understand you've been trying to reach me."

"Jacqueline, thank you for returning the call. How have you been?"

Jacqueline paused long enough to flick her eyes over the bay. "Fine. Just fine. What can I do for you?" she asked, dismissing any further pleasantries.

"I have some very bad news regarding your father, Jacqueline."

"Mr. Lawrence, I've not heard from my father in fifteen years. Don't preface something by saying you have bad news. Why don't you just say you have news regarding my father?"

A pause on the other end of the phone, then a subtle clearing of the throat. "You're right of course. I'm sorry, Ms. Keys. Your father was killed in an automobile accident yesterday. Your mother is in critical condition, although she is expected to recover. She is hospitalized with a broken pelvis, broken legs and back. She has a punctured lung from broken ribs, the most serious of her injuries."

Jacqueline stood quietly, her eyes still scanning the distant Santa Cruz Mountains. She regarded the news, acknowledging that she felt no sorrow, no regret. They were fifteen some-odd years removed from her life. Long ago, she had grieved for her lost family. She had nothing left to give.

"I see." She paused. "Mr. Lawrence, I'm wondering why you

felt the need to share this information with me. As I'm sure you are aware, my parents kicked me out of their life quite some time ago."

"It was your father's wish that I contact you. I'm simply following his directive."

"I see," she said again. "Well, thank you for the information. Good day." Before she could disconnect, his voice called to her.

"Wait! I was hoping I could persuade you to come to Pine Springs. Your Uncle Walter is making the arrangements, what with your mother in the hospital and all, but I think you should be at the funeral," he said in a rush.

"Why in the world would you think that? Mr. Lawrence, my parents put me on a bus when I was seventeen years old and shipped me out of town. I've not heard from them since. And I don't plan to attend any funeral."

"I really think it's in your best interest that you be here, Ms. Keys. If not you, perhaps you could send your attorney."

"My *attorney?*"

"Ms. Keys, you probably are not aware of the extent of your father's business holdings. Without revealing the contents of his will, which obviously has not yet been executed, I strongly suggest, Ms. Keys, that you come to Pine Springs."

Jacqueline closed her eyes, lightly rubbing her forehead with two fingers as she tried to ward off the fast approaching headache. *Go to Pine Springs?* She shook her head. It was a place she swore she would never set foot in again.

CHAPTER TWO

"Excuse me? You're *what*?" Ingrid demanded.

"Going to Texas," Jacqueline said again. She moved through her bedroom, phone tucked against her ear as she pulled out clothes and tossed them on the bed.

"Texas?" A pause. "*Texas!* Have you lost your mind? We have a deadline, in case you've forgotten! You can not possibly go to *Texas*, of all places," Ingrid yelled through the phone.

"My father was killed in a car accident," Jacqueline said easily. "There's some legal business."

"Your father? I'm sorry, Jacqueline, but you've never spoken of family. I'm sorry."

Jacqueline folded the soft jeans in her hand, wondering why she'd never told Ingrid about her childhood. Ingrid was her agent and nearly twenty years her elder, but still, they were friends. She wondered why it had never come up.

"I left home when I was seventeen. I've not been back."

"Why?"

Jacqueline stopped, turning around her bedroom, her eyes lighting on familiar objects, seeing none.

"I'm gay."

"Yes, I know. I am, too."

Jacqueline allowed the briefest of smiles. "I was gay, so I wasn't welcome in my home any longer," she explained. "I wasn't welcome in Pine Springs."

"Then why are you going back?"

Yes, why, Jacqueline? Why go back to a town that laughed at you? Why go back to a mother who said you were abnormal and a disgrace to the family?

"Closure," she said quietly. And it was true. She'd been whisked out of town so fast, she'd not had time to say good-bye to anyone. Kay, mainly. She'd not had time to reconcile her feelings, she'd not had time to even contemplate what was going on in her life. She'd just gotten up one morning and found herself on a bus, heading out of Pine Springs.

"Closure?"

"Yes, closure. And perhaps a chance to see my mother, to show her that I survived."

"Unless she's been living in a cave, I'm sure she knows you've survived, Jacqueline. Having two novels made into movies, even in Pine Springs, Texas—wherever that is—I'm sure they've heard of you."

Jacqueline walked back out into the living room, needing space, needing to see the bay. She slid open the doors, walking out, ignoring the fog and the cool wind that tossed the dark blond hair about her face.

"My father was mayor of Pine Springs when I was in high school," she said, leaning heavily on the railing of her deck. "My family owned the largest lumber mill in East Texas, so they were very visible. Having a gay daughter was, naturally, the talk of the town. They put me on a bus with a hundred bucks in my pocket and told me not to come back until I'd come to my senses."

"*My God.* Are you serious?"

"Very."

"Why in the world would you go back? Do you think you *owe* them something?"

"No. I don't owe them anything. Maybe I want them to see that I've made something of myself," Jacqueline admitted. Despite her mother's warning that she would come crawling back on bended knees, begging them to let her stay, she survived. And she was proud of that fact. No, she didn't owe them anything.

She heard Ingrid sigh, knew the older woman was twisting the gray hair above her ears into knots, knew she was counting to ten before she brought up the book.

"I don't mean to sound uncaring or anything, Jacqueline, but . . . but what about the book?"

"Don't worry, Iggy, I'll have my laptop. I can e-mail you anything you need."

"Jesus, Jacqueline, I hate it when you call me that."

"Yes, I know. And I promise I'll meet the deadline."

"You'll have your cell?"

"Of course."

"You think they have service out there?"

This time, Jacqueline did laugh. "Ingrid, I'm not going to a third world country, you know."

"Yes, I know. I'm sorry. It's just—"

"Have I ever missed a deadline?"

"No."

"Well, there you go. Quit worrying. I may be back within the week, anyway."

"Just keep me updated, please. You know my blood pressure is not what it used to be."

Jacqueline disconnected, still standing on her deck as the clouds swirled over the bay, letting her mind wander back to those carefree days of childhood.

"*Come on, Kay. You can make it.*"

"*I don't know, Jackie. It's pretty high.*"

8

"*I promise, I won't let you fall.*" *Jackie reached down and offered her hand to Kay. Kay didn't hesitate. She let Jackie pull her up the tree to the first limb, sitting across it like a horse, just as Jackie was.* "*See? Piece of cake.*" *Jackie pointed.* "*If we can just get up there, it'll be enough room for both of us to sit. And we'll be high enough so Sammy can't get up here to bother us.*"

"*Jackie, I can't go that high. Mama will have my butt if she finds out.*"

Jackie laughed. "*She'll only have your butt if you fall!*"

Jackie used Kay's shoulder to balance herself, shoving her dirty sneakers between branches and the trunk of the old oak, climbing ever higher. She looked down at Kay who was watching her in awe. "*Well, come on. Follow me up.*"

Their eyes met, blue on blue, and Kay's face set with determination as she followed Jackie up the tree. Jackie found the bend she was looking for, and it was plenty wide enough for the two of them to sit. She knelt in the crevice of the tree, again offering her hand to Kay.

They leaned back, both breathing hard after their excursion. Then Kay started laughing.

"*What's so funny?*"

"*I wouldn't do this for anybody else,*" *she said.*

"*What?*"

"*Climb up this high. You know I'm scared up high. Remember when I fell off the barn roof?*"

"*Yeah. But you made it. See? Here we are, at the top of the world,*" *Jackie said, waving her arms to the treetops.*

Jacqueline let a small laugh escape. It had been the first of many times they scampered up the old oak tree in Kay's back yard. The first time Kay's mother had caught them, she'd threatened them with a belt. And she couldn't blame her. They'd been all of ten when they started climbing that damn tree. She leaned against the railing, her eyes sliding closed when she remembered the last time they'd climbed up there. Seniors in high school. Jacqueline needed to talk, she wanted to tell Kay what was going on with her, how she was feeling. She felt like if she didn't tell someone, she was just going to explode with it. And where better than their tree? They'd had many a long talk in that tree. They'd made big plans, they'd gossiped, they'd hidden from Rose. And they'd talked about everything over the years. They had no secrets.

Except one. And in the end, Jacqueline couldn't bring herself to tell Kay that she was gay. She was afraid Kay wouldn't be her friend anymore, and Kay was her best friend, her only friend, really. The only one that mattered. But it was soon out of her hands. Only a few weeks later, she was on a bus out of town, never to return.

She stood up straight, her eyes looking out to the Pacific Ocean. Never to return, until now.

CHAPTER THREE

The flight to Dallas was crowded, even for this ungodly hour of the morning, and Jacqueline struggled to stretch her long legs, ignoring the young man next to her who was tapping his fingers nervously on his own legs.

"First time," he finally said.

"I understand," she murmured.

"You?"

"No." She pulled out her laptop, hoping that would discourage any further conversation. She was nervous, too, but it had absolutely nothing to do with flying. She brushed at the hair on her forehead, intending to work some, but her mind drifted. It had been so long since she'd thought of her parents, she hardly had a picture of them in her mind anymore. But she remembered clearly the day they sent her away. She, standing there in her faded jeans and scuffed athletic shoes; her mother, dressed for cocktails at the country club.

"We've purchased you a ticket to Dallas. Where you go from there is up to you."

"Why are you doing this to me?"

"You know perfectly well why, Jacqueline. We're the laughing stock of Pine Springs, not to mention the Women's League. We simply cannot allow it to continue, and you seem to think that you were born this way! Think of your father. He won't be reelected next year. The laughing stock, I tell you!"

Jacqueline closed her eyes, remembering the pain she'd felt that day. She vowed then and there that she would never return, no matter what. But here she was, on a flight to Dallas nonetheless.

She wanted to believe they sent her away to shock her, scare her perhaps. But she had been too proud and too stubborn for that. After her brave declaration to them a few weeks before, stating that she would not marry Daniel Thornton because she liked girls, her father had refused to even look at her, much less speak to her. No matter how hard she tried, her father simply turned away from her. Her mother, on the other hand, took every opportunity to tell her the devil had his hooks in her and surely Brother Garner could talk some sense into her. Jacqueline was forced to sit through two sessions with him as he attempted to *heal* her. That, she would never forget.

She let a ghost of a smile touch her mouth. It would have been very comical had it not been happening to her. The week seemed to last an eternity. It hadn't taken long for the rumors to spread through town and she felt all eyes on her, especially at school. Friends suddenly avoided her, and the girls' locker room was suspiciously empty when it was her turn to shower.

"Bunch of idiots," she murmured. All but Kay. She never avoided her. She seemed nearly puzzled by everyone's reaction. But she never once made mention of it.

Jacqueline purposely turned her focus to her laptop, resting her fingers lightly over the keys, refusing to allow any more memories to crowd in. It was from another life. It would do no good to dwell on it. But still, why in the world was she going back? Closure? To tell her mother off? To let the whole town know she'd made something of herself after she'd escaped from behind the pine curtain?

She doubted anyone would even remember her. Or care, for that matter.

Hours later, she found herself creeping along in Dallas traffic. Heavy, yes, but nothing like rush hour trying to get in or out of San Francisco. She managed to find the interstate without getting lost and by early afternoon, was heading east on I-20. She'd purposefully rented the most expensive car she could find, for comfort she'd told herself, but she knew better. The Lexus would definitely stick out in Pine Springs.

After stopping in Tyler for a bite to eat, she headed south. She had another three hours, at best. But it was a beautiful spring afternoon, and she was in no hurry. She was enjoying the drive, she admitted. Beautiful redbud trees, in full bloom, seemed to compete with the snow white of the dogwoods. Azaleas, just starting to show color, were proudly displayed by nearly every house she passed. Soon, the road was virtually swallowed by pine trees, and she felt an unfamiliar peace settle over her. The pine curtain. Why in the world would she feel peaceful heading back into it?

Time—and the miles—flew by. She checked her directions again, then turned off the main highway just past Rusk and headed even deeper into the Piney Woods. Tiny towns, just dots on the map, seemed stuck in the past, hovering in the mid-century. Old farmhouses tucked against the forest while cows grazed lazily on cleared pasture land. She took it all in, so different from the ocean condo she now called home. She drove aimlessly, her mind wandering as the miles passed much too quickly.

Her breath caught when she saw the sign. PINE SPRINGS. 20 MILES. Suddenly, it all became a reality. She was going back home.

And it was the time of day Jacqueline remembered well. The late afternoon hung on for a few more minutes before early evening would take its place. A time when, as a kid, Jacqueline would rush home on her bike, trying to beat the sun—and her curfew. Many a day she would come flying up the driveway, the gravel kicking up under her bike tires as she skidded to a halt before bursting through the kitchen door, just in time to catch her mother's scolding glance.

"Louise has dinner ready. Your father is already at the table, young lady."

"I'm not late."

"You're filthy. What trouble did you get into today?"

"No trouble. Baseball."

"Baseball? How many times have I told you? That is no sport for a lady."

"I'm not a lady. Besides, I'm better than them."

"You are too old to be playing with boys, Jacqueline. Now, go wash up."

The smile came without warning as she remembered the argument they'd had more than once over dinner. Her parents wanted her to try out for the cheerleading squad, but she adamantly refused. *Cheerleading?* Please. She wanted to try out for the basketball team. And she did, *over their dead body.*

She slowed as she reached the outskirts of Pine Springs, surprised that it was all still so familiar to her. Not much had changed over the years. She crossed the bridge into town, looking fondly down the river, and so many memories crowded in at once. Downtown hadn't changed a bit, she thought, as all the familiar structures came into view. The old courthouse building looked exactly as she remembered with giant magnolia trees on every corner. Across the street, the lone bank dwarfed the old five and dime store that surprisingly appeared to still be in business. There were few cars on the streets, but then again, she supposed the shops all closed up at five, everyone rushing home to kids and dinner.

It hit her suddenly. What the hell was she doing here? Familiar, yet alien. It had been fifteen years, a lifetime ago. She was no longer the scared kid getting on that bus. She was a grown woman, a successful writer. This town had nothing to offer her except painful memories, and she certainly had nothing to offer it. But that wasn't entirely true. Not all her memories were painful. She had a great childhood, and both her parents had spoiled her, giving her things that her friends' parents could not afford. She realized now that they'd only done that to prove they had more money than anyone else in town. But still, she'd been happy. She excelled in sports, not cheerleading.

Then it happened, that early spring day during her senior year of high school. She was finally able to put a word to what she'd been feeling for so long. Lesbian. *Gay*. Jacqueline remembered the loneliness she'd felt at that time as she tried to keep her secret. Even Kay had no idea.

But really, it was her feelings for Kay that had made her come to terms with her sexuality. It became obvious to her that it was Kay, not her so-called boyfriend, she wanted to be with. Kay was the one she thought about at night while lying in bed. And it was because of Kay that jealousy consumed her the night of their senior prom when she'd seen Kay and Billy Ray Renfro kissing behind the bleachers in the gym. It all became crystal clear that night. Jacqueline was different. She didn't fit in. So, little by little, she withdrew from Kay, keeping her secret to herself. She would be going off to college soon enough, and then she wouldn't have to worry about it. She and Kay would drift apart. But then, her parents brought up the subject of her marrying Daniel Thornton, saying they had already discussed it with Daniel's parents. No, Jacqueline definitely was not going to marry Danny Thornton.

And so it all came out. Her secret. Within a week, it was all over town, and a mere ten days before graduation, her mother put her on a bus and sent her away in shame.

The honking of a horn startled her, and she shook herself, realizing she'd been sitting at the traffic light, daydreaming. She pulled through the intersection just as the light turned red, no doubt pissing off the driver behind her.

The motel Mr. Lawrence directed her to was on the main drag, the sign chipped and faded, but still, it made Jacqueline laugh. *Pine Springs Motel. Take your boots off and stay awhile.*

"Why on earth would anyone want to do that?"

But she pulled in nonetheless, parking next to the faded vacancy sign that was nailed to an ancient pine tree. There were all of three cars in the lot, and she eyed the motel suspiciously. John Lawrence had offered a room at his home, but she'd insisted she would rather have her privacy. Perhaps she should reconsider. The motel hadn't seen an improvement in thirty years, she was certain.

The desk clerk was a scruffy, bearded man with a wad of tobacco in his cheek and he chose that moment to spit into a filthy cup. Jacqueline raised an eyebrow.

"Help ya, ma'am? Git ya a room?"

"Actually . . . no, thanks."

She turned and quickly retraced her steps, pausing beside her rental car to unclip her cell phone from her jeans pocket. She searched through her programmed numbers, finding John Lawrence, which she'd just added that morning. Leaning against the car as she waited, her eyes scanned the darkening sky, smiling slightly at the nearly full moon that rose over the pines.

"Hello."

"Mr. Lawrence? It's Jacqueline Keys, I hope I'm not interrupting dinner."

"Good evening, Jacqueline. No, no, you're not interrupting. I trust you made it."

"Yes. No problems. I'm actually at the motel right now." She cleared her throat as she glanced at the faded vacancy sign. "Well, I'm in the parking lot, anyway. I'm afraid to go inside."

His hearty laugh brought a smile to her face and she relaxed a little.

"I tried to warn you."

"I was wondering if maybe I could reconsider your offer."

"Mary has a room already made up for you. We've been waiting dinner. I'm sure you have lots of questions."

She let out a sigh of relief, finally opening the door and climbing in. "Great. I'm sorry, but I don't remember where you live."

"We've moved to the country club, not far from your parents' new home. Just off the ninth green. Do you remember how to get to the country club?"

"I think so. I played golf there enough, I should remember."

"We're on Fairway Lane, third house on the right, but call if you get lost. The streets are rather winding."

"Thanks. I'll see you in a bit."

Once back on the highway, she drove through the heart of town, the streets now dark and deserted. The only activity she could see was at the Dairy Mart. She imagined it was still the main hangout for the high school kids. She drove along, turned down familiar streets, surprised that she still remembered the way.

The entryway for the county club was as impressive as ever, although the electronic gate had not been there in the old days. She gave the guard her name, and, after checking the guest list, he let her through, giving quick directions to the Lawrence's house. Fifteen years ago, the country club was just getting started. There were only a handful of homes here then. She remembered her parents discussing whether they wanted to build a home out here. Apparently, they had. But even back then, they spent plenty of time at the country club. Much to her mother's delight, Jacqueline excelled at golf and had joined them frequently on weekends.

She found the Lawrence home easily and parked in the circular drive. Motion lights signaled her arrival, and she had no time for nervousness. The front door opened immediately. John Lawrence hadn't changed much in fifteen years, although his hair was no longer the salt and pepper she remembered. It was an attractive shade of white, and she recognized his wife, Mary standing behind him. She had aged more, and she looked nearly ten years his senior now. They both waved, and her uneasiness fled. Maybe it wouldn't be so bad.

Grabbing the one bag she had on the back seat, she flung the strap over her shoulder and walked up. She stopped, smelling a fragrance in the air that brought back many memories. Jasmine. She smiled slightly, then walked up, hand outstretched to greet them.

"Jacqueline Keys, my God, look at you."

"Mrs. Lawrence, how are you?"

"Call me Mary, dear. I'm so glad you came."

"Thank you for having me on so short notice. The motel was . . . well, a rat trap may be too kind a word."

They laughed and drew her inside their home. It was spacious, but still unpretentious and very homey. She'd always liked them. They never quite seemed to fit in with her parents' normal circle of friends. This house wasn't a showcase for their wealth, it was simply their home. She never could have said that about her own home growing up.

"When I called you, I was afraid you would turn me down. In fact, I expected it," John Lawrence said.

"To be honest with you, I'm not certain why I agreed to come. I don't feel that I owe them anything."

"I understand. But we have time to talk later. Let's get you settled, and we'll have dinner."

Mary gave her a quick tour of the house, and Jacqueline was thankful that her room was on the opposite end from theirs. At least she wouldn't feel in the way and would have some privacy. She tossed her one bag on the bed and turned, finding Mary watching her.

"Is that all you brought?"

"I've got another bag in the car with my suit, but I'll get that later."

Mary glanced once over her shoulder, then walked closer. "I know this must be very hard for you, Jacqueline. But we both felt like you had a right to be here, if you wanted. Of course, after all that happened all those years ago, I wouldn't have blamed you if you'd chosen not to come here. You may not believe this, but it wasn't your father's idea to send you away. Your mother just . . . well, she went out of her mind over it all. She blew it all out of proportion, thinking the entire town was laughing at her. Truth is, most people didn't really care. When word got out that she'd sent you away, well, most just felt sorry for her."

"Does she know I'm here?"

Mary shook her head. "John didn't think it was a good idea to tell her."

"How is she, Mary? Is she well enough to attend the funeral?"

"No. She's had two surgeries already. From what I understand, she'll be in the hospital for another week or so, until they move her home. Even then, she'll need a nurse to care for her for months yet."

Jacqueline tried to muster up sympathy, or some emotion, but nothing would come. Her mother was but a stranger to her, and she couldn't find it in her heart to feel sorry for her.

"What hospital is she in?"

"She's here in Pine Springs."

Jacqueline's eyebrows shot up. "Pine Springs has a hospital?"

"Oh, yes. Over on the west side of town, things have grown quite a lot."

Jacqueline frowned. "They have a hospital but no motel?" She watched as a slight blush colored Mary's face.

"Actually, John may have omitted a few things. There is a fairly new motel on the west side."

"And he sent me to the old Pine Springs Motel?"

Mary smiled. "He really wanted you to stay with us. He didn't want you to feel like an outsider, and that's exactly what you'd have been if you'd stayed at the motel. It wouldn't take long for word to spread."

"So, the town's grown, but gossip still flies?"

"Jacqueline, your father was a very powerful man in the county, so yes, gossip and speculation have been spreading like wildfire."

"I don't understand."

"Come on. Let's get dinner on the table. John will discuss business with you afterward."

CHAPTER FOUR

"Sit, please," Mr. Lawrence instructed, pointing to the leather couch in his study. He moved away, taking two glasses from the bar. "Scotch or brandy?"

"Brandy, please."

He handed her a glass, then joined her on the sofa. Jacqueline sipped her drink quietly as her eyes moved around the room. Legal books lined one entire wall, but the rest was filled with family pictures. She recognized his son and daughter in several along with who she assumed were his grandchildren.

"I mean this as a compliment, but you've changed an awful lot in the last fifteen years, Jacqueline. The tomboy I remember has grown into a beautiful woman."

"Thank you."

"Do you mind me asking how you managed back then? Of course, if it's none of my business, just say so."

She shrugged. "It was hard at first. Very hard. When I made it to Los Angeles, I worked as a waitress for a year, saving every penny I could. Then I started college, taking classes during the day and working nights." She shrugged again. "I made out okay."

"I think your father always hoped you'd contact him, behind your mother's back. He was beside himself, the first few years when they couldn't locate you. He blamed her totally. If not for his position in the community, I'm sure he would have divorced her. Over the years, their marriage deteriorated." He cleared his throat. "I'm sorry. You probably don't care to hear that."

"I don't really care one way or the other, Mr. Lawrence."

"Please, call me John."

"Of course."

"This may not mean anything to you, but your father was very proud of you."

"Proud? I disgraced the family. In fact, he wouldn't even speak to me the last two weeks I was here. Wouldn't even *look* at me."

"It was a . . . a shock to him, Jacqueline."

"I'm sure it was, especially since he and Mr. Thornton had my marriage all arranged."

John laughed before sipping from his drink. "Talk about ironic. Daniel went off to one of those Ivy League schools, pre-law. Next thing his parents knew, he'd moved to New York City and became an actor."

"Really? Danny?"

"Yes."

"How'd he do?"

"Had a couple of shows on Broadway, they tell me. But," Lawrence shrugged. "He died of AIDS probably ten, twelve years ago now."

"AIDS?"

"Yes. He was gay."

Jacqueline stared at him. "Talk about ironic. If not for his death, this would be funny."

"The situation, yes. I think, in your mother's mind, her world was crashing down around her. She sent you away because you were gay and refused to marry Daniel Thornton. And then, a few years later, it's made known that their chosen son-in-law is gay, too. Trust me, the news that the high school quarterback turned out to be gay was much bigger news than you."

She smiled, thinking back to the innocent dates she'd had with Danny. She should have known. She'd thought it was just her, but apparently Danny had been just as content to keep their relationship platonic as she was.

John stood and crossed to his desk, picking up a large folder, which he turned nervously in his hands. "I have something for you. And we have some things to discuss."

Jacqueline watched him, eyebrows raised as he opened the folder and took out a small white envelope. Her name was printed neatly on the front.

"Your father wrote this to you, years ago. As I said, he was proud of the success you'd achieved. And all without his help."

He handed the envelope to Jacqueline and she took it, staring at her name for a few seconds before laying the envelope in her lap. She couldn't possibly imagine what her father had to say to her. An apology, perhaps. Well, she would read it later, if at all.

"This is his will. We'll have a formal reading later, but I thought you should know ahead of the others. There'll be problems, no doubt."

"Problems?"

"Yes. He's compensated your mother nicely, of course. More than half of his assets. But the business—Keys Industries—and a couple of other holdings, the rest of his wealth, he left to you."

"*What?*"

"Your uncle, who has been managing the lumber mill for years, may contest the will. Of the original mill, your uncle owned less than forty percent. But you must understand, the mill was but a small portion of Keys Industries. And besides your uncle, you can be most certain that your mother will contest the will."

"Jesus Christ, John! Why would he even mention me in his will?"

"On the surface, it would appear that he was trying to make up for what they did to you. In reality, he truly loved you."

"Well, I can't take it. I don't need his money. I don't *want* his money."

"I understand. I'm simply his lawyer and the executor of his wishes. If you choose to sell the business or give it to your uncle or mother, that's your decision. You probably have no idea of his worth, but it is substantial, Jacqueline. His business holdings aren't limited to the mill. In fact, while it is common knowledge that he bailed the bank out all those years ago, no one really knows that the bank would collapse should he pull his money. Keys Industries controls the bank." He paused. "Perhaps, after you've had a chance to absorb this, you may decide to accept it."

Jacqueline stood, pacing nervously across the room. This, she was not expecting. Jesus, talk about ironic. If her mere presence in town didn't send her mother to her death, this most surely would.

"He controls the bank?" she asked quietly.

"Yes."

"How?"

"It goes back to the days of your grandfather. However, poor business decisions over the years left the bank in desperate need of capital. Your father obliged, using Keys Industries. In turn, he was able to secure loans for future plants at exceptionally low interest rates. Financially, the bank is extremely sound now. Your father hired a financial consultant from Houston years ago to oversee investments and such. He doesn't officially have anything to do with the bank, like the title of president—that honor goes to Mr. Wells—but he has the last say on everything. Your father trusted him completely."

Jacqueline was speechless. "And my mother knows none of this?"

"No. She thinks he had a small interest in the bank. I assume she believes it was all left to her, along with the mill and the business, of course."

"Jesus Christ," she murmured.

John smiled. "No, he left Brother Garner out of the will."

23

CHAPTER FIVE

Jacqueline had one free day before the funeral, so she took Mary's advice and drove into town, foregoing her original thoughts of playing a round of golf. You don't play golf the day before your father's funeral, even if the weather was perfect for it.

She found herself driving back toward the old downtown area, the buildings looking much drabber now in the light of day. And small. Pine Springs had not changed, not really. Dobson's bakery was still on the same corner. The meat market next to it. She felt a grin come on when she saw the sign for the café. *Garland's Café-Just Good Food*. God, did that bring back memories. Kay's family had owned it for as long as she could remember, and Jacqueline spent many a Saturday morning there, helping Kay and her sister Rose in the back with dishes much to her mother's dismay. A café was no place for the mayor's daughter. On impulse, she decided a cup of coffee was in order. Perhaps Mrs. Garland would be there. It would be nice to say hello, at least.

The bell jingled as she opened the door, and she looked up, certain it was the very same bell she remembered from all those years ago. A few curious glances were tossed her way by the lingering breakfast crowd, but the conversations never missed a beat. She walked confidently to the counter, sat on one of the old barstools and waited. A bell dinged and "order up" was yelled from the kitchen. A young woman grabbed the two plates and hurried off to a table to deliver breakfast.

"Well, butter my butt and call me a biscuit! Look what the cat drug in!"

Jacqueline turned, finding Rose Garland staring at her—an older, plumper version of the kid that used to tag along with her and Kay. She smiled slightly and raised an eyebrow, not exactly certain how her presence would be accepted.

"I'm surprised you recognize me."

"Darlin', there ain't another person in this world got baby blues like you." She laughed and walked closer. "Should I back away in case lightning bolts come crashing through the roof?"

"Might not be a bad idea."

"Never thought we'd see you again, Jackie. How the hell are you?"

"I'm . . . I'm good."

"Sorry about your father, but we didn't think you'd actually come for the funeral. Kay and I were just talking about you last night. We wondered if anyone would even contact you."

"Oh yeah? How is Kay?"

"Kay? Oh, Kay's doing fine. She owns the Hallmark shop out in the new strip center." Rose filled a cup with coffee and set it in front of Jacqueline. "So, you came back. Where'd they find you?"

"Monterey."

"Where's that? California?"

Jacqueline nodded. "South of San Francisco."

"Well, it must suit you. You look great."

"Thank you. You haven't changed much, Rose."

"Oh please. Who are you kidding? Having four kids before

25

you're thirty does this to your body," she said, pointing at herself. "That, and eating Mama's cooking."

"You look fine. You were always such a skinny little kid."

"Oh I was, but I ate that person several years ago," she said with a laugh. "Let me get Mama. She'll want to say hello."

Before Jacqueline could protest, Mrs. Garland hurried out of the kitchen, a delighted smile on her face.

"Jackie Keys, as I live and breathe! Give me a hug."

Jacqueline stood obediently and was enveloped by the larger woman.

"My goodness, you've grown up." Mrs. Garland held her at arms length, studying her. "A beautiful young lady you've become, Jackie. Your father would have been so proud."

Jacqueline's smile faltered. "I doubt that. I haven't changed *that* much, Mrs. Garland."

"Oh, pooh. That was all your mother's doing. As if we would have thought less of you or your family. It's not like we're living in the fifties, Jacqueline."

At that, Jacqueline laughed. Yes, Pine Springs was definitely caught somewhere between 1950 and 1970, she was certain. But she was pleased at her reception here in Garland's Café. She should have known better than to think that these kind people who had loved her as one of their own would have turned her away.

"How long will you stay?"

"I'm not sure. I haven't actually gone to see my mother yet. I'm sure that will be entertaining."

"I'd love to tag along and watch," Mrs. Garland said with a twinkle in her eye. "Or be a fly on the wall. Forgive my bluntness, but I never understood that woman, sending her only child away like she did. Why, I've hardly spoken to her in the last fifteen years."

"Mama, it's not like you frequent the country club, you know," Rose reminded her. "Or that she would ever set foot in here."

"Well, still. It wasn't the Christian thing to do, but she never missed a Sunday service. Let's hope she was silently begging for forgiveness."

Jacqueline smiled, knowing the thought would have never crossed her mother's mind. Madeline Keys had done nothing wrong, as far as she was concerned.

"Enough of that. I'm so glad you're back. You've got to look up Kay. She'll be thrilled to learn you're here."

"Yeah, I hate that I didn't get to say good-bye to her," Jacqueline admitted.

"Well, I won't say that she's forgiven you, Jackie. You were best friends. She took the whole thing pretty hard."

"Hard? That's putting it lightly, Mama. How many nights did I have to listen to her tirades?"

"I'm really sorry, but I didn't have a whole lot of choice. One morning I think I'm getting ready for school and instead I'm on a bus to Dallas."

Mrs. Garland shook her head sadly. "Crying shame, I tell you."

"It's okay. It was probably for the best. Who knows what would have happened if I'd stayed here. I've done all right."

"Yes, you have. And don't think it doesn't eat at your mother knowing you've made a success of yourself. I'm surprised she didn't have a coronary when your book made the bestseller list, not to mention a movie."

Jacqueline shrugged. Yes, professionally, she'd done quite well, much to her own surprise. She had Ingrid to thank for that. But personally, no. She lived a lonely life. Not much had changed in that regard. Oh, she had friends. Lots of them. Being a successful writer who had two novels turned into movies did that. Acquaintances suddenly became the best of friends. And it also brought never-ending offers for sexual favors. She thought that would be enough. But each time she brought another woman to her bed, the lonelier she became.

Jacqueline took a sip of her coffee that was now long cold. She grimaced, shoving the cup away, and both Rose and Mrs. Garland laughed.

"Let me get you a refill," Rose offered.

"How about some breakfast? I'll make you up a batch of those buttermilk pancakes you used to love," Mrs. Garland added.

"Thanks, but I had breakfast with Mary earlier."

"Mary? Mary Lawrence?"

"Yes. I'm staying with them."

"Well, that was kind of them," Mrs. Garland said. "I always thought they were good people."

"I should get going anyway and let you two get back to work."

"Would you join us for dinner, Jackie? Ralph would love to see you. We'll have the girls over, and it'll be just like old times."

Jacqueline considered the offer, remembering the numerous times she'd shared dinner with the Garland family. All eight of them. Yes, it would be nice.

"Okay. I accept."

"Great! I can't wait to show off my kids," Rose said. "And the hubby. He's a really nice guy. You might remember him. Greg Kubiac?"

"Geez, Rose. The little nerdy guy we all called 'four-eyes'?" Jacqueline teased.

"Yes. But he now wears contacts, and we've fattened him up nicely, haven't we, Mama?"

"Yes we have. He works out at the mill, Jackie. Graduated college with some computer degree and works in the office out there."

Jacqueline nodded. Yes, the lumber mill probably employed half the town, if not more. The mill. Soon to be her mill. Damn.

"Well, it will be nice to see him again."

"Now, you run along. Go see Kay. Did Rose tell you where she worked?"

"Strip center. Hallmark."

"Great. And come early. I only wish we'd thought to send someone to the county line for refreshments."

"Refreshments?"

"Beer and the like," Mrs. Garland whispered.

"County line?"

"Well, you know you can't buy alcohol in town. Not with all the

Baptists still in control," she said with a laugh. "Don't tell me you've forgotten this is a dry county?"

Jacqueline nodded. "Yes. Forgot prohibition still existed in these parts."

Jacqueline was surprised at the nervousness she felt as she pulled the Lexus into a parking space in front of the Hallmark store. She'd thought of Kay a lot over the years, especially at the beginning. In fact, she'd gone so far as to seriously consider contacting her when she'd graduated college, just to share her news. But, she'd convinced herself that Kay would want nothing to do with her, and she let the idea fade. Now here she was, fifteen years later, a grown woman about to see the first girl who had stirred feelings in her, feelings she had no idea what to do with at the time. The picture she had of Kay in her mind was as she'd been at seventeen. She wondered how much she'd changed. Had she grown like Rose? Jacqueline hadn't even bothered to ask who she'd married or if she had kids. Probably. She'd come from a large family. No doubt she tried to duplicate that, much as Rose had done.

"Come on, come on," she whispered, lightly tapping the steering wheel. "Can't hide in here all day."

She finally opened the car door and stepped into the sunshine, her eyes looking through the glass into the store, trying to find Kay. A few customers were milling about, but none looked familiar to her. She brushed at the hair over her ears, then nervously pulled at the collar of her shirt before walking purposefully to the door, hesitating only a fraction of a second before entering. An electronic tone announced her arrival, and she moved inside, pretending to look at a display near the door. She finally raised her eyes and surveyed the store, looking for Kay.

"Good Lord," she murmured quietly. Kay was at the register in the back of the store, talking to a customer, laughing at something she said. Her light brown hair was much shorter than she wore it in high school. It was styled nicely, barely touching the collar of her blouse now. Jacqueline remembered it as being long and straight. The easy smile that Jacqueline remembered was still there, but laugh lines now showed around the smooth skin of her eyes. She was as lovely as ever. And the sight of her caused Jacqueline's heart to beat just a little faster.

She waited until the customer left, then moved closer, standing with her hands shoved nervously in the pockets of her jeans. She watched as Kay straightened the pens in the jar next to the cash register, waiting for her to look up. Kay finally did, her light blue eyes moving slowly over Jacqueline, stopping when they reached her face. A slight frown as her eyebrows drew together, then a widening of her eyes as recognition set in. Jacqueline smiled.

"Oh my God. Is it you?"

Jacqueline shrugged. "You . . . who?"

"Jackie," she whispered.

Then Kay was walking slowly around the counter, moving toward her. Her steps increased, and before Jacqueline knew what was happening, the other woman flung her arms around her, squeezing her tight.

"My God. It's really you."

Jacqueline hugged her back, surprised at the familiarity of that simple embrace.

"In the flesh."

Kay finally stepped away, grasping her hands. Their eyes locked together as identical smiles touched their faces.

"I am *so* mad at you," Kay finally said.

"Oh yeah? What'd I do this time?"

A hard fist slugged her arm and Jacqueline stepped back, rubbing the spot where Kay had hit her.

"What's that for?"

"You know perfectly well what that's for. Not one word! Not a letter. *Nothing*. I didn't know if you were dead or alive!"

Jacqueline lowered her eyes. This, she was expecting. She'd expected it from Rose and Mrs. Garland, as well.

"I didn't have a chance to say good-bye, Kay. Later, well, it was too late. Besides, I wasn't certain you'd even want to hear from me."

"You were always so stubborn. I should have known."

"Stubborn? I was kicked out of town," Jacqueline reminded her.

"Bullshit. It wasn't like they had a gun to your head. You could have stayed with us. You know Mama would have welcomed you."

"I knew no such thing. I was scared. I didn't think you'd even talk to me, much less want to see me."

"Why? You were my best friend."

Jacqueline shrugged.

"Jesus. Stubborn. I swear."

They stared at each other, finally breaking down into laughter.

"I'm sorry. I haven't seen you in . . . in fifteen years and I'm fussing at you."

"It's okay. I deserve it."

"No, you don't. It wasn't like you ran away or anything. I'm sorry, Jackie." Kay again wrapped her arms around Jacqueline, pulling her into another hug. "It's just such a shock to see you. Couldn't call first, huh?"

"I wasn't certain I would even look you up. But Rose and your mother insisted."

Kay's eyes widened. "You've seen them?"

"Stopped by the café for coffee. In fact, your mother invited me for dinner tonight."

Kay laughed. "She would. She always loved you. Did she tell you she told your mother off?"

Jacqueline's eyebrows shot up. "You're kidding. When?"

"When we found out she'd sent you away. Mama drove right over to your parents' house, rang the bell and let her have it, right there on the front step."

"All this time, I imagined everyone hating me, glad I was out of their lives. I didn't think anyone would care," Jacqueline admitted.

"Oh, Jackie, you're not serious? We loved you, no matter what. You shouldn't have been alone." Kay paused. "Why didn't you tell me?"

"I thought you would hate me."

31

"Hate you? I loved you."

Jacqueline shrugged. "I was a kid. I hardly knew what was going on myself, Kay. I certainly didn't think you would understand. And I was scared to tell you."

Kay sighed. "You're probably right. I freaked out when I heard. I was angry with you for not telling me, but I was confused, too. And . . ."

"And all those times we slept together," Jacqueline supplied.

Kay blushed. "I'm sorry. That's not what I meant."

"Don't be sorry. I don't blame you for thinking that."

The phone rang, and Kay grabbed Jacqueline's arm. "Don't you dare go away." She hurried to the counter, picking up the phone in a smooth motion. "Kay's Hallmark." A smile. "Yes, she's here now."

Jacqueline grinned, then turned away to give Kay privacy. And herself. This wasn't anything like she'd imagined their reunion being. She expected anger, yes, but she was surprised that they'd picked up their bickering as if they'd not been apart for fifteen years. Oh, they could get into some arguments in the old days. But through it all, they were the best of friends. Until they got older, until Jacqueline started feeling things. God, it was all she could do to be around Kay then. And when they started dating boys, when Kay would go out alone with Billy Ray Renfro, it was all Jacqueline could do to not follow them to make sure that Kay was all right. Her eyes widened, wondering if Billy Ray was the one Kay had married. God, she hoped not. Billy Ray was a loser.

"Well, I'm officially invited to dinner. Mama is so excited you're back. She's got a cookout planned. I hope you're ready for that."

"That'll be great. It'll be good to see everyone again. Rose's got four kids, huh?"

"Oh yeah. And I spoil them rotten."

"Yeah? What about you? Any little Kays running around?"

Kay shook her head. "No kids."

"I'd have thought you'd have a house full by now. Why not?"

32

Kay shrugged. "Just didn't happen."

Jacqueline nodded. Wrong subject. Well, perhaps later she'd ask more. "I should let you get back to work. And I should check in with Mary. She's probably wondering what trouble I've gotten into."

"Mary? You brought . . . you brought someone with you?"

Jacqueline laughed. "No. Mary Lawrence. I'm staying with them."

"Oh. I see. I guess staying at your folk's place is out of the question, huh?"

"I haven't seen my mother yet. She doesn't know I'm here."

Kay lowered her head. "I'm sorry. I completely forgot the reason you're here."

"It's okay. It's not like I . . . I feel anything, you know. He was my father, but I lost my family a long time ago. Any grieving I did is well in the past."

Kay nodded sadly. "I understand."

CHAPTER SIX

"I knew if anyone welcomed you with open arms, it would be the Garlands," Mary said. "I'm glad you're going to see them. Such kind people."

"Yes, they are. They were my second family."

"Have you . . . have you thought about seeing your mother?" Mary asked hesitantly.

"Yes, actually. I thought I'd go today, but the time kinda got away from me. Maybe I should wait until after the funeral tomorrow."

"I'm sure word has already spread around town that you're here. In fact, I'm surprised I've not had a phone call yet."

"From her?"

"Yes. Despite everything, your mother is still a very powerful woman in this town. With your father gone, everyone assumes that your mother is in control of the mill now. Your father was a very fair man but your mother . . . well, she's perceived as a . . ."

"Bitch?"

"I wasn't going to use such a strong word, but—"

"I lived with her for nearly eighteen years, Mary. I know all about her."

"Well, I just think people are going to want to stay on her good side, is all. So, letting her know that you are back in town, to warn her, perhaps, I'd not be surprised if she's had several visitors already."

"So you're suggesting I go see her today?"

"We were always friends with your parents on a social level. That's all. If I had any advice to give you, it would be to not see her at all. She's a very vindictive woman. I can only imagine the words you'll exchange with each other."

Jacqueline laughed. "I'm thirty-three years old. I can handle myself. She's my mother in name only. I don't feel anything for her except maybe some long-harbored hatred. There's nothing she could say to me that could possibly hurt me any more than she did fifteen years ago."

"Don't underestimate her."

"Mary, I'm not scared of her. She has nothing I want."

"Okay. But if you intend to enjoy yourself this evening at the Garlands, I would recommend you not visit your mother today."

Jacqueline smiled at the other woman. "I agree. So, after the funeral tomorrow, I'll stop by. How's that?"

"I think that's a good idea. Can you imagine how she must be feeling? Missing out on this opportunity to be the center of attention? I'm sure it's killing her, being stuck in the hospital. No one can see her pain."

"Physical pain? Or emotional?"

"Physical. But she would put on a good show at the funeral, I'm sure."

"What are you saying?"

"Oh, I shouldn't gossip, Jacqueline. It's not common knowledge, but your parents' marriage ended long ago. When they moved out here, they both had separate wings in the house. They haven't had a real marriage in years."

"Not common knowledge? Come on, in *this* town?"

"Well, rumors, sure. It's not like the housekeepers don't all gossip. But still, it's just gossip."

Jacqueline shook her head. So much energy wasted on such bullshit. She was glad she'd left when she did.

"Enough of that. Go get ready. I'm sure you're looking forward to tonight. You and Kay were always such good friends. I bet you have a lot of catching up to do."

"Yeah. Yeah, we do." Jacqueline paused, then asked the question that had been on her mind all day. "What about her husband? When we talked, I didn't think to ask."

"Oh, Kay's been divorced years now. She married that Billy Ray Renfro about a year or so after high school, I think. But, well, it wasn't good."

"What do you mean?"

Mary lowered her head. "I hate to gossip about these things, Jacqueline. But, well, everyone could see what was happening."

"He beat her?" Jacqueline guessed.

Mary nodded. "It was bad. At the end, he put her in the hospital."

"Dear God," Jacqueline whispered.

"Did some jail time, then left town. Got into some trouble in Houston, last we heard."

Jacqueline felt her heart clutch painfully. The bastard. Kay was the kindest, gentlest person she knew. Who in the world could possibly hit her?

"Please, it's something she's put in the past. Don't tell her I said anything."

"Of course."

But later, as Jacqueline drove to the Garland's house, she was still wondering how she was going to act when she saw Kay. Her hands gripped the steering wheel hard, remembering the night she'd seen Kay and Billy Ray kissing under the bleachers. She should have known then. He had her pushed up hard against the railing, holding her there. But Jacqueline had been too consumed with jealousy to notice. All she could see was them kissing, touching. But it was Billy Ray's hands that were touching. Kay's hands had been at his shoulders, as if pushing him away.

"Goddamn! I should have done something, said something."

But no, they were just kids. Kids exploring their sexuality. And in a jealous rage, she couldn't have just gone up and pulled him off her. She shook her head. Two days ago, she was in California, not giving a thought to Pine Springs, Kay or her past. Now, here she was, wondering why she hadn't stepped in fifteen years ago when her best friend was sharing a passionate kiss with her boyfriend.

"Let it go. It's none of your business," she murmured.

She was going to have a nice dinner with very old friends, catch up on the past and then go home. In a few days, she'd be back to her life, and Pine Springs would go on as it always had. There was nothing she could do to change things.

She found the Garland's home without problems, and it looked exactly as she remembered, including the assortment of cars parked in the driveway. Ralph Garland was a mechanic, and there always seemed to be three or four cars around the house that he was fixing up. With six kids, no doubt he'd done that to give them all something to drive. Maybe that was just an excuse then or perhaps he was working on his grandchildren now.

The azalea bed in the front of the house was bursting with blooms, and Jacqueline paused to admire them. She never understood how Mrs. Garland could work all day at the café and still have time to tend to her yard. That was one thing Jacqueline remembered. No matter the time of year, something was always blooming.

From the shadows of the corner of the house, Kay stood, watching Jackie as she surveyed the yard. She still couldn't believe she was here. She had long ago given up hope of seeing her again. But here she was, as familiar to her as she'd ever been. Fifteen years hadn't changed her that much. Jackie was still taller than she was, but not by much. Her blond hair seemed darker now, her eyes bluer. And she looked every inch the tomboy Kay remembered and not the successful writer Kay knew her to be. She watched as Jackie brushed the bangs at her forehead, smiling as Jackie hesitated before going into the backyard.

Jacqueline listened to the voices, then followed the well-worn path that led to the backyard and the patio. The barbecue pit was already smoking, and kids were running around, dodging the lit citronella candles. Lawn chairs were placed in the grass and on the patio, and she stood, taking it all in. She'd missed this. This closeness of family, friends. Laughter rang out, and she recognized Sammy, Kay's kid brother, who was now well over six feet tall. He'd still been a little squirt when she'd left.

"Scared?"

She jumped, startled. Kay stood behind her, holding a covered dish in her hand.

"Just looking." Jacqueline tilted her head. "What you got there?"

"Potato salad."

"Ah."

"Mama intends to treat you to a back home meal, I'm afraid. She said you probably hadn't had a decent barbecue since you left."

Jacqueline fell into step beside Kay. "She's right about that."

"Jackie, there you are. Come, come. Sammy's been beside himself waiting to see you."

"He always had such a crush on you," Kay whispered.

Jacqueline blushed as she stood face to face with the now grown version of the kid she remembered.

"Jesus Christ, Sammy, you've grown three feet."

It was his turn to blush.

"Hi Jackie."

Then she walked closer, wrapping her arms around him for a tight hug. "Good to see you again."

"Yeah, you look great." Then he blushed again. "Here, meet

my wife." He pulled an extremely shy young woman to his side. "This is Tess."

Jacqueline politely shook her hand. "Nice to meet you."

"Thank you," came the quiet response.

"Don't mind her, Jackie," Rose said as she walked over and put her arm around Jacqueline. "She's heard all the horror stories about you. She's probably scared to death."

"Rose!"

"Oh, Mama, I'm just kidding." Rose turned to Jacqueline. "Tess doesn't talk much," she whispered.

"Well, with this crowd, who could blame her."

Rose laughed. "Look at Sammy. Can you believe how he shot up?"

"No, I hardly recognized him. What about Eric and the others?"

"Eric works offshore. He's here a month, then gone a month. And Bobby, you remember Bobby? He's over in Austin, coaching football at one of the high schools there."

"I remember Bobby, of course. He was a pain in the ass, even at ten years old."

"Still is. Becky is the only one of us girls to leave town. She married a boy she met in college, and they live in Oklahoma City." Rose tugged Jacqueline's arm. "Come on over here," Rose said, leading Jacqueline to her father and who she assumed was Greg, her husband.

"You remember Pop."

"Mr. Garland, how are you?"

"Great, Jackie, great. So good to see you again."

"And this is Greg, my husband."

Jacqueline shook his hand. He looked nothing like the young boy she remembered. He'd grown into a handsome man, his neatly trimmed mustache lifting on one corner as he smiled. "Nice to see you again, Greg."

"Jackie, you too."

"Four of the little monsters running around here are my kids, but I'll introduce you later," Rose said. "Grab something to drink." She pointed to the pitchers of iced tea sitting on the picnic table. "I'm going to see if Mama needs help."

Jacqueline dipped a plastic cup into the ice, then filled her glass, looking around for Kay. "Want one?"

"Please."

Jacqueline handed Kay a glass, then took her first sip of sweet tea, her eyes slamming closed at the memories that taste recalled.

"Good?"

Jacqueline smiled. "Very." She glanced over at Rose. "I see Rose hasn't changed a bit. She's still as bossy as ever."

"Yes. She should have been the oldest girl in the family, not me. She's always just taken charge of things."

"As I recall, she tried her best to take charge of us back then. Our saving grace was that she couldn't climb that damn tree."

Kay laughed, pointing at the very tree. "Still here."

Jacqueline met her eyes. "I have a lot of fond memories of that tree," she said quietly.

"Me, too. Remember that time you took a six-pack of beer from your parents' fridge?" Kay asked. "We hauled it up the tree with us and spent the afternoon attempting to drink it."

Jacqueline nodded. "I thought your dad was going to kill us both."

"Well, at least we saved him one."

They were quiet, both remembering other times that some mischief Jacqueline concocted had gotten them into trouble. Mostly from Kay's parents, though. They hadn't spent a whole lot of time at Jacqueline's house.

"So, what have you been doing for the last fifteen years, Kay?"

Kay shifted uncomfortably, her eyes not quite meeting Jackie's. When they were young, they could talk about anything, share thoughts, feelings. But fifteen years had passed. She wouldn't just blurt out her life's failures, hoping they could pick up where they left off. So, she lied.

"Nothing much exciting. I've had the store now six years. It keeps me busy."

Jacqueline nodded. "And?"

"And what?"

"That's it? That's all I get? What about after high school? Did you go off to college?"

Kay shook her head. "No. I . . . I worked in the café for awhile. And then . . . well, I got married."

"Yeah? Who was the lucky guy?"

Kay met her eyes, then looked away. "I really don't want to talk about this now, Jackie. Okay?"

"Hey, sure. I'm sorry. Just trying to catch up."

"What about you?" Kay asked, changing the subject. "I've read your books, by the way. You're very talented. I don't remember you ever writing when we were in school."

Jacqueline blushed slightly. In fact, she'd always written, she just never shared her stories with anyone, afraid they would laugh at her.

"I secretly dabbled in it," Jacqueline admitted. "When I started college, I had no idea what I wanted to be when I grew up, so I took some writing classes, and it just fell into place. I was very lucky."

"And your love life?" Kay surprised herself with the question. It was something she'd thought about often, in the beginning, when she'd first found out.

Jacqueline smiled. "You want to talk about my love life? What? I'm the only lesbian you know?"

"Actually . . . yeah."

"No closeted spinster women hanging around town?" Jacqueline teased.

"Well, you know, Ms. Cutter never married. Does that count?"

"She's still here? Damn, she must be in her eighties by now."

"She was only in her forties when we were in school. In fact, she's still teaching."

"And lived alone all these years?"

"Well, she does go out of town on weekends quite often."

"There you go. She's probably sneaking off to some deviant affair she's been having. Some other spinster woman in another town, maybe."

They laughed and Rose walked up, linking arms with both of them.

"What's so funny?"

"Nothing," Kay said. "Just catching up."

"Uh-huh. You two cannot hide over here all night talking. God, I used to hate that when you were together. You'd lock me out of your room, and I could hear you talking and laughing for hours."

"It was big-girl talk and you were just a little squirt," Jacqueline said.

"I was not. I'm only four years younger than you guys."

"That makes you twenty-nine. God, Rose, you're twenty-nine and you've got four young kids? You know what causes that, right?"

"Very funny. But I'm certain *you* don't," Rose teased. "And anyway, Mama's given up on Kay giving her grandkids, so the rest of us are all having one extra."

Kay playfully punched her arm. "Thanks a lot, sis."

"Hey, I can't help it if you didn't get my maternal instincts."

"Girls? Come on over and be sociable. We didn't drag Jackie all the way over here so only you two could have her."

"Come on. Mama's put her foot down."

"I want to hear all about Jackie's life in California. It must be very exciting."

Jacqueline turned and winked at Kay. "Should I leave out the part about my love life?"

Kay smiled, watching as Jackie was absorbed into her family once again. For the first time in years, Kay felt true happiness.

CHAPTER SEVEN

"It was so great seeing Jackie again, wasn't it?" Rose asked while they were helping their mother cleanup.

"Yes, it really was. Almost like old times," Kay said. She found it very surprising that after fifteen years of separation, they could talk and tease like they hadn't missed a day.

"Did you . . . did you tell her anything?"

Kay shook her head. "We didn't have much time alone. Besides, do I really want to bring all that up?"

Rose grabbed her arm as she walked past, squeezing lightly. "You told me yourself, Jackie was the only one you'd ever been able to talk to. And I know for a fact you haven't talked to *anyone* about this."

"It's been what? Six years? I think I'm over it by now," Kay insisted.

"Bullshit. You've kept it bottled up inside, as if you could put the cork back on a bottle of bad wine, hoping it'll turn into a nice chardonnay someday."

"You're comparing my life to a bottle of bad wine?"

"You know what I mean, Kay. You've got to get it out, pour it out and start over. Have you even thought about dating again? You can't live your life alone just because some asshole did that to you."

"Pine Springs is not exactly crawling with eligible men, Rose, even if I did want to date. Which I don't," she added.

"And that's my point. You don't want to. Something's wrong with that, Kay. You've got to find yourself someone. You're already thirty-three. It's time you had your own kids so I can try to undo the damage you've done to mine."

"And what do you mean by that?"

"You know exactly what I mean! You spoil them rotten. I can't even control them anymore. Have yourself a couple, and I'll return the favor."

Kay laughed, pausing to kiss her sister on the cheek. "Thanks, sis. But I like this arrangement just fine. I won't have to pay for college this way."

"Well, if you're not careful, I'll send Lee Ann to live with you."

"Don't forget to blow the candles out, girls."

"I'll get them, Mama." Kay walked to the picnic table, blowing out the two tall candles that were still burning.

"Do you know how long she's staying?"

"Jackie? She didn't really say. I assume through the weekend. Although, if she goes to see her mother, she may decide to skip out early, which I can't say I blame her."

"No kidding. Wonder how many candy stripers she's made cry?"

Kay paused. "Do you think anyone's gone to see her? I mean, did she have any friends?"

"Of course she's got friends. There's the Women's League, the country club, all the women that drive those big fancy cars. Those friends."

"Ah. Of course. What was I thinking?"

"Don't tell me you feel sorry for her."

"No. No, I don't. I think it's a shame that he was the one that died, you know? He was a decent man."

"Practically a saint to have lived with her."

"Girls? What are you gossiping about now?"

"Nothing, Mama. We're coming in."

Later, as Kay drove home, memories of her childhood flooded her, and she laughed as she recalled one of the many adventures Jackie had dragged her into.

"We're not going to get in trouble, Kay, 'cause nobody's gonna know."

"Only the big kids come down here," Kay insisted.

"We're big kids."

"We're twelve."

"Yeah. And I can still beat the snot out of Jim Bob, the big pussy."

Kay imagined Jim Bob Pearson catching them at his spot on the river. He was three years older than them, and took delight in tormenting Kay, for some reason. On more than one occasion, Jackie had come to her rescue, the last time, bloodying Jim Bob's nose with a fist square to the face.

Kay laughed out loud in the car. She hadn't thought of that in years. And yes, they did get caught that day at the river. The water was shallow and muddy in most places, but there were spots along the slow moving river that were deep, perfect for swimming on hot summer days. And most of those swimming holes had been claimed by the high school kids. Much like gangs protecting their turf, every group had their own spot, and no one shared. Especially with two twelve-year-old brats! But Jackie had pulled Kay through the woods after leaving their bikes hidden in some brush. The best swimming hole was claimed by Jim Bob's older brother, and Jackie had been adamant about crashing their party.

It had been a Saturday morning, still early, and no one was about. They both stripped down to their underwear and jumped in, enjoying the cool water on that hot summer morning. It hadn't lasted long. Jackie heard them first, nearly yanking Kay from the water. They struggled to put their clothes on when Jim Bob came walking up with two of his friends.

"Well, look what we've got here. Brat one and brat two. Get 'em, boys!"

Kay grabbed her shoes and started running, but Jackie held her ground. At the edge of the woods, Kay stopped, her eyes wide.

"Jackie? Come on!"

"No! I ain't scared of 'em."

It was then that Kay realized just how tall Jackie had gotten over the summer. She stood up straight, still barefoot, but clothed. The three boys surrounded her and Jackie started laughing. They were all smaller than she was.

"This hardly seems fair, guys. Maybe I need to tie one hand behind my back," Jackie goaded them.

Kay laughed again. She could still picture Jackie standing there, tossing one after the other into the river, fully clothed. Of course, it wasn't long before Jim Bob's brother could be heard, and this time Jackie did run. They were on their bikes, riding fast down the dirt road, still able to hear Jim Bob screaming at them.

Yes, Jackie had talked her into more things, but God, they'd had fun. And she realized she would have followed Jackie anywhere. Did follow her, she corrected. It was only when they got older, that last year of high school, that things started to change between them. Jackie was seeing Danny Thornton and Kay was going out with Billy Ray. The two boys didn't like each other, which meant there were no double dates. Not to mention Jackie *hated* Billy Ray. On more than one occasion, Jackie had told Kay to dump him, that he was no good for her. Turns out, she was right.

CHAPTER EIGHT

Jacqueline stood before the mirror, smoothing the skirt around her hips. She hated suits. She hated the confinement of hose and skirts and jackets and fucking pumps.

But she couldn't help to smile. She looked nice. Ingrid would hardly recognize her. Then she curled her toes, hating the tight-fitting shoes. She had a moment of defiance earlier, and thought of just wearing slacks and let tongues wag, but it'd hardly be worth it if her mother was not there to see. So, she'd donned the pressed suit, hose and all, and even applied a little makeup.

"If this had happened a couple of months later, they could have seen the butch haircut," she murmured. Her hair had been very blond when she was young, but had darkened some over the years. She remembered when she'd first chopped it off. God, had that caused a scene. She'd started playing sports, and her long hair was just in the way. She'd asked her mother to take her to get it cut, but she'd adamantly refused, saying some nonsense about being a cheerleader. So, Jacqueline talked Kay into cutting it. After the initial damage, Mrs. Garland had tried to straighten it up, claiming the whole time that Mrs. Keys would have her hide if she found out. As it turned out, it was Jacqueline's hide that suffered the damage.

She kept her hair longer now, but not by much. She brushed the layered strands over her ears and met her blue eyes in the mirror. Now what? She was here, she was going to a funeral in a few hours, she'd met up with some old friends. Now what? See her mother? Jacqueline rolled her eyes. Not looking forward to that.

Behind her, on the bed, she saw the image of her laptop in the mirror. She hadn't even opened it. No doubt Ingrid had been e-mailing her, reminding her of the deadline. She had asked Ingrid not to call unless it was an emergency, and so far, her agent had kept her word. She would take the time tonight to check in, maybe do some work. She had not decided how long she would stay, even though Mr. Lawrence had requested she stay through the next week to tend to the will, as he put it. That was something else she was not looking forward to. She didn't want to face her Uncle Walter, not over something like this.

A light tapping on the door brought her around, and she walked to open it. Mary, still clad in a robe after her shower, stood there, her eyes widening.

"What?"

"My, my. You look lovely, Jacqueline."

Jacqueline colored slightly, but managed a nonchalant shrug. "Thanks."

"John wanted to make sure you knew you could ride with us. And sit with us, of course. I'm sure your Uncle Walter and his family will claim the first few pews."

"Well, he is my father's only brother."

"No one has called us, by the way. Perhaps they don't know you're in town."

Jacqueline raised her head. "Well, they're about to. I've decided to go by the hospital first." She shrugged again. "Get it over with."

"Are you sure?"

"Yes. I'll be fine." Then she smiled. "Just want to let her know I'm here."

"And that you'll be at the funeral and she won't?"

"Yeah. Something like that." Jacqueline moved back into the room, opening her briefcase to toss in her phone and wallet. "I doubt I'll stay long." She snapped the briefcase shut and picked up her keys. Glancing at her reflection in the mirror, she thought she looked more like she was going to a board meeting than a funeral.

"If you need anything or if there's trouble, you'll call of course."

"There won't be trouble, Mary. I can handle her. I'll meet you at the church."

But for her brave words, Jacqueline's apprehension grew as she neared the small hospital. She'd attempted to stand up to her mother on numerous occasions as a teenager and more often than not had lost. Even then, her father had been unable to intervene. Her mother's wishes were normally always followed. Well, not anymore. Jacqueline was her own person. She owed her mother absolutely nothing. In fact, she owed neither of them.

"And why exactly did you come?" she asked herself out loud. She had no answer. Over the years, she'd resolved herself to the fact that she had no family, no parents. She never thought she'd see them again. In all truth, she never *wanted* to see them again. She'd made good. She didn't need them for anything. But when she got the phone call, she'd hardly hesitated at all before agreeing to come back to Pine Springs. Perhaps it was as she'd told Ingrid. She needed closure. Perhaps then, she could get on with her life, maybe find a meaningful relationship instead of the one-night stands that seemed to dominate her life now.

The hospital was busy on this Saturday morning, she noted as she parked. A woman with a small child preceded her inside, and she waited as they made their way to the reception desk, asking directions. She stood back, surveying the hospital lobby. It was only then she saw the sign, signifying her father's money.

Keys Maternity Ward.

"May I help you?"

Jacqueline looked back the desk, nodding at the nurse. "Madeline Keys's room, please."

The nurse glanced quickly at her computer, then smiled. "Upstairs. Room two-nineteen."

"Thanks."

Jacqueline walked confidently to the elevator, waiting only a few seconds before the bell rang and the doors opened. Once inside, she took a deep breath to settle her nerves. She wondered what her mother would look like, laying there in the hospital bed. She always remembered her being dressed and made up for the country club or church, never relaxed and casual. No doubt it was killing her being locked up here.

Once in the hallway, she glanced around, seeing the nearest room number. Then she turned right, walking only three doors down before finding her mother's room. The door was ajar, and she listened absently to the television for a second before knocking lightly on the door. She ducked her head, trying to see inside. Then a quiet voice beckoned her to enter.

"Here goes," she whispered.

She stepped inside, leaning casually against the door as she met her mother's eyes. She got the reaction she was hoping for. An audible gasp, then the remote her mother had been holding fell helplessly to the floor.

"Hello, Mother," Jacqueline drawled. "You're looking well."

"*You*," her mother hissed. "What the *hell* are *you* doing here?"

Jacqueline pushed off the wall, walking slowly toward the bed. The woman she'd feared most in her life lay helpless, a full-body cast prohibiting her movements. But, from the neck up, she looked exactly like the woman she remembered. Dark hair, perfectly coifed, makeup applied to perfection—you'd never guess she'd been four days in here.

"Well, I've come to bury my father, of course. Your husband." Jacqueline bent down and picked up the remote, tossing it back onto the bed just out of her mother's reach. "I hate that you won't be able to attend. I'm sure it's breaking your heart."

"You have no place here. You ceased being a daughter to us long ago."

"Oh, yes." Jacqueline casually crossed her arms. "Would that be the day you ran me out of town?"

"You made your bed. You had a choice."

"A choice? Oh, that's right! Daniel Thornton. That would have been a great marriage, both of us gay and all. Were you actually hoping for grandchildren?"

"Get out of my room!"

"That's all you have to say? I'm disappointed, Mother. You always had such a vicious tongue."

"I'm sure John Lawrence is behind this. And the first thing I'm going to do is remove him as counsel for this family. He had no right contacting you."

"Yeah? He's a good man. I'm actually staying with him and Mary. They've been very gracious hosts."

"I should have known. What do you want? Did you come back to stake your claim to your father's fortune? Well you're sadly mistaken, young lady. Your father despised you and your perverted lifestyle. You'll not get a penny of his money. You made a laughing stock out of him."

Jacqueline smiled. "Actually, I think it was you that made him a laughing stock, Mother. But no, I didn't come back for money. I have plenty, thanks. And I owe that to you. My first novel, you may have heard of it. *No Place For Family*." At her mother's wide eyes, Jacqueline nodded. "Yes. I should thank you. The mother in the story was a carbon copy of you. I think they portrayed you well in the movie. It was such a tragic death, though."

"Get out of my room! Now, before I call security!"

"Security? They have security in Pine Springs?"

"You disgrace this family, and then you have the gall to show up at his funeral? As if you are a part of this family? How dare you? Can you imagine what the talk will be?"

Jacqueline laughed. "You know, that was always your problem, Mother. So concerned with what everyone thought about you, about us. In fact, most people didn't give a damn about our little family."

"Your father owned this town. He was the mayor. He employed half the county. Of course we had to set an example for the people here."

"An example? So as an example, you send your only daughter away because Brother Garner couldn't *heal* her?"

"You are the devil's child and I refuse to talk to you another second." Her hand moved, and she pushed a button several times. "And I will instruct them not to let you back inside this hospital again."

"Don't bother. I won't be back. I just wanted to come by and let you know that I was in town. I'm sure Uncle Walter will fill you in after the funeral."

A nurse rushed in, moving past Jacqueline to the bed. "Mrs. Keys, what can I do for you?"

"What you can do is escort this . . . this *person* from my room."

"I don't need an escort, Mother. I can find my own way. I always have."

With that, Jacqueline turned and walked confidently from the room, wondering why she'd even come in the first place. What had she hoped to accomplish? Had she expected her mother to have a change of heart after all these years?

She was shaking by the time she got back in her car, and she gripped the steering wheel hard, trying to calm her nerves. What purpose had that served? None. Her mother was the same callous woman she'd always been. A part of Jacqueline had hoped that perhaps her mother had changed, that she would be glad to see her after all these years. But no. Her mother still wanted no part of her.

"Fine. Just fine with me," she murmured, turning the key in the ignition and driving away in one motion, the tires squealing on the pavement as she accelerated. She glanced in the mirror and smirked. "Very childish, Jackie."

CHAPTER NINE

Jacqueline turned onto the street that would take her to the First Baptist Church of Pine Springs. Through the trees, she saw it, perched on top of the hill, overlooking the town as always, watching the townspeople as they went about their daily lives. Brother Garner had the best view in town, sitting up here, judging people. Oh, she remembered his sermons on Sunday. She'd lived in fear of him. He seemed to know everything about everybody. And when her mother had hauled her up here, confessing to him that her daughter was a sinner, Jacqueline very nearly retracted the whole thing, just so that she wouldn't have to sit and listen to him, face to face.

But in the end, she didn't. She couldn't. In fact, she told him to go fuck himself. She was nearly certain it was Brother Garner who suggested the bus to Dallas.

She parked away from most of the other cars, wanting to give herself some time to prepare. She should have made arrangements to meet Mary and John somewhere. The last thing she wanted was to walk into the church alone, imagining all eyes on her. But her trepidation lifted somewhat when she saw two familiar faces walking up the sidewalk. She quickly got out of her car, hurrying to catch up.

"Hey guys."

"Holy shit!"

Jacqueline smiled. "What?"

"No offense, Jackie, but seeing you in a dress and makeup is kinda like seeing my daddy in women's underwear," Rose teased.

Kay covered the smile on her face with her hand, but her shoulders shook.

"Very funny. I'd forgotten about your warped sense of humor, Rose."

"But, you look cute. Doesn't she, Kay?"

"Adorable." Then Kay touched her arm. "Where will you sit?"

"With Mary and John, I guess. You guys want to join me?"

"I wouldn't miss it. Can you imagine the talk at the café come Monday morning?"

"Rose!"

"It's okay. She's probably right. Besides, I wouldn't mind having some friendly faces around," Jacqueline admitted.

"Are you sure it's safe to walk in with you?" Kay asked. "Lightning bolts and all."

"Ah, you're both comedians today. But I think you'll be safe."

The three of them walked up the long flight of stone steps to the front door of the First Baptist Church, and Jacqueline ignored the curious glances they were receiving.

"Your reputation might be shot to hell, though," she whispered to Kay.

"Truth is, I don't actually make it to church all that much, Jackie."

"No? Why?"

Kay shrugged. "Long story."

"Well, it seems you have several long stories to tell me. Wonder when we'll find the time?"

"Speaking of that. How long are you staying?" Rose asked.

"Into next week. I haven't really decided. Of course, Mary may be tired of having a house guest by then. I think I may check out the new motel she was telling me about."

"You can always stay with me," Kay offered, the words out before she knew it.

"You're just dying to become the town's gossip, huh? Can you imagine? The Keys's long lost lesbian daughter comes home for the funeral and stays with little Kay Garland, no doubt trying to convert her in the process," Jacqueline said, eyebrows rising mockingly.

"Oh, please. You got me into so much trouble when we were young, I doubt anyone would even notice now."

"Jacqueline. There you are."

Jacqueline looked up as Mary Lawrence walked over. Jacqueline took her hand, then pointed at her two companions. "You know Kay and Rose, right?"

"Of course I do. How are you, ladies?"

"Fine," they said in unison.

"I've asked them to sit with us. I hope you don't mind," Jacqueline said.

"Not at all. There is safety in numbers, after all," Mary said with a smile.

"Kinda what I was thinking."

"Your uncle is sitting for the family. He's also doing the eulogy."

Jacqueline nodded. "Good. Does he know I'm here?"

"Yes. John told him. Other than being surprised, he didn't have much to say. Or not anything John chose to repeat."

"Then maybe it won't be such a big deal. I mean, it's a funeral. And my mother is not here to cause a scene."

Mary linked arms with her, leading her away. Jacqueline glanced over her shoulder, motioning for Kay and Rose to follow.

"How did that go, anyway?"

"About as I expected. She had me thrown out."

"Why am I not surprised?"

Once inside the church, quiet music was playing as people filed up the aisle. Jacqueline stopped. The casket was at the front, opened.

"You don't have to go up," Mary said.

"No, I should. I need to." Despite everything, she wanted to at least say good-bye to him. And she needed closure.

"I'll go with you," Kay offered.

Jacqueline met her eyes, smiling gratefully.

"We're sitting right there," Mary whispered, pointing.

Jacqueline and Kay walked down the aisle with Rose following a few steps behind them. Jacqueline heard quiet murmurs, and she envisioned all eyes on her. Much to her relief, Kay reached out and linked arms with her, squeezing lightly on her hand.

Jacqueline was surprised at the emotion she felt upon seeing her father. He looked nothing like the man she remembered. He had aged dramatically in fifteen years, the dark hair now mostly gray. She stood still, unaware that she was tightly holding Kay's hand, squeezing almost painfully.

"It's okay," Kay whispered.

Then she felt Rose walk next to her, felt Rose's hand at her elbow, and she relaxed.

"He looks much older," she finally said, quietly.

"Yes."

She wanted to reach out and touch him, but she dared not. Instead, she lowered her head and closed her eyes. *I wish we'd had some time to talk. I think maybe you'd have liked me now. I . . . I made out okay.*

Kay watched the woman beside her, wondering what thoughts were going through her mind. She also wondered what most of the congregation was thinking. She could hear the whispering. No doubt Jackie heard it, too. But Kay didn't care what they were thinking. She only knew she had this overwhelming urge to offer Jackie comfort, strength. Not that she thought Jackie needed strength. She exuded nothing but confidence. She always had.

Jackie felt Kay's hand squeeze her own and she straightened up, looking at Kay, meeting her blue eyes and nodding. They turned and made their way back down the aisle. Jacqueline looked around, seeing vaguely familiar faces and noting that, indeed, all eyes were focused on her. And on Kay, who still held her hand tightly. She wondered what they all must be thinking. But she didn't care in the least what they were thinking.

She sat down next to Mary, and Kay and Rose followed suit. She was very thankful for their support, doubting that she could have done this without them. Before long, a hush fell as Brother Garner walked to the pulpit. He, too, had aged, but that voice, she would never forget it.

"We are here today to say good-bye to a great man, Nicolas Keys, taken prematurely from this life, only to be reunited with his God."

Jacqueline shifted uneasily. She felt out of place. She didn't belong in this town or this church. In fact, she'd not stepped foot inside a church since the last time she'd been here, fifteen years ago. She listened absently as Brother Garner read the obituary, noting without surprise that her name was not included with the surviving family members. Then her Uncle Walter walked to the front, unfolding a piece of paper that he took from his coat pocket. He began to read, listing off the great attributes and accomplishments of her father, all stated without emotion. And this was his only brother. God, what a screwed up family.

She felt a soft hand take hers, felt fingers entwine with her own. She turned, meeting Kay's eyes.

"You okay?"

Jacqueline nodded, then bent closer to whisper into Kay's ear. "Thank you for being here. I think I may have already run out if you weren't."

"They can't hurt you."

"No, they can't."

The service was all a blur to Jacqueline—the eulogy, the singing, the sermon. She was aware of Kay's presence, of the hand that took hers occasionally, of eyes on her. Then it was over, and she stood with the others, walking silently out of the church. Some people turned to stare, those vaguely familiar faces. She thought she recognized Rene Turner. The Turners had been friends of her parents and Rene had been a cheerleader, a path her mother had hoped Jacqueline would follow.

"You remember where the cemetery is?" John asked.

"Not really, no."

"You can follow us."

"I'll ride with her," Kay offered.

"Thanks."

"It'll all be over soon," Mary promised, lightly patting Jacqueline's arm as she walked past.

"I'm going to beg out of this part," Rose said. "I'm sure the café will be busy with everyone in town. I better get back to help Mama."

"Thanks for coming, Rose."

"No problem. I always liked your father. You'll make sure my sister gets home okay?"

"Of course."

Jacqueline and Kay watched the others walk away, then looked at each other.

"Come on," Jacqueline said, motioning with her head toward her car. "I can't wait to get out of these clothes."

"Yeah? Not used to the suits, are you?"

"Shorts. Jeans. Not much else."

"Why doesn't that surprise me?"

Jacqueline stopped next to the shiny black car, gallantly opening the passenger door for Kay.

"Wow," Kay murmured, running her hand over the smooth leather.

"It's just a rental."

"Showing off?" Kay guessed.

"Maybe."

They crept along in line with the other cars, Jacqueline obediently turning on her lights like the others.

"Was that hard for you?" Kay asked.

"Odd. Not necessarily hard." Jacqueline glanced at Kay. "I felt out of place."

"I imagine you did. Could you hear the whispers?"

"Oh, yeah. Loud and clear."

"Did it bother you?"

"No. I came for the funeral out of a sense of duty, I suppose. I don't really give a damn what anyone thinks of me."

"No, I don't suppose you do."

"Do you blame me?"

"Of course not. Actually, I'm surprised you came back at all. I'm even more surprised you're going to the cemetery."

"Isn't it expected?" Jacqueline asked.

"Expected? The immediate family, yes. Most people go out of curiosity. With your mother not being there, a lot of the drama is gone."

Jacqueline paused, drumming her fingers on the steering wheel. "I hardly consider myself immediate family. I wasn't even mentioned in the obituary. Fifteen years removed from their lives, nearly the same amount of time I lived here, I really feel nothing, Kay."

"I don't blame you. I take it your mother wasn't exactly thrilled to see you today?"

"Despite being in a body cast and lying there helpless, she was her usual bitchy self. In fact, she threatened to call security to have me tossed out."

"Amazing. To think you're her only child."

"Amazing, yes." Jacqueline looked in the mirror, then back at Kay. "Listen, I don't really want to listen to more bullshit from Brother Garner. Let's skip the cemetery."

"Skip it? Jackie, we can't skip it. For one thing, we're already in line."

"Well, then let's get out of line." Jacqueline turned sharply left, cutting across the other lane to take a side street. "Where the hell are we, anyway?"

"You are *so* bad! Can you imagine what they are saying about us now?"

"I don't really care. I just want to get out of this damn suit and into jeans." Jacqueline turned again, going back toward the church. "If I remember correctly, there's a back road."

"Yes. It comes out behind the high school."

"Ah, yes. I remember now." Jacqueline sped up, the road deserted now as the funeral procession had left. "So, who's manning your store today?"

"Frannie. A high school student who helps me on Saturdays and during the summer."

"You make a good living?"

"I do okay."

"Is she expecting you this afternoon?"

"I told her I would stop by later. Why?"

"Wanna play hooky?"

"And what? Go swimming out at Blue Hole?" Kay laughed. "I got grounded two weeks because of that."

"And I got my car taken away."

"For only one week, if I recall."

"That was torture enough, having my mother drive me to school every day."

Kay smiled. "I would like to spend some time with you, though."

"Me, too. Got any ideas?"

"Well, it's sunny and warm." Kay raised her eyebrows mischievously. "Wanna go to the river?"

"Kay Garland, you are a troublemaker! The last time you talked me into going to the river, we got caught drinking beer and smoking pot."

"*You* brought the beer *and* the pot!"

Jacqueline laughed. "God, it's so good to see you." She reached across the console and lightly squeezed Kay's arm.

"Yeah, I know. I've really missed you."

"Yeah. We never got a chance to say good-bye, you know. It was like . . . like I was just ripped away from here and . . ."

"I know, Jackie. I . . . I cried at first. I didn't understand how you could just leave without saying anything to me. But Mama . . . she explained everything. About your mother and why they sent you away. And then I got pissed that you'd let them do that. And when you didn't write or call, I got angrier. I felt like our friendship didn't mean anything to you."

"Oh, Kay. I'm so sorry. It wasn't like that. I thought about contacting you so many times over the years, but . . . well, the more time that passed, the more I convinced myself that you wouldn't want to hear from me. Hell, for all I knew, you wouldn't even remember me."

"I know you don't truly believe that, not after all we shared. You were my *best* friend."

"Your best friend who turned out to be gay and didn't have the courage to tell you."

"We were just kids. But Jackie, you could have trusted me with anything."

Anything? She wondered what Kay's reaction would be if she confessed it was sexual feelings she had for Kay that finally opened her eyes. Jacqueline looked at her old friend, the light brown hair hanging loosely over her expressive eyebrows, shadowing the blue eyes that Jacqueline used to know by heart. Without thought, Jacqueline reached over and brushed the hair away, revealing those eyes to her. They were the same caring, honest eyes she remembered.

"I was scared to tell you," Jacqueline finally admitted. "Hell, I was scared about everything. And with good reason, it turned out."

Jacqueline slowed as they reached the country club, the guard waving her through. Kay got out when Jacqueline parked, her eyes moving over the manicured lawn and up to the house. She silently followed Jackie to the door, waiting as she unlocked the front door and motioned for Kay to enter.

"Nice."

"Yeah, it is. Look around. It will take me a second to change."

Kay watched Jackie walk away, then moved into the living room, looking around at the pictures and personal items there.

She'd known the Lawrences all her life, but had never once been inside their home. The Lawrences and Garlands had not exactly moved in the same social circles. In fact, she found it odd that she and Jackie had even become friends in the first place. The Keys were the most powerful family in Pine Springs. Hardly the kind of family Kay would feel comfortable with. But she and Jackie had just clicked, ever since they were kids. At first, Mrs. Keys had tried to keep Jacqueline away, steering her toward the kids whose parents were members of the country club. But, as Kay had said several times, Jackie was stubborn. Finally, Mrs. Keys had given up, allowing Jackie to stay overnight often on weekends with the Garlands. It was a habit that continued all through high school. Kay had been content having Jackie as her only friend, shunning most of the other girls to spend time with Jacqueline. She remembered how jealous she felt when Jackie started dating Danny Thornton. That was the only reason she ever agreed to go out with Billy Ray Renfro in the first place.

She groaned, not wanting to bring up those memories. Not yet. Despite what she'd told Rose, she was not over it. She doubted she ever would be. It was the most horrible time in her life, a time when she needed Jackie the most. But Jackie had vanished, without a word.

"Why are you frowning?"

Kay turned, finding a more familiar Jackie standing there in jeans and T-shirt. She was so comfortable looking. She always had been. The cute teenager she'd known had grown into a very attractive woman. However, the teenager she knew would never have ironed a T-shirt or tucked it into jeans. She smiled. "Feel better?"

"Much." Jacqueline walked closer. "Why the frown?"

"I was just thinking."

"About?"

"You. Me. High school."

"Ah. Well, how about we pick up some *refreshments* before we go to the river, huh? We can talk. It'll be just like old times."

"Yes. I'd like that."

CHAPTER TEN

The river road was as Jacqueline remembered it. Bumpy. The Lexus took every pothole in stride, and she drove them down to the end, turning off on a side road that followed the river a ways before ending.

"It looks exactly the same," Jacqueline said. "Just more trash."

"Yeah. More trash. But I don't think the high school kids come here as much as we did in those days."

"Well, they don't know what they're missing."

Instead of beer, they decided on wine, both agreeing they'd grown up enough to progress to wine when sneaking off to the river. Jacqueline grabbed the bottle and the corkscrew they bought, and Kay brought the blanket she'd tossed in the back seat when they'd stopped by her house to change. They both smiled as they walked down the same path they'd taken hundreds of times before. As Jackie had said, not much had changed. The forest opened up right at the river's edge and they found a spot under one of the large pine trees. Kay spread the blanket and they both sat cross-legged, looking out over the water.

"Listen," Jacqueline whispered. "So quiet." The gentle flow of the river was silent in the forest, and above them, cardinals sang.

"You miss this? The quiet?"

"Yes. Although I don't really live in the city. I bought a condo in Monterey, so my quiet is listening to the ocean."

"It must be beautiful."

Jackie smiled. "Some days beautiful, some days foggy. But the sound is always the same. Once you've lived by the ocean and fallen asleep to the sound of waves crashing on shore, you find there is no more comforting sound than that. It's endless," she said quietly. "The day that sound stops is the day the world ends."

Kay watched as Jacqueline opened the wine while she spoke, her quiet words echoing in the forest. She then poured wine into the plastic cups they had snatched at the liquor store. She took one from Jackie, smiling before taking a sip.

After only a few moments, Jacqueline reached over and tapped Kay's leg. "Now, we're alone, no interruptions. It's time you told me one of those *long stories* you've been holding back on."

"I see you're as impatient as ever."

"Why don't you go to church anymore?"

"Why don't you?" Kay countered.

"Well, let's see." Jacqueline leaned her head back, looking to the top of the pines and into the blue sky beyond. "How about because my mother took me to Brother Garner to have him heal me of my sickness, to have him pray the devil out of me? Now *that* was a fun time, let me tell you. Or how about the fact that I'm destined to spend eternity in hell, paying for my sin of loving women instead of men?" Jacqueline met Kay's eyes. "Or maybe I'm just afraid of lightning bolts!"

"Okay. You got me beat."

"Tell me, Kay."

Their eyes held, blue on blue, and Kay felt the weight lift somewhat from her heart. For so long, she'd kept it all inside, never talking it out with anyone, just skimming over the surface with

Rose, with her mother. She'd always insisted she was fine, just fine. But the crystal blue eyes she remembered were there, looking into her soul as they'd always been able to do, seeing things no one else was ever able to see.

"I . . . I was dating Billy Ray Renfro when you left, remember?"

"Yeah, I remember."

"Well, I guess about a year after high school, everyone started asking when we were going to get married. He was the only one I'd ever dated."

"Why? As beautiful as you were, as you are, I never understood why you picked him."

Kay shrugged. She didn't remember ever being overly interested in boys then. There was just Jackie. That was enough.

"I don't know why, Jackie. It just happened. And when he asked me to marry him, I thought, what else did I have? I was still stuck here in Pine Springs, you were gone, and there was no one else. He was working at the mill then, had a steady job, so I said yes."

"Forgive me, but I always thought he was a loser."

Kay laughed. "Well, you were right."

"I'm sorry. If I'd been here, I would never have let you marry him."

"Oh, yeah? At the wedding, when Brother Garner asked for objections, you'd have stood up?"

"Absolutely."

Kay laughed. "Yes, I believe you would have."

"I'm sorry. Go on."

"Oh, Jackie, this is hard for me, you know."

Jacqueline reached over and took her hand. "Tell me what happened."

Kay watched as their fingers entwined, remembering all those other times when they'd come here to talk, how easy it was to talk to Jackie, to tell her things she would never consider telling anyone else. She looked up then, meeting blue eyes. How was it that she felt so comfortable telling Jackie things, but Jacqueline had been terrified to talk to her about the most important thing in her life?

"Why couldn't you tell me, Jackie?"

Jacqueline frowned and nervously brushed the hair over her ears. "I thought this was your time to talk."

"It is. But we always talked about everything, Jackie. *Everything.* Why couldn't you tell me about that?"

"You know what? Maybe some day I'll tell you about it. But not now. Now we're talking about you."

Kay nodded. "Fair enough." She leaned forward. "Don't think I won't hold you to it." She cleared her throat and took a deep breath. "Billy Ray was violent," she blurted out. She felt her fingers being squeezed by Jacqueline, and she squeezed back. "It's okay, Jackie. I knew it going in, I think. He was . . . he was never gentle, you know. And it just kept getting worse and worse. I couldn't seem to do anything right. Nothing was ever good enough. Dinner was late, and he got mad. I had dinner ready early, and it got cold. Just little stupid things, but he'd get angry and . . . hit me. At first, a slap here and there. Then, well, it just kept getting worse."

Jacqueline swallowed the lump in her throat, watching her friend as tears escaped and slid down her cheeks. Jacqueline reached out and brushed them away.

"You never told anyone?"

"No. I was too ashamed. If I had bruises, I made up some excuse."

"Bastard," Jackie whispered.

"He came home really drunk one night. Which wasn't unusual. But he wanted to have sex. I couldn't sleep with him. I hadn't been able to sleep with him since, God, since nearly the beginning. I wasn't in love with him. I couldn't stand his touch. And I should have left, I should have told someone . . . Rose, my mother, someone who would have talked to me and made me leave him. But I didn't. I stayed because that was what I thought I should do."

"Jesus, I'm so sorry I wasn't here for you."

"That night, when I refused, he took a chair and smashed it over my head. And he kicked me and hit me and . . . and then he raped me," she finished in a whisper.

"Oh, sweetheart." Jacqueline moved to her, taking Kay in her arms and holding her tight.

Kay clung to her, crying. She'd never told anyone he'd raped her. She'd begged the doctor not to tell her mother. Just the assault was enough to lock him up, just the assault was enough to make her hang her head in shame. She didn't want the whole town to know her own husband had raped her.

"I don't remember a whole lot of that night. When I came to, I was in the hospital, and he was in jail. I spent one week in the hospital, and he spent two years in prison."

"Where is the bastard now?"

"I'm not sure. His family moved away after it happened. I know he was in Houston for awhile. I think he got into some trouble there, too."

"That son of a bitch. If I'd been here, I would have killed him."

Kay smiled through her tears. "Yes, I think you very well might have." She pulled completely out of Jacqueline's embrace, but didn't release her hands. Kay cleared her throat, then continued. "You asked me why I didn't go to church anymore. I don't go to church because of Brother Garner."

"I don't understand."

"When the hitting first started, I went to see him. I thought I could talk to him confidentially, perhaps get some advice."

"And?"

"And the advice I got was to be a better wife and to obey my husband."

"Well fuck. That's it? You were the cause, not the victim?"

"Yeah. It was my fault that he hit me." She smiled weakly. "I wasn't a good enough wife."

Jacqueline just shook her head, watching Kay as her eyes shimmered with tears. She knew in her heart that if she'd stayed, she never would have allowed Kay to marry Billy Ray. But how arrogant is that? As if she could control these things. She wondered, if she'd stayed, if she would have been able to continue seeing Kay, being friends with her, without confessing her feelings? And then what? Kay would have been shocked, no doubt. She probably wouldn't have wanted to see Jacqueline anymore, would have kept her at a distance until their friendship faded into the past. And Jacqueline would have ended up leaving anyway.

"What are you thinking about?"

Jacqueline looked up, unafraid to meet Kay's eyes. "Nothing."

"Nothing?"

"Okay. I was thinking that if I'd stayed here, I never would have allowed you to marry him. And then I was thinking that I didn't control you and you could marry whomever you damn well pleased."

Kay looked down at their hands that were still entwined. She pulled hers away finally, brushing the hair away from her eyes. "Not that I blame you in the least, Jackie, but the only reason I began dating Billy Ray in the first place was because you were seeing Daniel Thornton."

"What? I wasn't really seeing him, Kay."

"Of course you were. Friday nights when you and I used to be together, you were with him. After football games, you went out with him and his friends." Kay shrugged. "I was—" *Jealous? God, how would that sound?* "I was lonely."

"I went out with him because it was expected. Our parents pushed us together. But, it was then that I realized I didn't like boys. Oh, we kissed a few times, made out, but I never slept with him. He really didn't try all that hard."

"Well, I guess we know why. Did you know then that he was gay?"

"Are you kidding? I hardly knew *I* was."

"You heard what happened to him?"

"Yeah. Mr. Lawrence told me. We were talking about how my parents had my marriage all arranged, and he told me that Danny had died."

"Yes. His parents took it very hard. I've always wondered if it was because he died or because he was gay and the whole town knew. People can be funny about those things, you know."

"You're telling me!"

Kay laughed. "Tell me about your love life."

"Change of subject?"

"I told you about my awful marriage. What about you? Is there someone waiting for you in California?"

"No, I . . . no. I live alone."

Kay raised her eyebrows. "Surely there's been someone?"

Jacqueline shook her head. "I haven't met anyone that I wanted to . . . live with, be with. I mean, I date, but . . ."

"You haven't fallen in love?" Kay guessed.

Jacqueline drew her knees up, resting her cheek there as she looked at Kay. She recalled how her heart would race when they were together. How, when they slept together, she would ache with the longing to wrap herself around Kay, to touch her. And how, at times like this, when they were alone, talking, the desire to kiss Kay was nearly too much for her. In love? Maybe. Or maybe just the feelings associated with that very first crush. But God, at night, she would dream of them together, dream of Kay coming to her with as much desire as Jacqueline had for Kay.

"Or maybe you have," Kay said quietly.

Jacqueline blinked. "What?"

Kay smiled. "Your eyes got all dreamy. Were you thinking about her?"

Jacqueline blushed and looked away. "Yes, actually, I was."

"Who is she?"

"No, it was someone from a long time ago. I never . . . I never was . . . shit, it doesn't matter." Jacqueline poured more wine.

Kay was quiet, thinking. All those years ago, she had been devastated to lose her best friend, knowing in her heart that she would never be as close to another woman as she'd been Jackie. Now, here she was, sitting at their favorite spot near the river, sharing wine in plastic cups with the one person she was certain she would never see again.

"You know, I took a lot of heat after you left," Kay admitted.

"How so?"

"Well, it was no secret that you spent most weekends at our house. I was teased mercilessly for weeks afterward."

"I'm so sorry, Kay. I can imagine what they were saying to you."

Kay laughed. "That's just it. I was so naïve about things, I didn't really know *what* they were saying. Mama had to explain to me exactly what a lesbian was." She laughed again. "I told her she was wrong. You couldn't possibly be a lesbian because you'd never once tried to kiss me."

Jacqueline spit out the wine she had just sipped, coughing as she swallowed wrong. Kay tapped her back until she caught her breath. Jacqueline turned slowly, knowing her face was red with embarrassment. But Kay's eyes twinkled in amusement and Jacqueline relaxed.

"Funny."

Kay laughed, punching Jacqueline's arm, enjoying her embarrassment. She never once had known Jackie to be flustered. "For awhile afterward, I always wondered why you hadn't," Kay finally confessed. In truth, it had bothered her a lot. She and Jackie were so close, closer than sisters.

"I . . . I would *never* have done that, Kay. Hell, I was confused but not . . . not like that," she lied. *Shit*. "You know that, right? You were my best friend. I would never have destroyed that."

"I know, Jackie. We were just kids."

"It's probably best that I left. Your reputation would have been shot to hell if I'd stayed."

"Like I cared what this town thought."

"Rene Turner?"

"Rene? Yes, she was the worst. I couldn't even possibly repeat everything she said to me after you left." Kay smiled, meeting Jackie's eyes. "Rumor was you'd made a play for her, and she turned you down."

"Are you kidding me?"

"She said you ripped her blouse in the locker room."

Jackie nodded, then started laughing, the long ago memory surfacing.

"Well, well, well. Jackie Keys. Or should I say Jack Keys?"

Jackie tossed her towel into the bin, ignoring Rene.

"I guess this means Kay is your girlfriend?"

Jackie turned on her, her eyes flashing. "You leave Kay out of this."

"Protective, aren't we? How sweet."

"What do you want, Rene?"

"Why nothing. It's just that everyone is all surprised. I say, why should they be? You and Kay have been inseparable for years. I guess pretending to date Danny and Billy Ray, you thought no one would know."

"I don't know what you're talking about. Kay and I are friends."

"Oh, please."

Jackie stood up straight and took a step toward Rene. "You leave Kay alone. If you don't, I'll tell everyone that you and I knew each other really well, Rene. Really well."

"What are you saying?"

"I'll tell them I fucked you right here in the locker room, that's what I'm saying. You leave Kay alone."

Rene laughed. "Like anyone would believe you."

"Oh, yeah?" Jackie lunged forward, grabbing Rene's shirt. "I was an animal, Rene. You couldn't resist." She ripped opened Rene's blouse, revealing the lacy bra beneath.

"You bitch!" Rene stepped back, away from Jackie. "You pervert, how dare you?"

"I can spread rumors just like you can, Rene. So unless you want the town to think you were my first, you leave Kay out of this."

"You're sick. Sick!"

Jackie smiled. "And you're a fucking bitch. Get out of here."

"Why are you laughing?"

"I did rip her blouse. And if I remember correctly, she was wearing a very attractive lacy bra."

Kay covered her mouth. "Are you kidding? You really ripped her blouse?"

Jacqueline nodded. "She came into the locker room that last week. She was talking about me and you. I didn't want her spreading rumors about you, so I told her I'd tell everyone that she and I went at it in the locker room if she said anything about you."

Kay smiled sweetly and took Jackie's hand. "Well, you must

71

have scared her. She didn't say a word about me until after you were gone."

"What a bitch she was."

"Still is. She married Jonathan Wells. He's vice president at the bank."

"So she thinks she's hot shit?"

"They built a house at the country club last year. I see her at Christmas when she comes to the store to buy new ornaments."

"Well, that's big of her to patronize your store."

"Yes, it is." Kay tilted her head, squeezing Jackie's fingers with her hand. "Tell me, Jackie."

Jackie shrugged. "What do you want to know?"

"Tell me what really happened. All I know is, I went to school one morning and you weren't there. And then the rumors."

Jacqueline leaned back against the pine, her eyes closing as she remembered the scene in her mother's kitchen.

"I know you want to move away to go to college, Jacqueline, but you must think about your future here. Daniel Thornton's parents have agreed, once you marry, to give you twenty acres of their property. You can build out there. I think it's acceptable if you want to commute to the junior college until the marriage, but after that, there's really no need. Daniel will work in the mill. Your father will make sure he's promoted, of course."

"Excuse me? You have not only my marriage planned, but also my future husband's employment? Well, that's really romantic, Mother."

"Romantic? Jacqueline, your father is the mayor of this town. The mill employs more than half of the men in the county. There's no time for romance. The Thorntons, as well as owning thousands of acres of timber, are the wealthiest family in the county, besides our own. It's only natural that we merge."

"Merge?" Jackie tossed her sandwich on the table. "I don't know what you've been planning, Mother, but I'm not marrying Danny Thornton. I don't love him."

"Love? Jacqueline, it's high time you realize that love has absolutely nothing to do with it. It's all a business."

Jackie shook her head. "No. I'm not marrying him. I'm not staying in this town. I'm going off to college. I have my own dreams, my own life. I'm sorry, but it doesn't involve Danny Thornton and Pine Springs."

Her mother smiled, the smile that Jackie had grown to hate over the years. The victory smile.

"You don't really have a choice, Jacqueline dear. You have no money. Your father will simply refuse to send you to college." She nodded. "You'll marry Daniel Thornton."

"The hell I will! I don't even like boys! I'm not going to marry one." Jackie fled out the door, childishly grabbing her bike instead of her car keys.

She slowly opened her eyes to blue sky. The river flowed past, sloshing quietly against the bank. The gentle breeze rustled the pines, muting the calls of the birds. All except the jays. They flew low over the water, congregating on the other side, disrupting the silence along the river bank.

"Tell me," Kay said again.

Jacqueline looked at Kay, their eyes locking.

"Tell me what happened."

Jacqueline shrugged. "My mother was planning my wedding to Danny Thornton. She was telling me how *beneficial* it would be to both families. I told her I wanted to go to college, I wanted to move out of Pine Springs. It didn't matter. My future had already been decided." Jacqueline poured the last of the wine into her cup, looking apologetically at Kay.

"I'm good. Go on."

"I told her I wasn't going to marry him. I told her I didn't like boys." Jacqueline sipped from her cup, her eyes watching the river as it flowed past. "I left, got on my bike and rode for miles, it seemed like. When I got home, my father was there. They wanted to know exactly what I meant when I said I didn't like boys." Jacqueline shifted, moving against the tree. "I told them I was gay." Jackie closed her eyes, remembering her mother's shocked expression and the disappointment in her father's eyes.

"At first, my mother accused me of making it up just to punish her. My father said there was to be no discussion on the matter. I *was* marrying Daniel Thornton and that was final." Jacqueline was aware of Kay's soft hand taking her own. "I told him it wasn't final. We talked . . . well, mostly they screamed at me," Jacqueline said. "I went to school like normal. It was just a couple of weeks before graduation. Then one day, my mother hauled me off to see Brother Garner. He was going to cure me, to exorcise the evil within me."

"I'm sorry," Kay whispered.

"I was scared to death," Jacqueline breathed. "Scared of him, scared of what was going to happen to me."

"Why didn't you tell me?"

"And I was scared of you too," Jacqueline admitted. "I was scared you'd leave me, abandon me."

"Oh, Jackie." Kay moved closer, wrapping her arms around Jacqueline. "I would never have abandoned you."

"One morning, I'm dressed for school, and my mother comes into my room with this little backpack. She tossed it at me and told me to pack some clothes. Told me that since I wasn't *normal*, they had no use for me. She drove me to the bus stop over in Cherokee. I guess she didn't want anyone in Pine Springs to see her. She bought me a ticket to Dallas and gave me a hundred dollars. She told me not to come back until I'd come to my senses."

"My God," Kay murmured.

Jacqueline shook her head, burying her face against Kay, accepting the comfort Kay's arms offered. "I was so scared, Kay. I had no idea what I was going to do."

"You could have called me."

Jacqueline pulled away. "Kay, I wasn't even eighteen. My parents had just disowned me, had sent me away in shame. There was no way I was going to call you. For all I knew, it was all over town, all over school. And I didn't want you to hate me."

"I swear, you were always so stubborn."

Jacqueline shook her head. "I just couldn't take a chance with you."

"So you just left me," Kay stated quietly.

Their eyes held, both questioning. Then Jacqueline's cell interrupted the silence. She grabbed the phone from her jeans and checked caller ID. She grinned. "Busted."

"Who?"

"It's the Lawrence's number," she said before connecting. "Jacqueline Keys."

"Jacqueline? It's Mary Lawrence. Are you okay?"

"I'm fine, Mary. Just . . . Kay and I are catching up."

"We were worried when you didn't show up at the cemetery."

"I'm sorry about that, but Kay convinced me to play hooky."

Kay punched her arm. "I did not," she hissed.

"I decided to skip out, Mary. I'm sorry, but I'd had enough. So, we came down here to the river where we used to come when we were kids. Just wanted to visit some, have some time alone."

"I understand. You might have Kay call the café. John called there looking for you when you didn't show up. I think he got Rose and her mother worried."

Jacqueline nodded. "We're about to head back. We'll swing by there."

"What?" Kay asked when Jacqueline had disconnected.

"Oh, they were rounding up a posse. Didn't know anyone would miss us."

Kay rolled her eyes. It was just like old times. She took Jacqueline's offered hand and let herself be pulled to her feet.

"Come on, Miss Garland. Let's get you back before your mother has my hide."

On the drive back, Kay again brought up the subject of Jacqueline staying with her. "You know, my offer still stands."

"What's that?"

"If you want to stay with me. I've got an extra room that's just going to waste."

"Not afraid of the local gossip?"

"Just the fact that you're back in town is gossip enough. I doubt anyone will care where you're staying."

"Well, you know, I think I might just take you up on that, if you're serious."

"I'm very serious. I would love for you to stay with me. It'll give us more time to catch up. Because, first of all, you've not told me a thing about your life."

"Haven't I?"

"No, not really. You're very good at skirting questions."

"Okay. I'll let you grill me with questions if you'll cook. I haven't had a home-cooked meal in years."

"Well, you may regret that. I'm afraid Rose inherited all my mother's culinary skills."

CHAPTER ELEVEN

Kay waved as the black Lexus pulled away, then walked into the café only to be confronted with both Rose and her mother.

"Where the hell have you been?"

"I wasn't aware that you were keeping tabs on me, Rose."

"Of course not, Kay, we were just worried," her mother said, taking in her jeans and the blanket that was folded under her arm. She raised her eyebrows.

"We went to the river."

"The river? You're not in high school anymore, Kay! You can't just go sneaking off like that and expect us not to worry."

"If you use this tactic on your kids, Rose, no wonder they like me better."

"Her father was being buried, and you skip out to go to the river?"

"Yes, actually. And it wasn't my idea."

Her mother laughed. "It never was. Always Jackie's fault, if I recall."

"She's been back two days, and you're already grounded," Rose tossed over her shoulder as she walked back around the counter.

Kay turned to her mother. "We just wanted to talk." She paused. "I told her about Billy Ray."

"Oh my. What did she do?"

Kay smiled. "Threatened to kill him."

"Yes, she was always your protector. But you talked? That's good. Rose seems to think that you've kept it all inside. You certainly haven't told us all that happened. That can't be good, Kay, keeping it inside like that."

"I know, Mama. But some things, I didn't want to share with you or Rose. I've always been able to talk to Jackie."

"Even after all this time?"

"Yeah. Obviously, we've both changed, but that . . . that connection is still there. In fact, she's going to stay with me while she's here."

"She is? Well, good. It'll be nice for you to have company."

"We need a cook back here," Rose called.

"The boss is cracking her whip," her mother said with a wink. "You going to stay?"

"I was hoping Rose would run me home."

"It'll be another hour before we get cleaned up," her mother warned.

"That's okay. I'll help."

Later, as Kay was helping Rose load the dishwashers, Rose nudged her. "Mama says you told Jackie about Billy Ray."

"I swear, you can't keep anything from the two of you."

"I can't believe you went to the river," Rose said. "When's the last time you've been out there?"

Kay smiled. "The last time Jackie took me there, I guess."

"You've missed her, huh?"

"Yeah. More than I thought. It's like we just picked up where we left off, you know?"

"I was always jealous of your relationship," Rose admitted. "I never had a close friend like that. Not like you two." Rose closed the door to the dishwasher and turned it on, the swooshing sound of the water familiar to both of them. "And I know that since Jackie left, you haven't had another close friendship."

"No, I haven't."

"It's strange. Greg and I have a handful of friends, other couples with kids, but you've been my closest friend. For you, well, I couldn't replace Jackie. You've been more or less alone. I worry about you. I wish you would go out, date—something."

"I'm fine, Rosie. Quit worrying about me."

"Your highlight of the week is when you get to babysit my kids. You're going to end up like old Ms. Cutter, I just know it."

"Why does everyone call her that? She's barely sixty."

"She's been here forever, and she's always been alone, that's why."

"Maybe she just doesn't date anyone here in town. Maybe she's got someone outside of town."

Rose put her hands on her hips. "What are you saying?"

"Nothing. Never mind."

Rose narrowed her eyes. "You've met someone in another town? Who is he?"

Kay rolled her eyes. Rose had a one-track mind. "I've not met anyone, Rose. Trust me, if I do, you'll be the first to know."

"Uh-huh." Rose took her apron off and wadded it up, shoving it in her bag. "You want to come over? Greg was picking up a pizza."

"Can't. I'm having company."

"Oh?"

"Jackie. She's going to stay with me."

"Yeah?" Rose watched her then smiled. "You can both come over."

"What? And fight your kids for pizza? No thanks."

Rose smiled. "I'm glad your friend is back, Kay. But you know she'll be leaving again, right?"

"I know. It's just good to see her."

"Yeah, it is. Well, come on. I'll drop you off."

CHAPTER TWELVE

"I like your house," Jacqueline said. She pulled her chair closer to Kay's up on the back deck and sat down. "How long have you had it?"

"Two years this summer. I rented after . . . well, after the thing with Billy Ray. Mama wanted me to stay with them, but I needed some place of my own. The store was doing well, and I managed to save quite a bit." She took a sip of the sweet tea that Jackie made for her and continued. "I never told anyone this, but I seriously thought of moving out of town and starting over, you know. But, my whole family is here. I'd just be lost."

"Where were you going to go?"

"I'd thought about Dallas. But then, what would I do? My store's doing well here, and it just didn't make sense to sell it."

"You remember how we used to crawl up into that big oak tree at your parents' house? We talked about what we were going to do when we got out of this town. We had such big plans."

"Yes, we did. And you made it out and have done quite well for yourself. I was so proud of you. When we went to the movies and I saw your name up there, I was so happy. And sad."

"Sad?"

"Sad that you weren't in my life anymore. Sad that we didn't get to say good-bye."

"Ah, Kay, you didn't cry for me, did you?" Jacqueline asked quietly.

"For you or myself, I don't know which. But yes."

"I was . . . I was so scared when I got off that bus in Dallas. I'd had almost four hours to think about it, but I still didn't have a clue as to what I would do. Part of me wanted to go back home and beg them to let me stay. But the stubborn part of me wouldn't allow it." Jacqueline stretched her legs out, enjoying the coolness of the evening. Her eyes scanned Kay's small backyard, noting absently that Kay might not have gotten her mother's culinary skills, but she most certainly got her green thumb.

"What did you do?"

"Got a cheap motel. I think the guy there thought I was a runaway. I'm surprised he didn't call the cops. But I only had a hundred dollars and knew that wouldn't get me far. I spent that first night alone, hungry and scared. I had the TV on, and they were doing this piece on some actress in Hollywood. I don't even remember who it was now. But she was saying how she'd come to Los Angeles without a dime in her pocket and how she worked as a waitress while she tried to land a role." Jacqueline shrugged. "I thought, hell, I can do that."

"In Dallas?"

"No. I thought if I was really going to get away, hell, might as well go for the top. So, I got a bus ticket as far as Phoenix. That was all the money I had, except twenty bucks. I wanted to keep something to eat on, you know. When I got to Phoenix, I hitched a ride to Los Angeles. Took me three more days to get there."

"Oh, Jackie. Anything could have happened. You could have been—"

"I know. But, I didn't really care at the time. Besides, luck was on my side. The last guy to pick me up owned a restaurant. He put me to work right away."

"Where did you live?"

"I stayed at the Salvation Army shelter for awhile, but it was kinda scary. Finally, one of the girls there at the restaurant let me bunk with her." Jacqueline blushed. Her first sexual experience. God, it had been awful. She didn't even like the girl all that much.

"What?"

"Nothing. We . . . well, we kinda became involved. But it was a disaster. I moved about six months later, moved in with this gay guy I'd met. Christopher. We're still good friends, actually. He's a cartoonist."

"So? Tell me about college."

"Not much to tell. Started out going to class at night so I could still work. Then, got a night job at a bar so I could go full time. Any spare time I had, I wrote. It was mostly therapy, I think. Christopher knew all about my family, and he liked what I was writing. He was friends with this guy who was friends with Ingrid. She's my agent. He hooked us up and, well, it took off from there."

"*No Place For Family?*"

"Yeah. But it literally took years to finish. Ingrid was pushing, wanting me to get it done right then, but I'd worked too hard with college. I wasn't about to quit. I continued working, going to school and writing when time allowed. Of course, with studying, it didn't leave much time. I finally finished it three months after I graduated." She grinned. "Did I do a good enough job of portraying my mother, you think?"

Kay laughed. "When I was watching the movie, I thought so."

"So, eight years after leaving Pine Springs on a bus, I had enough money to get my own apartment and quit my job and write. End of story."

"End of story?"

"I live in a very nice condo now up the coast in Monterey."

"What else aren't you telling me?"

Jacqueline smiled. "There's no exciting love story, if that's what you're getting at."

"Why not?"

"I told you, I just never met anyone that I wanted to be with."

"Why? Afraid?"

"Afraid? What do you mean?"

"You didn't exactly have a role model to go on. Were you afraid your relationship would end up like your parents?"

"You know, even back then, I think I knew their marriage was rocky. I mean, surely my father couldn't have been happy living with her. At first, I just kinda lumped them together, you know. But as I got older, I realized my father was pretty much in the same boat as I was, being controlled by her. Here he was, the largest employer in the county, the mayor of Pine Springs, and he had to come home to *her*. God, Kay, she was so . . . so superficial, I guess is the word I'm looking for. Everything she did, everything she said was just an act she performed, as if everyone was watching her."

"I know. And for all your brave words, you were terrified of her."

"Yeah, I was. I wanted a family like you had. There was such love there. I mean, even in front of us, your parents showed affection to one another. I can't remember my parents even touching. And you know, they never once told me they loved me. My mother tried her best to teach me how to be a lady, how to be a *Keys*. You know, if you and I hadn't been friends, if I hadn't seen how a real family interacted with one another, I may have thought it was perfectly normal the way my parents were. God knows, most of their friends were exactly the same."

"I know she practically despised me. I was scared to death to go to your house. I was never good enough to be your friend."

"I remember once, she told me that the Garlands weren't of the same social class as us. I didn't understand what she meant. In my young mind, I enjoyed being with you and your family much more than my own. She used to tell me she wished I was more like my cousins who knew their place in this town. It wasn't until we were in high school that it clicked with me what she was trying to tell me, when the Thorntons' kept coming over. I know now that Daniel must have hated it as much as I did."

"Did you ever talk about it?"

"It? No, we were practically forced into dating. And I guess on some level it made sense to me. Until, well, until I realized I didn't really like kissing him."

"When did you know?"

"Know what? That I was gay?"

"Yeah. I mean what, one day you just realized it?"

Jacqueline smiled. "Something like that."

"There's something you're not telling me." Kay leaned closer. "Who was she? One of the girls on the basketball team?"

"No, of course not! Jesus, Kay."

"Then who? Why won't you tell me?"

"Some things are meant to be private."

"Oh, please. We didn't have one single private thing between us."

"Yeah, well, we had this."

Kay laughed. "I got it. Becky Thompson?"

"Good God, no. Becky Thompson?"

"She went off to college in Austin and seldom came home. And as far as I know, she's never married. She's comes home for Christmas and that's it."

"You're reaching here." But Jacqueline laughed. "She's never married, huh? She's not a coach somewhere, is she?"

"As a matter of fact, she is."

"Well, I'll be damned. Becky Thompson." Truth be known, Jacqueline did suspect that Becky was hiding her own secret back then. She was just too scared to approach her.

They were silent for a moment, both shaking the ice in their now empty glasses. Jacqueline finally stood, taking the glass from Kay's hand.

"Another?"

"Yeah. That was good. But you must be starving. I know I am."

"I doubt there are any good restaurants open," Jacqueline teased. "What'd you have in mind?"

"Pizza."

"Pizza? In this town?"

"Of course. We have a pizza place now. And they deliver."

Jacqueline shook her finger at Kay. "I think you promised you'd cook."

"And I warned you, it wasn't my strong suit."

"Okay. Pizza. But tomorrow night, we cook."

"We? Don't tell me you've learned to cook?"

"I can cook quite well, thank you."

"This I can't wait for."

Kay leaned back, relaxing as Jackie went back inside for more tea. God, it was so good to have her back, she thought. She hadn't realized how much she'd missed her. Rose was right. She didn't really have friends. A few from high school that still lived in town. She was friendly enough with them, she supposed. She knew practically everyone in town, in fact. But close friends? No. She had her family, that was it. If she needed something, they would be there, no questions asked. But, after her disastrous marriage, she had retreated even farther, being content with her business and her house and Rose's kids. In reality, she hadn't given a thought to dating. As she'd told Rose, there wasn't anyone in town she was even remotely interested in. Not that some hadn't called. Secretly, she feared she would end up like Ms. Cutter, sixty and still alone. But was it so bad? It beat the hell out of living with Billy Ray Renfro. She would enjoy her time with Jackie, even if it was only for a week. And maybe now, they could keep in touch. Who knows, maybe she would venture to California for a visit, if Jackie offered.

"You look relaxed."

"Mmm. It's a nice evening, isn't it? I don't sit out here much."

"No? I'd be out here all the time. I have a nice sized deck that looks out over Monterey Bay," Jacqueline said as she handed Kay her tea. "On a clear day, I can see across the bay to the Santa Cruz Mountains. But even on foggy days, which are often, I still enjoy sitting out there."

"I remember how much you always liked being outside. Even at night, Mama would have to run us in."

"Yeah, I do miss this. Ingrid's got this great house, up near Santa Rosa. Whenever I'm there, I make her cook outside so we can enjoy the gardens. I've thought about buying something like that, but I just haven't gotten around to it."

"When did you move from Los Angeles?"

"When Ingrid moved to San Francisco. I didn't realize how much time I spent with them. Other than Christopher—and he still lives in LA—they were my social connection. But I didn't want to move to the city, which is where they moved to first. So, Monterey is south of San Francisco, north of LA. Close enough to both. Although, when Ingrid moved to Santa Rosa, that's quite a trek for me now. But I usually spend at least one weekend a month with them."

"She's your agent still?"

"Yeah."

"Are you involved?"

"Ingrid? God, no. I mean, she's a really good friend and even if she was single, no. But she's got a lover. They've been together as long as I've known her."

Kay sighed. "It's a different world, isn't it? I mean, here I am, still so naïve about things."

"It's a different world from Pine Springs, yes. I was thinking, as I was driving out here, that most of the towns were still stuck in the last century. But is that such a bad thing?"

"Isn't it? It's like we haven't grown. We still have the same prejudices that our parents had, that their parents had. It just goes on and on. Change is very slow to come."

"Well, on some levels, I guess it's not necessarily a good thing. But think of Rose's kids. They'll get to grow up in a small town, enjoying pleasures that most city kids have never even heard of."

"But they'll miss out on so much more."

"But they won't really know they're missing out on it, you know. I mean, we didn't know what was out there. We didn't care. But TV and the Internet, that's changed everything. Kids know a lot more now."

"Yeah. They know there's more out there than just Pine Springs. Each year, more and more kids leave, go off to college and don't come back."

"And you wish you were one of them?"

"Sometimes."

Jacqueline studied her. "Why didn't you go to college? It was all we talked about that last year."

"Truthfully? Because you weren't here. I was afraid to go alone."

"Ah, Kay."

"I know. It's silly."

"If I had to do it over again, I'd have called you from Dallas."

"Part of me wishes you had. And part of me is glad you didn't."

"Why is that?"

"You wouldn't be where you are today if you'd called. Everything happens for a reason, Jackie. Here you are, a successful writer. You wouldn't be if you'd stayed. We both know that. You'd be working at the mill, alongside your cousins."

"You're right about that, I suppose. Should I go thank my mother?"

Kay smiled. "No, let's leave her out of this. But speaking of calling, I should order a pizza."

"Actually, I already did. I hope you don't mind."

"Found the number, did you?"

"Plastered right next to the phone. I take it you call often."

"I'm quite friendly with Joni, yes. Although they are probably wondering why a strange woman was calling from my phone."

"I told them you were out on your deck trying to get drunk on spiked tea, and I needed to feed you."

"Funny. I wouldn't doubt it if they called Mama to report me."

"Is it really like that? I mean, does everyone still keep tabs on everyone else?"

"Oh, yes. Right now, in fact, my neighbors are all wondering about the black car in my driveway. First, they'll assume someone in my family bought a new car until they see that it's a Lexus. Then, they'll think I must have a gentleman over. A wealthy gentleman at that."

"And if the car is still here in the morning?"

"Then someone will call the café and casually mention to Mama that a strange black car was at my house *all night*."

"Man, you can't get away with anything."

"No. It drives me crazy sometimes, but I'm used to it."

"It would drive me nuts. I like my privacy."

They saw car lights flash across the trees and a short time later, the doorbell rang.

"Dinner."

"Good. I'm starved," Jacqueline said.

They ate the pizza in the living room, sitting on the floor as they flipped through the channels, never stopping long enough to watch anything. They were just content to be in each other's company. Kay realized once again that Jackie was the one person in the world that she was most comfortable with, even after all this time.

"Can I tell you something?"

"Of course," Kay said, putting her piece of pizza down and wiping her mouth with her napkin. "What is it?"

"Mr. Lawrence gave me a heads up on the will. Seems my father found a way to get back at my mother."

"Oh yeah?"

"Yeah. He left the lumber mill to me, among other things."

"Jesus Christ! Are you serious?"

"Afraid so."

"Oh my God." Then she laughed. "Can you even imagine what your mother will do?"

"Oh, yes. Vividly."

"What about your uncle? Hasn't he always owned a part of it?"

"A part, yes, but my father had controlling interests. I think it was like sixty-forty or something like that. I'm not sure how that came about, though. I mean, their father started it, but my father was the oldest so I assume he left it to him. It wasn't really something that was talked about at home."

"What are you going to do?"

"Officially, the will won't be read until Wednesday. Then, I'm assuming that Uncle Walter will contest it, or so John says. I'm not really sure if he will. From what I remember of Uncle Walter, he didn't really have the business sense that my father had. He ran the operation, and my father took care of the business end of it." Jacqueline shrugged. "He may not even think to contest it. I'm sure my mother will."

"Is that legal, though? I mean, I thought naturally everything just went to your mother."

"Everything would go to the surviving spouse if there was no will. He left her more than fifty percent of his liquid assets, and the house, of course, but left me his portion of the mill and the rest of his estate. I'm sure the fact that I've been estranged from the family gives her something to stand on, but John seemed to think that everything was fine, legally. But, the problem is, I don't want anything, certainly not the lumber mill. I mean, Jesus, I hate logging. Not to mention the fact that I would not have the first clue about the business of running it."

"So? What will you do?"

"I don't know. I haven't really had a chance to absorb it. Part of me wants to take it all, just to piss my mother off."

"You could always sell it," Kay suggested.

"I would only sell it to Uncle Walter. I mean, half this town relies on it for their income. If I sold it to some corporation, who knows what would happen to the jobs."

Kay reached over and squeezed Jacqueline's arm, smiling gently at her. "After everything that's happened to you, you still care about this town, huh?"

"The mill was here long before me. I don't want to be vindictive about it and sell it and not give a damn about the people who depend on it."

"That's what I always loved about you, Jackie. You had more money than anyone else in town and you never once acted like you were any better than anyone else."

Jacqueline looked away, embarrassed.

"I sometimes forgot where you came from. You were just one of us."

"Just because my family had money, didn't make me better. If anything, it made me worse. I didn't learn to appreciate things. It wasn't until I became friends with you, and your family treated me like one of their own, that I realized how precious things were. You never took anything for granted, Kay. Me, I had anything I wanted, anything I asked for. I think the only reason I survived when I was on my own was because of things I learned from your family."

"I can't imagine how you felt, them sending you away with a handful of dollars when they had millions."

"Yeah. Don't think the thought never crossed my mind. My mother spent that much on dinner at the country club, yet she expected me to survive on it."

"Maybe that was the plan. She figured you'd come running home."

"I'm sure of it. And that's why I refused to ever ask them for a penny. I pinched and saved and ate my meals from leftovers at the restaurant, swearing I would never ask them for anything. I struggled, Kay, I won't deny it. And it's not like I'm wealthy now, you know. But I've learned to appreciate money, not take it for granted. I don't live exorbitantly. I mean, I have a modest condo, I drive a car that's five years old. I can afford better, but why? Just to prove it?" Jacqueline shook her head. "If there's one thing I'm working for, it's to buy a house outside of the city, in the foothills, maybe. That's it. Just some . . . *space*. I don't need a bunch of fancy stuff. And I don't need my father's fortune."

"You're afraid it'll change you?"

"Maybe. I don't ever want to be my parents, where the most important thing in life is money, and having more of it. Jesus, Kay, look how much money they had. Did they ever think to build a new library for the town? A youth center? Something to benefit the town? No, they kept it for themselves. And for what? So they could have a bigger house than anyone else? So they could drive a new car every year? And even then, it didn't put a dent in their money."

Kay smiled. "Got you on a roll, huh?"

"I'm sorry. It makes me angry. They had more money than they could possibly spend in two lifetimes, but they didn't do any *good* with it. And now, my mother is going to go absolutely crazy, knowing that part of that wealth is being taken away from her. Not because she needs it. Lord knows, she'll still have plenty."

"Jackie, you need to stop. You're making yourself nuts over this."

"I know. That's why I didn't even want to think about it. I knew this would happen. I'm sorry."

"Don't apologize to me. I agree with you. I always admired your values, Jackie. It was one of the things that drew me to you in the first place."

"I thought it was the fact that I beat up Tommy what's-his-name when he pushed you off the swing."

"Haskell. And yes, you were protecting me."

"The first time of many. You got into more trouble, Kay."

Kay laughed. "I think it was mostly you getting me into trouble."

Jacqueline relaxed, letting the tension of talking about her parents dissolve. Kay was right. She'd gotten on a roll. She reached over and lightly rubbed Kay's knee.

"Kay, I've got to be honest with you. It means so much to me that you've accepted me for what I am. You can't know how good it feels to be back here with you, sharing thoughts and feelings and knowing you won't judge me or think less of me. I have *so* missed talking to you."

Kay felt her eyes mist over at Jacqueline's sincere words. She was the one who should be thanking Jackie. For so many years, she'd felt alone. And now Jackie had been back two days, and she felt so much like her old self again.

"I would never ever judge you, Jackie. And I know who you are and what you are, and I think you're one of the best people I've ever known." She leaned over and kissed Jacqueline's cheek. "And I have missed you like hell."

Jacqueline felt her heart catch as those soft lips touched her cheek. She thought it amazing that, after all this time, Kay still had the power to affect her. "Thank you," she murmured.

CHAPTER THIRTEEN

Jacqueline settled under the covers in Kay's spare bedroom, still wide awake. There were so many thoughts running through her mind, she couldn't seem to relax. He'd left her the goddamned mill. And the *bank*. She couldn't believe it. Then she turned her head, glancing at the white envelope she'd left out, propped up against the clock on the nightstand. She had intended to read it, but changed her mind. Truthfully, she was scared to read it. What if it was an apology, a heartfelt confession of how he really felt about her? Then what? She'd feel guilty as hell for not trying to reconcile with him. But, at the same time, he obviously knew where she was living. He could have contacted her if he'd desired. In fairness though, he would have no idea what her reaction would have been. In fact, she wondered that herself. Obviously, since her success, they would have known where she was and what she was doing. Not that she was a household name by any means, but writing a book about a small East Texas town and having it made into

93

a movie would have caused some heads to turn in tiny Pine Springs, Texas. Surely.

She took a deep breath and closed her eyes, willing sleep to come. She relaxed, thoughts of her father replaced with thoughts of Kay. Jesus, after all this time, she thought she'd be over that by now. But just being around Kay conjured up all the old feelings she'd had as a teenager. It struck her suddenly that she'd never had those feelings for anyone else. The women who had paraded through her bed were just substitutes. She'd been looking for someone to make her feel the way Kay did—and none had.

Now what? Here she was, back in Pine Springs, reunited with the one woman who made her feel alive, who made her feel *something*. Now what?

"Leave it alone," she whispered. Just leave it alone. There was no need for Kay to know. It was enough just to rekindle their friendship. There was no reason to tell Kay that she still had a silly teenage crush on her. Soon, she would go back to California and resume her life, and Kay would still be in Pine Springs. At least they'd reconnected. Now, they could keep in touch, talk. Perhaps it would be enough.

CHAPTER FOURTEEN

Kay tossed the covers off, the restless sleep she'd been fighting finally chasing her from the bed. It was still very early, but she remembered from the old days that Jackie was an early riser. She'd start coffee then grab a shower. She covered her nightshirt with a robe and walked barefoot into the living room, not bothering to turn on any lights. She was startled when the spare bathroom door opened and there stood Jacqueline, naked head to toe, her beautiful body outlined by the bright light over the vanity.

Kay stood rooted to the spot, her eyes slowly traveling over Jackie's body as she walked into the hallway. Her breasts were still small, her body as lean as ever. Kay swallowed, realizing she had stopped breathing. Then Jackie looked up, her eyes finding Kay's.

"*Christ!* I'm sorry. I thought you were still asleep." She hurried back into the bathroom, grabbing the discarded towel to cover herself.

Kay smiled. Jackie had always been shy around her. Apparently, that hadn't changed. "It's okay. I was just going to make coffee."

"Yeah, but . . . I'm sorry."

Kay laughed. "You used to always hide from me in high school, too. Relax, will you? I've seen you before, Jackie."

Jacqueline blushed, then hurried into the spare room, closing the door forcefully and leaning back against it. She'd hidden from Kay in high school because she was certain that her body would give away her desire for the other girl. Innocent Kay had paraded around half-naked in front of Jacqueline all the time. It had been torture, pure torture.

Kay was still smiling as she scooped coffee grounds into the filter. Jacqueline had a beautiful body. For the life of her, she couldn't understand why she was shy about it. Then her hands stilled, her thoughts going back to high school. Kay had never been ashamed of her body, had never been shy about dressing in front of Jackie. And really, in the beginning, neither had Jacqueline. But that last year it seemed, Jackie avoided undressing in front of Kay, avoided being there when Kay was dressing.

Then it hit her. Jackie had already known that she was gay, and she'd been embarrassed. And Jackie thought that, if Kay knew, then she'd stop being friends with her.

"Oh Jackie," she murmured. She shook her head, wondering what all had gone through Jacqueline's mind during that time. She'd been scared, no doubt. Scared of losing their friendship. Kay wondered what she would have done had Jackie told her she was gay. Would she have been afraid of Jacqueline? No way. Jackie was her best friend. She would have never turned her away, no matter what.

"I'm decent now, in case you were wondering," Jacqueline said from behind her.

Kay turned slowly, finding Jackie's eyes, holding them captive.

"You've always been decent, Jackie." Kay walked closer, finally taking Jacqueline's hands in her own. "We're friends. No matter what, that's not going to change." Then she smiled. "So lighten up, will you?"

"Yeah. Yeah, I'm sorry. It's just, well, I . . ."

"Don't be embarrassed. You have a beautiful body, Jackie. I've always thought so." Kay dropped Jacqueline's hands and walked away before Jackie could reply, leaving her standing there with her mouth open.

Sunday afternoon found them sitting outside on Rose's patio, a tight card game being played between the four of them.

"You never could beat us," Kay boasted. "This time will be no different."

"Yeah? Well I doubt you and Jackie will remember the secret codes you used to cheat with," Rose countered.

"Cheat? Rose, we didn't have to cheat to beat you. Geez, you and Eric sucked."

"It wasn't me. It was Eric. And now Greg and I will kick your ass!"

Jacqueline smiled at the banter between the sisters, watching as Greg dealt the cards. She had not played Spades since . . . well, since the last time she'd played with Kay and Rose. It had nearly been a ritual on Saturday nights when Jacqueline had stayed over.

"Mommy? I want to play."

The child tried to climb on Rose's lap but Rose put her right back down. "You're supposed to be babysitting, Lee Ann."

"I'm six. I'm too little to babysit."

"They're sleeping. How hard can it be?"

"You want to sit in my lap and watch?" Kay offered.

"Goody."

Rose rolled her eyes. "See? I can't wait until she has some," Rose told Jacqueline. "I'm going to turn them into spoiled brats, just like she's done mine."

"What's spoiled?" Lee Ann asked innocently.

"It's what you are when Aunt Kay is around."

"Aunt Kay says I'm sweet."

"And that you are," Kay said. She positioned the child in her lap, then looked at Jacqueline and winked.

Jacqueline smiled at her, then gathered the cards in her hand, hoping she remembered how to play. To her surprise, the ace of spades peeked back at her. *That's good, right?* She looked at Kay and raised an eyebrow. What was the signal for the ace? Ah, yes. A tug on the right ear.

Kay burst out laughing and Rose glared at her. "What?"

"Nothing." Her eyes twinkled as she looked at Jackie, and she nodded slightly.

"What are you two up to? We haven't even started yet. Greg, watch them like a hawk! They cheat."

"I'm not sure I even remember how to play," Jacqueline said. "But I'll go six."

"Six? Geez." Rose studied her cards. "Two."

"Gonna get set," Kay told her. "I'll go four."

"Greg?"

"Two."

"Two?" Rose leaned on the table. "There are only thirteen tricks."

"Gonna get set," Jacqueline echoed. She tossed out the two of clubs to start the game. They all followed suit, and Kay gathered in the first trick. She was amazed at how quickly it all came back to her. She and Kay were on the same page from the start and not only did Rose and Greg get set, they only managed one trick.

"I had forgotten how much I hated playing with you two," Rose grumbled as she shuffled the cards for the next hand.

"Very good, Jackie. I haven't had a decent partner since you left," Kay said.

"I make *her* have Eric now," Rose said.

And so it went, Kay and Jacqueline easily winning the first game, only to be challenged to another by Rose and Greg.

"I thought you promised us dinner," Kay said. "And drinks? I think I'm past tea."

"I made up lasagna this morning. It just needs an hour to bake," Rose said. "Jackie? Lasagna okay with you?"

"Sure. Wouldn't mind a beer, though."

"Me too," Kay added.

"I'll get them," Greg said, taking Lee Ann with him.

"Check on the kids," Rose called. "He's so good with them. I really lucked out."

"He's seems like a good guy," Jacqueline said. "Doesn't talk much though."

"With Rose around? He doesn't get much of a chance," Kay teased.

They played another game, which ended up being much closer than the first, but still, Kay and Jacqueline won, much to Kay's delight and Rose's chagrin. By the time the lasagna was ready, all four kids were up and loaded with excess energy. Kay seemed right at home with them but Jacqueline, who had never been around small children, was a nervous wreck.

Rose surprised them all by pulling out a very expensive bottle of wine. She handed it to Greg to open.

"When did you get this?" he asked.

"I've been saving it for a special occasion. I thought having Jackie back was special enough."

"Thank you. I'm honored," Jacqueline said sincerely, touched by the gesture.

Four adults and four children crammed around the table made for six and Jacqueline passed around the garlic bread after grabbing two slices for herself. She had missed this, she noted. Informal group dinners were a rarity in her life now, except when Ingrid and Cheryl included her in their get-togethers. Which was quite often, but it wasn't the same as sharing a meal with the Garland clan. She always felt like one of the family in the old days, snatching food from Eric's plate just to piss him off. Kay's older brother had pretended to be annoyed, but Jacqueline knew, even back then, that he'd had a crush on her for years. Unfortunately, her crush fell to his sister.

She watched Kay as Lee Ann and little Denny fought for her attention. She could tell Kay had a soft spot for Lee Ann, no doubt because she was the oldest. Kay looked up and caught her staring, raising her eyebrows questioningly.

"Want one?"

"No, no. You're doing just fine."

"How long will you be here, Jackie?" Rose asked.

"Haven't decided. Mr. Lawrence is reading the will on Wednesday. After that," Jacqueline shrugged, "we'll see."

"But your mother won't be able to attend?"

"Thank God, no. But Uncle Walter will be there, I'm sure." Jacqueline turned to Greg. "How well do you know him?"

"Walter? Oh, he's right at home in the plant, doesn't make it to the office much. But, he's a nice enough guy. I worked much more closely with your father, actually."

"Really? I'm afraid I don't know a whole lot about the mill."

Kay met her eyes, wondering if Jacqueline would tell them about the will. Probably not, since she hadn't decided if she even wanted to keep the lumber mill.

"Over the years, your father turned the sawmill into quite a large corporation. It's no longer just about how much board feet we turn out. We've got a plant now that makes plywood. One that makes particleboard. In the last five years, we've opened up a fiberboard plant."

"So instead of selling the waste wood to other companies, you use it yourself?" she asked.

"Yes. In the old days, it was simply lumber and maybe trim, wood siding, things like that. We sold all of the by-products. But, your father was a smart businessman. Why sell all of the waste for practically nothing and let other companies make millions? So, he built the plywood plant first. It's just taken off from there. The latest addition was the creosote plant."

Jacqueline couldn't envision it all. She'd never spent much time at the mill, but all she remembered was the large building where the logs went in and nice, evenly cut boards came out. Now, all of this? Creosote? She could only imagine the pollution.

"How many employees?"

"Oh, gosh. I don't know." He shrugged. "Fifteen hundred, I'd say, here at the plant. That doesn't include the logging company."

"Wow. He owned a logging company? I would have thought he'd contract out for that."

"Yeah. I think years ago, they contracted out. Keys Industries is now the largest employer in this area, by far."

"So Pine Springs Lumber is separate from Keys Industries?" Jacqueline asked, glancing at Kay.

Greg looked at her, then at Rose. "Well, the mill still sells under the name of Pine Springs Lumber, but the rest, it's all under Keys Industries."

Jacqueline took a deep breath. "I guess I'm confused. You're saying the lumber mill, which my father and Uncle Walter owned, is a completely different company from Keys Industries?"

"Well, yeah. Sort of. I mean, the plants are all there where the sawmill has always been. The whole operation is on two hundred acres. But Keys Industries is all your father, not Walter."

"How is that possible if he's using the sawmill?"

"I don't know about all of that, Jackie. I'm sure Mr. Lawrence and the accountants can tell you."

Jacqueline looked at Kay. "Damn."

"What?" Rose asked.

Kay gave a slight shake of her head and Jacqueline nodded. "Nothing. I just . . . well, I had no idea it had grown like it has."

"With your father gone, everyone is speculating what will happen now. Your Uncle Walter, he can run the plants but he didn't have your father's vision," Greg said. "Oh, there are people that can carry on, no doubt. Managers and such, but everything still went through your father. People are probably going to turn to Walter now, but I think he's in over his head. No offense, just my opinion."

"Greg, I haven't seen Uncle Walter in more years than I can count and even then, it wasn't like we were close. So, no offense taken." Jacqueline's mind was racing. The first thing she was going to do tomorrow morning was pay John Lawrence a visit.

"Enough shop talk, huh?" Rose asked. "What I really want to know is if Jackie will still be here Friday night."

"Why?" Jacqueline asked hesitantly.

"Mama said Eric should be back in town. I thought we could all get together here and grill burgers or something. I know he'd love to see you."

Jacqueline hesitated. Ingrid would kill her. Then she glanced at Kay, seeing the expectant look in her eyes.

"I guess that depends if I still have a place to stay," Jacqueline conceded. Yes, Ingrid would definitely kill her.

Kay smiled. "Of course. Just don't expect me to cook for you every night!"

CHAPTER FIFTEEN

"No, I don't have an appointment. But I'm sure he'll see me," Jacqueline said politely to Mr. Lawrence's secretary. She waited patiently as the woman walked into his office, closing the door pointedly in Jacqueline's face. It took only a few moments before the woman reappeared.

"He'll squeeze you in."

Jacqueline controlled the urge to laugh, simply nodding at the woman. Apparently, she took her job very seriously.

"Jacqueline, welcome. Come in, sit."

"Thanks for seeing me, John."

"Of course. How have you been enjoying your stay with Kay Garland?"

"It's been nice. I had Sunday dinner with her sister Rose and her family. We've had a chance to visit and catch up."

"Good, good." He resumed his seat behind his desk, closing a file he'd apparently been reading. "Now, what can I do for you?"

"Keys Industries. What the hell is it? I thought it was just another name for the lumber mill."

He cleared his throat, shifting uncomfortably in his chair. "Your father started Keys Industries probably fifteen years ago. It was just a name at the time, yes. He wanted something that was separate from his brother. But, he was majority owner of the lumber mill, and he used that to open up the various plants that are now there, all owned by Keys Industries, not Pine Springs Lumber."

"How could he do this? Obviously he used the lumber mill to his benefit. How did he compensate Uncle Walter?"

"He didn't compensate Walter, he compensated Pine Springs Lumber, which in turn, compensated himself as well."

"And Walter just went along with this?"

Lawrence shrugged. "What could he do? Besides, the money that the new plants were bringing to Pine Springs Lumber was not exactly small potatoes. He's made out quite well for not having to do anything except continue managing the sawmill."

"So my father's real wealth was not in the sawmill at all."

"No. Keys Industries is big enough to warrant a CEO, a board of directors, etc. But your father didn't want to go public. At least, not yet. He could have doubled his fortune if he had, but why? He was content being in control of all aspects of the operation. He hired managers for each plant, people he trusted, but still, he made all the decisions. He was still in control of everything."

"Well, that was all great at the time, but he's not here now. Who's going to make the decisions? The managers?"

"There is no president to appoint someone, no. The new . . . the new owner will most likely need to make some decisions concerning all that."

"Me?"

He nodded. "Now you see why I insisted that you come to Pine Springs."

"So when you said that Uncle Walter might contest the will, he really has no grounds concerning Keys Industries," she said.

"No. But your father also left you his portion of Pine Springs Lumber. That, I'm sure, Walter will contest."

"And my mother?"

"I doubt your mother knows the extent of Keys Industries. For that matter, I doubt she knows the extent of your father's wealth. I know for a fact that she believes he only controlled about twenty percent of the bank. As I said, he left her a rather large cash settlement, as well as the house, of course." He shifted again in his chair. "Jacqueline, I really shouldn't discuss all of this with you without all parties here and their attorneys. Unless of course, you choose to retain me."

Jacqueline sighed. Bullshit. Just bullshit. "Isn't that a conflict of interest? I mean, you represent my mother, don't you?"

"I worked for your father. And I'm still retained by Keys Industries. I handled his business dealings as well as personal matters. Your mother has already called me. She's not happy that you're here, that you came at my calling. In fact, she was particularly distressed that we'd opened our home to you. With that said, I no longer represent your mother."

Jacqueline leaned forward, frowning. "Why do you think that she is so upset that I'm here? Surely, she's over the embarrassment factor by now. I mean, she's practically nuts by it. You should have seen her at the hospital."

"Your parents' marriage . . . well, I won't go into all that, but suffice it to say it was not exactly an ideal relationship. Your father blamed your mother for what happened with you, and rightly so. I'm sure you remember that not much happened in your household without your mother's approval. The situation with you was no different. She thought it best to send you away. Your father had little say in the matter. But, it was the beginning of the end. He started devoting all his time and energy to the business. It was the one thing your mother had no say over. In fact, he rarely discussed Keys Industries with her at all. That's why I'm certain she has no idea of his wealth."

"None of that explains why she's so unnerved over the fact that I'm here. And please don't tell me she's still worried about what people may think."

"Your mother is still the most prominent woman in Pine

Springs. I'm sure a part of her is concerned with what people will think. It's common knowledge that she sent you away and why. To have you come back now while she's stuck in the hospital is more of an embarrassment to her than anything."

"If she's the most prominent woman in Pine Springs, why does she even *care* what people might think?"

"It's also common knowledge that you've become a successful writer without any help from them. And, that your first book and subsequent movie was based on your mother and this town."

Jacqueline smiled. "My mother, yes. Not necessarily the town. It could have been any small town in East Texas. I doubt they differ very much."

"Very well. However, your portrayal of your mother was . . ."

"Award winning," Jacqueline supplied. "And so she's *pissed*?"

"Embarrassed. So, she's trying to keep the upper hand."

"And let me know that she's still the boss," Jacqueline guessed. "You know what, John? I don't really care."

"No, I don't presume that you do." He stood, walking to his file cabinets. He opened one and pulled out a thick folder. "Do you wish to retain me as counsel?"

Jacqueline shrugged. "Yeah. Sure."

He smiled and nodded. "Very well." He again sat across from her, shuffling through the papers in the folder. "Have you had a chance to read the letter from your father?"

Jacqueline shifted uncomfortably. "No. I . . . well, no, not yet."

"I was just wondering how much of all this he might have told you, if any. I have no idea what the letter is about, whether he explains Keys Industries or if there was just some personal items he wanted to share."

"I'll read it tonight," she promised.

"I would advise that you at least read it before Wednesday, in case there's something of importance in there that even I didn't know." He handed her a piece of paper. "There at the top," he instructed.

She glanced at the legal document, not knowing what she was

looking for. Then she saw it. Keys Industries. Owners: Nicolas M. Keys, Jacqueline L. Keys.

"What the hell?"

"Your mother may contest the will and she may win, although I seriously doubt it. But this, this she cannot contest. You are sole owner of Keys Industries. The affidavit states that, upon either of your deaths, complete ownership reverts to the surviving party."

Jacqueline tossed the paper on the desk. "I . . . I never agreed to any of this. I never signed this," she said. "Not knowingly."

"I'm not at liberty to say how your signature was obtained."

"Oh? I thought you worked for me now."

"Sorry. The promise goes back a long ways."

"And what if I don't want this?"

"Well, you could say that you were not privy to this document and that is not your legal signature. In all likelihood, Keys Industries would then go to your mother."

"Great. Just great," she murmured. "He certainly knew what he was doing."

"Yes. And at the time, I thought he was crazy to have done it this way. But, over the years, I've come to realize that his marriage was all but over. There was no way he was going to leave his life's work to her."

"Well, John, this ought to be fun," she said as she stood. She reached out to shake his hand. "I hope you're ready for it."

"Oh, don't worry about me. Your father and I have faced tougher opponents than this. Your mother will most likely retain one of the Gentry twins. They've only been practicing a few years. I doubt they have any idea what this is all about."

Jacqueline studied him. "Why do I get the feeling that you've only been pretending to be a small-town attorney?"

"I learned a lot from your father, Jacqueline. He threw me up against some big shot lawyers from Houston one time. They damn near had me for lunch. That night, he told me everything I'd done wrong, as if he was the attorney, not me. We went over strategy all night. The next day, we blew their socks off."

"I take it your practice here is mostly for show?" she guessed.

He nodded. "Your father compensated me well, yes. Mary has no idea, of course. She thinks we can afford to live at the Country Club because I do legal work for the bank and a handful of other small businesses in town."

"I see. So, keeping secrets from wives is a common thing around here?"

He shrugged. "Women tend to talk."

She smiled. "And some things are best kept quiet?"

"Exactly."

CHAPTER SIXTEEN

Kay smiled when she saw Jackie's black Lexus parked in her driveway. She'd left early that morning, before Jacqueline was even up. She was behind on her bookkeeping and thought she'd work before she opened at eight. Bookkeeping was something she usually reserved for Sundays, but she had been happy to forego it this time. She'd enjoyed their day at Rose's, and she knew that Jackie had, too.

She found Jacqueline at the table, tapping away on her laptop.

"You're home," Jacqueline said, her fingers never stopping.

Kay grinned. "Glasses?"

Jacqueline shoved them tightly against her nose. "I need them with the computer. Nerdy, huh?"

"No. Cute." She peered over Jackie's shoulder. "New book?"

"No. Edits. I'm just doing some touch-ups. Ingrid's been badgering me for them, even though I still have a couple of weeks before my deadline. I thought I'd send them to her early and get her off my back." She finally stopped and looked back at Kay. "How was your day?"

"Great. Yours?"

Jacqueline took a deep breath. "I went to see John Lawrence. And it's just so overwhelming, I don't even know where to start."

"I see. Keys Industries?"

"Yeah. I'll skip all the bullshit and just tell you that I've been part owner of Keys Industries all these years."

"What the hell?"

"And now that my father is gone, sole owner, thanks to an affidavit I allegedly signed about ten years ago."

Kay sat down, staring. "What are you talking about?"

"It's a long story, Kay. And honestly, I'm tired of thinking about it."

Kay stood. "I understand."

But Jacqueline grabbed her arm as she moved to walk past. "Kay? I'm sorry. I didn't mean to be short."

"It's okay. It's really not any of my business."

"Don't say that. There are no secrets, Kay. Later, after you've fed me and I've had something alcoholic to drink, I'll tell you all about it."

Kay relaxed. "But that would mean I'd have to cook."

"Yes. No pizza."

"I'll see what I can whip up."

After Kay changed into a comfortable pair of sweats, she again found Jacqueline typing on her laptop. She walked by without disturbing her, intent on fixing something suitable for dinner. She didn't know why she hadn't thought to stop by the grocery store. Well, she knew why. She was in a hurry to get home. But now, as she stared into her near-empty freezer, she wished she'd taken time. She moved a box of frozen corn aside, finding a lone package of ground beef. She shrugged as she took it out. There were a hundred things you could do with ground beef, surely.

She stood staring into her pantry for a good five minutes, her eyes moving over the cans of vegetables and beans, to the bag of rice and the one potato that . . . well, that needed to be thrown out weeks ago.

"This is all Rose's fault," she mumbled. As children, Rose was the only one who showed any interest in cooking. So, Mama had taught her everything she knew, much to the delight of Kay who would have much rather been outside playing with Jackie. She gave up her search of the pantry. Instead, she perched on the counter, phone in hand.

"Mama? I need help," she said quietly, glancing quickly across the bar, making sure Jackie wasn't listening.

"Kay? What's wrong?"

"I have to cook dinner," she said.

"And?"

Kay rolled her eyes. "And, this is *me*, not Rose."

"And Jackie is . . ."

"Expecting dinner."

"I see. Pizza?"

"Can't. Did that Saturday night."

"Okay. Well, do you have any chicken?"

"No. Ground beef."

"That's it?"

"Yes. It's frozen."

"Well, you can make a casserole. Do you have any pasta? If you have cheese, you could make a cheesy white sauce and . . ."

"*Mama*! Please . . ."

"I told you one day you would regret not learning to cook. Remember?"

"Yes, I remember. Consider me properly chastised."

She looked up as Jackie stuck her head around the bar, eyebrows raised. Kay slid off the counter.

"Smells good."

"Be quiet." She turned her back to Jacqueline, talking quietly. "Mama, I've got to go. Thanks for *all* your help." She hung up on her mother's laughter.

Jacqueline walked into the kitchen, leaning against the counter with her arms crossed. They stared at each other, then both looked at the lone package of frozen ground beef sitting on the breakfast table.

"That it?"

Kay nodded. "Afraid so."

Jacqueline walked closer. "You promised you'd feed me."

"I lied."

"Yeah?"

"Uh-huh."

"I see." Jacqueline took another step closer, stopping only a few feet in front of Kay. The mouth that she knew better than her own hinted at a smile and Jacqueline stared, waiting. Then the lips parted, breaking into a full grin. Jacqueline met blue eyes, her own smile matching Kay's. "Good thing Rose gave me the heads up then."

"*What?*"

"She said you couldn't throw a meal together to save your life." Jacqueline reached around Kay to turn the oven on, grinning. "So, I picked something up."

"Picked something up?"

"Well, your mother put together some stuff for us. I picked it up when I had lunch there. She said just to warm it in the oven."

"Mama *knew*? She let me make a fool of myself on the phone, and she knew all along?"

"Why were you calling her?"

Kay reached out and slugged Jacqueline in the arm. "I was calling her for help, that's why."

"Why'd you hit me?" Jacqueline asked innocently, rubbing the same spot Kay had hit last week.

"Ah, you're right. I'm sorry." Kay brushed Jackie's hand away, rubbing her arm softly. "I should be thanking you for getting us something to eat."

"Yes, you should." Jacqueline watched Kay's hand, motioning with her head. "A little higher."

"Uh-huh." Kay intended on stopping, but Jackie's flesh was warm, soft. Her arms firm, muscular. Her hand stilled, and she looked up, right into the crystal blue eyes that, as a kid, she used to love staring into. She finally dropped her hand and moved away, embarrassed.

Jacqueline saw the slight blush that crept up Kay's face, wondering what the other woman was thinking. "Thank you. Maybe the bruising won't be so bad now."

"Very funny." Kay moved to the fridge, finding the two takeout plates her mother had fixed. "What would you like to drink?"

"Actually, I bought some stuff."

"Yeah? What?"

"Well, I didn't know what you liked. I got some scotch, and rum, and a little beer. Oh, and a few bottles of wine."

Kay smiled. "That about covers it. Why don't you surprise me?"

"You're too easy. You don't drink much, do you?"

"Actually, no. For one thing, it's not really convenient having to drive to the county line to buy it. And, well, Billy Ray drank too much. It got scary."

"I understand. We don't have to have anything. Tea would be okay with me," Jacqueline offered.

"After the day you had, you probably want something other than tea. It's okay, Jackie. Fix us a drink."

Later, with plates piled high, they both sat cross-legged on the floor, using the coffee table instead of the dining room table, just like they used to do as kids.

"Mama would have a fit if she saw us, you know."

"Yes, two grown women acting like kids."

"This is great. I see she packed all my favorites, including a pork chop."

"I didn't care about anything but the meatloaf," Jacqueline said as she shoved a fork into her mouth. "God, this is the best."

"I thought you liked her chicken and dumplings best?"

"I do. But I ate the last of it at lunch."

Kay laughed. "Stay around here too long, and she'll have you fattened up in no time."

"Yeah. I couldn't eat like this every day, that's for sure. Maybe tomorrow night, I'll fix us a big salad, maybe some baked chicken."

Kay nodded. She could get spoiled having Jackie here. Not only did she have company, but also someone to cook for her. "You feel like telling me about your day?"

"Not much to tell, other than I own Keys Industries, and my mother has no idea. Or how about the fact that Keys Industries controls the goddamned bank? That was the highlight of my day."

"The *bank*? What are you going to do?"

"I have no idea. My choices are to challenge the legality of the affidavit, since I did not knowingly sign it, and then hand the business over to my mother or I can keep it."

"Not much of a choice, huh?"

"What would you do?"

"Me? God, Jackie, I can't even begin to know. If my mother had done to me what yours did—"

"That's not a fair equation. Your mother would *never* have done that to you."

"Well, you're right."

"Mr. Lawrence said that my parents' marriage was a farce, had been for years. He said my mother has no idea the extent of Keys Industries or the value. He said my father didn't want her to have it, which is why my name is there as owner."

"So, I guess you don't really have a choice, do you?"

"No, I don't."

Kay looked up shyly. "Does this mean you're going to stay?"

"Stay? Here? In Pine Springs?" Jacqueline laughed. "You've got to be kidding?"

Kay looked away. No, why would Jackie consider staying? This town meant nothing to her anymore.

Jacqueline realized how that sounded, and she reached over and took Kay's hand. "I'm sorry. I didn't mean to sound so harsh. It's just I . . . I can't see coming back here, not after all that's happened. Not with my mother still here. Can you imagine the hell that would be?"

"I understand. I was being selfish."

"Selfish?"

Kay squeezed Jackie's hand, then pulled away. "I love having you here. It's nice to have you back in my life."

"That doesn't have to change, Kay. We'll keep in touch, no matter where I am. Right now, I have no idea what I'm going to do with this business."

"Can't you just keep it, and let it go as is?"

"Well, that's the problem. As Greg said last night, my father still ran things, still made all the decisions. Now that he's gone, who is going to take his place?"

"Surely the managers that he hired are capable?"

"I don't know. Maybe."

"And you're tired of thinking about it?"

"Very. I've got to e-mail Ingrid and let her know I'll be here longer than I expected. She's going to kill me. She has this fear that I'm going to disappear into deep East Texas and miss my deadline."

"It must be exciting, your life."

"Exciting?" Jacqueline shook her head. "No, I'd not really call it that. At first, when they made the movie, it was exciting. It was all new and suddenly I was at parties with famous people, acting like I belonged there. Christopher kept me grounded, though. He made me keep writing. I think that I was content after that first one, you know. I was satisfied. It was hugely successful, the book and the movie, and I thought that was all I had in me. But," Jacqueline shrugged. "Four books later, I'm still at it."

"And another movie."

"Yeah. But I think I'm out of movies."

"What are you working on now?"

"It's something different, actually. Cops. Murder. That sort of thing."

"Tired of writing about the South?"

"I think I got it all out of me. Therapy, you know."

"The first one, sure. The others, I didn't get that feeling," Kay said.

"Oh, it was there. I think I was trying to write this town out of

115

my system. And I have, I guess. There was a time when, no matter how much John Lawrence had begged, I never would have come here."

"But I'm awfully glad you did now."

"Yeah. Me, too. Despite all the complications my life is about to encounter, I'm glad. I think maybe I needed to do this, Kay. I needed to come back to prove that I could. To prove that I'm over all that."

"Are you really over it?"

Jacqueline nodded. "Yes. I'm not afraid of my mother anymore. And I think I still was, even though miles and miles separated us. But not anymore."

"But you have regrets?" Kay asked gently.

"I regret that I didn't get to reconcile with my father, yes. But it's too late to dwell on that now. He . . . he left a letter for me."

"He did? What did it say?"

Jacqueline shrugged. "I haven't actually read it yet."

"Why not?"

"I was afraid of what it might say."

"What do you mean?"

"What if it's an apology? I'm going to feel guilty as hell for not trying to contact him."

"Oh, Jackie. What if it *is* an apology? Would that be so bad? Don't you think you deserve one?"

"Well, yeah, I think I do. But from her, and I know I'm never going to get one."

"Why just her? Your father knew what she was doing and he let her. And then later, he obviously knew where you were, but he didn't get in touch with you. I think you deserve one from both of them." Kay paused. "You know what bothered me the most? That first week in June, your eighteenth birthday. I kept thinking how you must be all alone. It made me very, very sad."

"Funny you mention that birthday. I was very much alone that day, sleeping in a dirty bunk at the Salvation Army. Isn't it all so weird, Kay? Who in their right mind sends their daughter away because she's gay? In this day and age? I mean, it's like it was the sixties and their daughter got pregnant by the town scum and they sent her away in shame. We've all heard of that happening. But, you're the mayor of the goddamned town, for Christ's sake! You don't just ship your daughter off and disown her. You don't just send her out into the world like she never existed."

Kay finally understood the pain and loneliness that Jackie had endured. Shunned by her family, forced to leave home and make it on her own, alone. God, she couldn't imagine. But she could see the pain in Jackie's eyes plain as day. She moved to her, taking her friend in her arms and holding her. She felt Jacqueline's shoulders shaking, heard the quiet tears.

"I'm so sorry," she whispered.

"I was so . . . so scared. So scared, Kay." Jacqueline let herself be comforted, relishing the security she felt in Kay's arms. She let her tears fall, tears she'd kept inside for all these years.

"It's okay, Jackie. I'm here. You're safe."

"Yes. I know. I always felt safe with you."

Kay tightened her hold, leaning them back against the sofa, gathering Jacqueline closer to her. It was she who had always felt safe with Jackie. She had no idea the other woman felt the same. She closed her eyes, relishing the closeness she felt right now with Jackie.

Jacqueline thought she should feel embarrassed, but she didn't. It felt too good to cry, to talk about it. And this was Kay, who knew everything. Kay, who was holding her so gently. Jacqueline became aware of the arms around her, the fingers lightly stroking her hair, her own hand that rested comfortably against Kay's waist. She finally pulled away, afraid she would do something that would embarrass them both.

"I'm sorry." She rubbed lightly at her eyes before looking at Kay.

"Jackie, you don't ever have to apologize to me." Kay reached out and brushed the hair off of Jacqueline's forehead, looking into eyes that were still filled with pain . . . pain and tears. "I'm just guessing here, but this is the first time you've shed tears. Right?"

"I was too angry to cry. It was the only way I could survive. If I had given in to the loneliness, they would have broken me. I would have begged to come home, I would have agreed to anything. And I knew in my heart that I couldn't do that. So I kept the anger there, right out front to remind me daily of what they'd done. And I was going to win." Jacqueline drew her knees up, wrapping her arms around them and resting her chin there. "Those first few years when I worked two jobs and went to school full time, it's just a blur. I was exhausted. But I had no time to think, you know? And really, it seems like it happened so fast. After I graduated, I intended on looking for a real job but by that time, Christopher had already introduced me to Ingrid, and she'd found a publisher for the manuscript I'd been working on. A few weeks later, she had a contract for me to sign. I just had to finish the damn thing. It all happened so fast."

"And now here you are," Kay said lightly.

"And here I am, back where it all started. Ironic, isn't it?"

Kay smiled. "What goes around, comes around?"

Jacqueline laughed. "Yeah, really." She finally relaxed, sitting up again and grabbing the last piece of meatloaf from her plate. "You didn't finish your pork chop."

"And keep your hands off it."

"You know, earlier when I said I couldn't stay here, I meant no offense by that, Kay."

"Oh, I know. It was silly of me to think that you would stay. I mean, this isn't your home anymore. You've got a life back there, a career."

"Yeah. But after all these years, it still doesn't really feel like home there. This might sound strange, but being around you, your family, that feels like home. Not necessarily this town, but here," she said quietly.

"Thank you. Maybe it's just being around people that love you. Loved you then and still love you."

"I appreciate you saying that."

"It's the truth." Kay pointed at the glasses Jackie had tossed on the table earlier. "How long have you had glasses?"

Jacqueline grinned. "Must be an age thing. Last couple of years, I've used them for reading and the computer."

"They're very attractive on you." Kay again brushed the hair away from Jackie's eyes. "But I like this better. Your eyes are too pretty to hide."

Later, after Kay had gone to bed, Jacqueline sat staring at her laptop, her fingers absently drumming the keys, wondering what to make of Kay's words, her actions. Oh, hell, it meant nothing. They were friends, and amazing as it was, they'd simply picked up right where they'd left off all those years ago. And even though she may still harbor that old attraction, it didn't mean that Kay was suddenly discovering feelings toward her as well. Because, truthfully, if Kay were, Jackie knew with certainty that she could not handle it. Kay was Kay, this perfect young girl that Jackie had placed so high above everyone else. And Kay had grown into the woman that Jackie always imagined she'd be. A compassionate, gentle woman. A woman who Jackie still measured others against.

She closed her laptop without e-mailing Ingrid. She just wasn't up to it. Instead, her eyes moved around the room, resting on the envelope still propped up against the clock. No sense putting it off any longer. She fluffed the two pillows behind her and leaned against the headboard, holding the envelope lightly in her hands. Then, before she could change her mind, she tore it open. It was handwritten, and she moved the lamp closer, staring at the words her father had written four years ago.

My Dearest Jacqueline:

I don't know if I can find the words to tell you how I feel, but I must try. You probably feel nothing but hatred for me, and I don't blame you. I have no excuse, other than I was weak. Honestly, I thought that you would come back to us, and we could make things right. But you were stronger than either of us imagined. I tried to find you, looking in Dallas first, thinking you would have stayed there. When I got word that you were in Los Angeles, two years had already passed. I went to see you, without your mother's knowledge, of course. It pained me to see where you lived, where you worked. But I was proud of you. You'd survived. It occurred to me then that you didn't need or want me in your life. And I can't say I blame you. But know that I kept tabs on you, just to make sure you were okay. If anything had happened, if you were in trouble, know that I would have come immediately.

It eases my pain somewhat to know that you've made a success of your life. I knew, of course, that you were writing. As I said, I kept tabs on you. But your mother, it was a complete surprise to her. To say that she was shocked and embarrassed by your first book is an understatement. Even to her cold eyes, she knew the book was about her. I applaud you. You got it right on. Which leads me to the business at hand.

Since you are reading this, I am no longer in this life. I'm sure you know of Keys Industries by now. And also know that it belongs to you. I worked all these years to turn it into something that you could be proud of, something that I could leave to you and you alone. Know that my heart and soul went into it, all for you. I owe you so much, Jacqueline. No child should ever be deserted by her family, no matter what the cause. There is no apology I could extend to you that would make up for that. All I can offer you is my life's work. What you choose to do with it is your decision. I only ask that it not fall into your mother's hands. My punishment was having to live with her all these years. Don't think I never thought about divorcing her. I did. Many times. But as I said, it was my punishment. Please trust John Lawrence to guide you with the business. He has been nothing but faithful to me over the years.

With that said, please find it in your heart to forgive me. I never stopped loving you, Jacqueline. You were always in my thoughts. My wish for you is to find happiness in this life, someone to share your love with and your life with. I know you've been alone. Don't be afraid to open your heart. You've suffered enough pain for one lifetime. It's time to live and love again. I just want you to be happy. I just want the best for you.

With all my love.

Jacqueline stared at the letter, aware that tears were streaming down her cheeks, blurring the words on the paper. She impatiently wiped them away, rereading the letter again. All this time, he knew where she was, he'd been keeping an eye on her, just in case. Perhaps he knew that she wouldn't welcome his presence in her life, not after two years had passed and she'd managed to survive somehow. But he'd been there all along.

Christ. It was her stupid pride that had kept her from contacting him. She'd known in her heart that it was her mother, not him, who had sent her away, but in her young mind, she'd lumped them both together. She pulled her glasses off and rubbed her eyes. *And you couldn't even bother to go to the cemetery when they buried him.*

"Goddammit."

But it was too late now. She could sit here and feel guilty, and hell, she did. But it didn't matter. What was past was past. They all had a part in it. Any one of them could have extended the olive branch at any time. But no, she was too intent on showing them that she didn't need them, that she was just fine in this world without them. So much energy wasted, so much time just down the drain, never to get it back again.

Her hands fell limply to her waist and she stared at the ceiling, unseeing. Now what? She really had no choice, did she? The least she could do was honor her father's wishes.

"What the hell am I going to do with a goddamned lumber mill?"

CHAPTER SEVENTEEN

Kay held the letter in one hand and a coffee cup in the other, her eyes misting over at the words. She looked at Jackie, then back at the letter, finishing.

"I . . . I don't know what to say." Kay put her coffee cup down, wiping at her eyes. She stared at Jacqueline. "How do you feel?"

Jacqueline shrugged. She'd had all night to think about it, but the guilt she'd first felt had not subsided.

"You have no reason to feel guilty, Jackie. He knew where you were. Hell, he even went to Los Angeles. He could have seen you if he'd wanted."

"I know. But I think he knew that I didn't want him to."

"And you feel guilty because you didn't want him to?"

"I know, it's crazy."

Kay nodded. She could think of nothing to say that would change that. Jacqueline had to reconcile this herself. But she hated that her friend was beating herself up over something that was out of her control. Her mother put the wheels in motion fifteen years ago, and

Jacqueline went with it instead of fighting it. Kay reached across the table and squeezed Jacqueline's hand. "None of this is your fault, Jackie. You were a kid. You just have to accept what happened and go on."

Jacqueline looked down at their hands, at the fingers that were entwined. Without thought, her thumb moved lightly across soft skin, gently caressing. She felt Kay's hand tighten and she looked up, meeting blue eyes across from her. She cleared her throat and pulled her hand away, finally realizing what she'd been doing.

"What do you have planned today?" Kay asked. She folded her hands in her lap, her fingers moving over the spot where Jacqueline had touched. It felt different, nice. She and Jackie had always been affectionate with one another, and suddenly she recalled a time in high school when Jackie's touch had caused her heart to pound—like it was now. It was on a rare occasion when they had double-dated. Billy Ray took them to the local pool hall, a place none of them wanted to go.

"I don't know how to play pool, Jackie. You know that."

"It's easy. I'll show you."

Kay looked up, afraid Billy Ray would intervene, but he lit his cigarette and moved back to the bar, sneaking beer from some of his older friends. Danny sat stiffly on a stool near the pool table, his eyes darting around the room nervously.

"I don't think Danny likes it here," Kay whispered.

"Who could blame him? We're in redneck hell."

"We can leave," Kay offered.

"Unfortunately, it's your boyfriend's car. And I think he's plenty at home here."

Jackie took a cue stick and held it out, eyeing the straightness before she tossed it on the table and rolled it. "This one will do." She handed it to Kay, then grabbed another. "Danny? You want to play?"

He shook his head. "I'll watch."

Jackie took the blue chalk cube and rubbed the tip of her cue stick then walked over to Kay. "Here, rub the tip. Keeps it from slipping when it hits the ball."

Kay watched intently as Jackie put all the balls in a triangle thing, moving them around, one by one. "What's that?"

123

"We're racking 'em. They're sort of in order." Jackie shrugged. "Good enough." She tossed the white ball in her hand. "Cue ball. We use this to break."

Kay looked again down the bar, watching as Billy Ray gulped down a beer. She slid apologetic eyes to Jackie.

"Don't worry about him." Jackie held up a ring of keys. "I swiped his keys."

Kay's eyes widened. "He'll be pissed, Jackie."

"Big deal. No way I'm letting him drive us home." She bent over, eyeing the table, her cue stick sliding back and forth between her fingers. Then she drew the stick back, slamming it hard into the cue, causing the colorful assortment of balls to scatter.

"Good one," Danny said.

"Sure you don't want to play," Jackie offered.

"No, thanks. I'll just watch."

Kay eyed the table. "Now what?"

"Well, since none went in on the break, the table's open. You can either have solids or stripes." Jackie raised her eyebrows teasingly. "Not the eight ball. That bad boy gets to be last." She pointed to a blue one near the back corner pocket. "The two ball will be easy for you."

"I've never done this before."

Jackie pulled her close. "I'll show you." She stood behind Kay, the hands on Kay's hips moving her at an angle to the table. "Eye the ball, Kay."

Kay's vision blurred as Jackie folded herself around her, hips tucked intimately against her buttocks, arms mirroring her own as Jackie's hand closed over her fingers.

"Watch the ball," Jackie whispered into her ear.

Kay was only dimly aware of her arm sliding back. She was vividly aware, however, of the warm body pressed against her own—and the small breasts pressing against her back. She relaxed totally, letting Jackie take over. The cue stick moved in her arms, the two ball slamming into the corner pocket, disappearing from sight. She still didn't move.

"Good shot," Jackie whispered against her ear.

Kay was aware of her heart pounding and not much else. She turned, *her eyes meeting Jackie's—blue on blue—and she felt shaken by what she saw there. Then Jackie moved away, giving her room.*

"You're a natural," Jackie said.

Kay nodded. "Let's do it again."

Kay blinked, bringing herself back to the present, focusing on Jackie as she spoke.

"I've got to call Ingrid and tell her what's going on. Then I've got to e-mail her the edits before she has a coronary." Jacqueline smiled. "And I need to go grocery shopping so we don't both starve to death."

"Good. That means you're going to cook for me tonight."

"Yes, I'm going to cook, seeing as how you can't."

"See? It has its advantages."

"Uh-huh."

Kay stood, taking her empty coffee cup with her. "I need to run. Try not to get into trouble today."

"I'll behave," Jacqueline murmured, her eyes locked on Kay's backside as her hips swayed beneath the khaki pants she wore. *Damn, Jacqueline, you're worse than a guy.*

After a third cup of coffee and one last look at the edits, Jacqueline finally picked up her cell phone to call Ingrid. She couldn't put it off any longer.

"Where the *hell* are you?" Ingrid demanded.

"I'm still here. Actually, I'm about to send you the final draft now."

"Can you work there, Jacqueline? I mean, if they're not ready, don't do it. We can just be late on our deadline."

"No, they're finished, they're good to go." She paused. "Some things . . . well, there have been some developments, and I have a few things to take care of. I'm meeting with my attorney tomorrow and then I should be able to head back in a few days."

"Your attorney? David's flying out?"

"No. My attorney here."

"Why do you have an attorney there, Jacqueline? What's going on?"

125

"Well, seems I own a lumber company and the various operations that go along with that."

"A lumber company? Your father's mill?"

"Sort of. I'm part owner of that, unless my mother contests the will. My father owned another business, Keys Industries. I've been part owner of that for ten years now and upon his death, full owner."

Silence. "Why haven't you ever told me this?"

"Because I just found out about it."

"You own a lumber company? How is that possible? You hate logging."

"Yeah. Ironic, isn't it?"

"None of this really makes sense to me, Jacqueline. What I want to know is when you're coming back?"

"I'll touch base with you on Thursday and let you know my plans."

"Fair enough. Now, is there anything you need me to take care of here for you? I know you thought you'd only be gone a couple of days."

"No. There's nothing. You might give Christopher a call. I think this was the weekend he was going to come visit."

"Of course. Well, keep me posted, please. And hurry back. Cheryl's planning a dinner party for the weekend after next. She'll expect you to be there."

"Sure." But the thought of one of Cheryl's dinner parties was enough to make her want to stay in Pine Springs. She enjoyed the informal cookouts that Ingrid arranged, but Cheryl's tended to be dress-up affairs with people Jacqueline had little in common with. And of course, there was always the one single woman that Cheryl invariably invited to keep Jacqueline company. And, she admitted, on more than one occasion, she had taken advantage of that, because sometimes it beat going home alone. Sometimes.

Despite everything that had happened, she felt somewhat relaxed. So, to keep her mind off the impending reading of the will, she pulled a lounge chair into the sun and sat on Kay's deck, her laptop humming as she worked on the new novel she'd started. Surprisingly, she was able to focus and before she knew it, the afternoon was upon her. She stood, stretching her back and neck, then brought everything inside. She still needed to go to the grocery store, and if she wasn't careful, she'd work right through the afternoon.

She bought enough to restock Kay's bare pantry and fridge, enough for several meals, as well as some breakfast items. Perhaps she would get up early in the morning and surprise Kay.

"Next thing you know, you'll be making her lunch for her," she murmured.

"Excuse me?"

Jacqueline blushed as the checkout girl stared at her. "Talking to myself. Sorry."

After Jacqueline had everything put away, her eyes lighted on the bottles of wine. She still had ideas flying through her mind. She should work. And she worked much better with a glass of wine. But she was in Pine Springs, and it was three thirty in the afternoon. And she knew Kay wouldn't like it. Hell, her husband was an abusive drunk, so who could blame her. She settled on iced tea, adding an obscene amount of sugar before she had it just right.

She actually was on a roll. Her fingers flew over the keyboard, her mind clear. Ingrid would be pleased. But at five, she made herself stop, hating the interruption but she wanted to have dinner started before Kay got home.

As she prepared the chicken breasts, she did indeed open a bottle of wine. Earlier, she'd sorted through Kay's limited CD collection, finally settling on something familiar, an old Bruce Springsteen. She moved around the kitchen, the Boss blasting from the stereo as she prepared dinner. Nothing elaborate, but not pizza, either. Fresh asparagus that she would steam, a wild rice pilaf and chicken. Simple, yet elegant. She rummaged through drawers, finding cloth placemats and napkins, which she guessed were seldom used. She set the table, bringing in a couple of candles from the living room as a centerpiece.

"Not bad." Then it occurred to her that Kay might think it was some sort of a seduction dinner. The candles, wine. *Jesus, you're going to scare the poor girl to death*. Then she looked down at herself. Jeans and T-shirt were hardly the clothes for a seduction dinner. She shrugged. Maybe lose the candles.

But she ran out of time. She heard the garage door go up, heard the kitchen door open.

"Jackie?"

Jacqueline grinned, listening as Kay moved about in the kitchen.

"God, that smells good."

Jacqueline walked in, leaning against the counter as Kay opened the oven door and peered inside. Jacqueline couldn't stop herself as her eyes followed Kay's length as she bent over. *Such a guy*.

"You really *can* cook." Then she spotted the wineglass still half full and raised an eyebrow. "Started without me?"

"Just barely. Would you like one?"

"Please."

Kay walked closer, pausing beside Jacqueline. Then, to Jacqueline's surprise, Kay leaned over and kissed her cheek.

"Thanks for cooking."

Jacqueline felt the blood rush to her face. "The least I could do. I mean, you're giving me a place to stay."

"Ah. But that's been my pleasure." Kay moved away, giving Jacqueline some space. "Let me change."

Jacqueline reached for her glass of wine as soon as Kay left the room. *Idiot.*

"Wow. The table looks nice," Kay called over the music.

Jacqueline went into the living room, turning down the volume. Yeah, the table looked nice. Nothing fancy. Hell, she wouldn't even need to light the candles. She shook her head. Kay was her friend. She needed to get over this silly crush. Actually, what she should really do is tell Kay and then they could have a good laugh about it. But she doubted Kay would laugh. Kay would most likely feel responsible for all this, for Jacqueline leaving, for the abandonment. And she would wonder why Jacqueline hadn't said anything earlier, when they could have talked about it and sorted through it all. Well, as Jackie had said, she'd been scared. Hell, she was still scared. But, now that she was older, she understood that Kay would never have stopped being friends with her, just like she wouldn't now. They would deal with it. And go on.

"What are you thinking about?"

Jacqueline realized that she was still standing there, staring at the table, lost in thought. "I . . . well, I thought that maybe . . . well, you know, candles and wine. I thought maybe you might think it was some sort of . . . seduction." *Damn*.

"Is it?" Kay asked quietly.

Jacqueline's eyes widened. "No! Of course not."

Kay only smiled, squeezing Jacqueline's arm as she walked past. She returned with both their glasses of wine and handed one to Jacqueline.

"Did you write today?"

"Yeah, I did. It was a good day."

"Can I see?"

"Oh," Jackie stared. "No."

"No?"

Jackie shook her head. "You can read my outline, if you want. It's rather lengthy. But the chapters that I have so far, no."

"Do you ever let anyone read them before they're finished?"

"The first one, yeah. Christopher read it as I went, then Ingrid. I learned my lesson. I can't write on demand, and they expected me to churn out pages each day. So now, no."

"How does it feel to write something, knowing that after it's published, thousands of people will read it?"

"I don't think of it that way. When I'm writing, I'm really writing for me. I don't hesitate over words, afraid I may offend someone if I word it one way or the other. I don't think about someone's reaction to it, I'm just trying to weave a story together."

Kay drew her into the living room. "I really did enjoy all your books. Your depiction of the south and the small towns was right on. I'm surprised. You've been gone so long. I can't believe that while you were here, you were gathering all this information and locking it inside."

Kay relaxed on the sofa and Jacqueline followed, both putting their feet up on the coffee table.

"You'd be surprised at how much I remember. A lot of it was just being at the café and listening. The old-timers would come in and tell stories, remember? Or they'd sit with their spouse of fifty years and talk about the same thing, over and over again. And they knew exactly what the other's answers would be and when they'd laugh." Jacqueline smiled, thinking of one couple in particular. She couldn't remember their names, but he always wore overalls and a flannel shirt, no matter the time of year. She would wear slacks, and Jacqueline remembered some of the others talking about her as if she'd committed a horrible crime.

"Remember the old couple, the guy that wore overalls all the time?"

"Yeah. Mr. and Mrs. Arnold."

"That's them. I couldn't think of their name," Jacqueline said. "Anyway, remember how they'd sit there and talk, and she'd pretend to be surprised by something he said, and you and I had heard him saying the same thing the week before and the week before that."

"Oh, yeah. They were married sixty-two years when he died. She was just devastated. Sixty-two years, Jackie. She probably couldn't recall a time in her life that he hadn't been in it."

"I don't suppose she's still around?"

"No. She passed on not even a year after him. It was sad. Their only son had been killed in Vietnam. The only other family lived over in Crockett. After he died, they wanted to put her in a nursing home, but she refused. She wanted to stay here, where they'd lived together all those years. And she got around okay, but ladies from the church would go by, make sure she had meals and clean and do laundry for her. But she just wasted away, you know? Like she didn't want to be here without her husband."

"Do you ever wonder if you'll have that with someone? That deep, lasting love that only death can separate?"

Kay shrugged. "I don't know. I hope I have that bond with someone, someday. I used to think . . ." She closed her eyes. *Don't go there.*

"What?"

"Nothing. It was nothing." She cleared her throat. "What about you?"

"Oh, I don't know, Kay. You're the only person I've ever felt close to, you know. When we were younger, I used to think that I could read your thoughts and you mine," Jacqueline admitted. She met Kay's eyes. "And we were just friends. I don't know if I'll ever find that with a lover. Obviously, so far, I've not met anyone."

Kay held her eyes. Jacqueline had just spoken the words that Kay had been afraid to voice. The only person she'd ever felt a bond with was Jacqueline. She wondered what would have happened if Jackie had stayed? She wondered if they would have become closer. Would they have become lovers? Strangely, that thought was not at all unsettling to her.

Jacqueline stood, taking Kay's empty glass. "I need to start the asparagus." Then she stopped. "You like asparagus, right?"

"Yes, although I doubt you're going to boil it in bacon drippings until it's limp," Kay said with a smile.

"Please don't say that's how your mother makes it. That would be a sin."

"*Everything* is cooked in bacon drippings, don't you remember?"

"Yes, I do. And I can't say I've missed it. Although the green beans your mother gave me yesterday were mighty tasty," Jacqueline called from the kitchen.

Kay wrapped her arms around herself, so very glad that Jacqueline was back. She hadn't felt this happy since, well, since Jackie had left. But, she warned herself, Jackie would be leaving again. She still found it amazing that they had this . . . this connection between them. She doubted seriously she would ever find it with someone else. And she was certain she would never find it with a man. Her husband, for instance. She hadn't even liked him as a friend. Why did she think she could be married to him? And what if he hadn't turned out to be such an asshole? Would they still be married? Would they have children by now? God, just the thought brought an ache to her heart. Perhaps she should be thankful he'd beat her. At least then, she had reason to divorce him. What if he'd turned out to be a nice guy? But that wasn't fair. If he'd been a nice guy, maybe she would have loved him.

She turned, watching Jackie walk back into the room with two full wineglasses. She was a beautiful woman. But, Kay admitted, she'd always been attractive. Her blond hair and blue eyes had attracted her share of the boys in high school, but Jackie never gave them a second look. Only Daniel. Of course, Kay knew now it was because Jackie was gay and wasn't interested in boys. And Daniel had been forced on her. And, as it turned out, she had been forced on Daniel.

"It won't be much longer. Are you hungry?"

"Yes. I skipped lunch."

"Why?"

"Mrs. Cartwright didn't work today. She wasn't feeling well."

"I didn't know you had help during the week," Jacqueline said. She resumed her seat on the sofa, handing Kay her glass. "How many employees do you have?"

"Just the two. Mrs. Cartwright has been with me since I opened. I rely on her a lot. She's widowed and doesn't mind working Saturdays. So, I usually have the weekend. Frannie is a senior now, and she's planning on going off to college, so I guess I'll be looking for someone else after summer."

"You really love it here, don't you?"

Kay shrugged. "It's home. It's familiar."

"And you're content."

"Yeah, I guess I am. I mean, I've grown to love this house. It's mine, at least. And, I make a comfortable living."

"But?"

"But?" Kay sighed. "Oh, I don't know. There should be more, I think. I mean, I'm happy, yes. Happy enough. But, years from now, will it still be enough?"

"You're only thirty-three. Way too young to be an old maid," Jacqueline teased.

"I really can't see myself marrying again, Jackie. The first one was so disastrous, but that's not the only thing. I just don't *see* it."

"You see yourself being alone?"

"I have this fear that Rose is going to send Lee Ann to live with me, and we'll grow old together, she shipping me off to a nursing home eventually."

"Are you serious?"

"Why do you think I'm spoiling her so much?"

"You'll meet someone."

"You think so? I know nearly everyone in this town and trust me, there is none I want to be with. And, it's not like new people move here, you know. No, I think I'm destined to be alone. I had my shot and I failed."

"The men in this town don't know what they're missing then. You're beautiful, smart. Hell, you own your own business. You're a good catch."

"Maybe I don't want to be caught."

"One strike and you're out?"

"It's not just that, Jackie. I knew, that day in the church when we were saying our vows that it wasn't right, that it wasn't what I wanted. But, I didn't see an alternative. I was young and working at the café. What future did I have?"

"And look at you now."

"Yeah. A success story," Kay said dryly, not able to keep the sarcasm out of her voice.

"You are, Kay. You could have folded. But you bought a business, you bought a house. You survived."

"Yeah. I survived." Kay reached over and took Jacqueline's hand. "Oh, Jackie, at first, I didn't think I would survive. I was humiliated. It wasn't so much what people were saying. I mean, they were sympathetic, how could they not be? But I was so disappointed in myself, for the choices I'd made, the decisions. Everything I did seemed wrong. When I opened my business, I thought, is this wrong, too? Is this another mistake?"

"But it wasn't."

"No. It was the best thing I could have done. I had something to focus on, something to work for. It's turned out okay. And, you know, I'm happy."

Jacqueline saw the doubt in Kay's eyes. She wondered what was really wrong, what regrets Kay had. Obviously, she regretted her marriage. But what else? Was it arrogant of her to think that perhaps Kay regretted their lost friendship? That her leaving had affected Kay somehow?

Jacqueline leaned forward. "Let's eat, huh?"

"Good. I thought you'd never ask."

They both stood, only feet apart. When their eyes met, Kay smiled and moved into Jacqueline's arms, holding her.

"Thank you for talking. I never get to voice my feelings to anyone. No one would understand."

Jacqueline let her arms wrap around Kay for a second, then pulled back, afraid her body would give her away. "You can always talk to me, Kay."

"I know. I've always known that." Kay moved to the stereo. "Want me to put on some more music?"

"Sure. You pick."

They fixed their plates in the kitchen and carried them into the dining room. Jacqueline went back for the wine, her body moving to the light jazz CD that Kay had chosen. She noted that the candles had been lit and she smiled at Kay, tipping her glass in the other woman's direction.

"Very nice."

"Yes, it is. Thank you."

Their conversation over dinner was more relaxed, Jacqueline telling Kay about her writing, her condo and her handful of friends in California.

"I don't think you should buy a house in the hills," Kay finally said. "Do you know how many times you've mentioned the bay and the ocean and the sounds of the water? I think maybe you like it there more than you think."

"When I was in LA, I lived in the city. I was surrounded by buildings and concrete. So, moving to Monterey and having a view of the bay is like moving to the country for me. And I have grown to love it. Besides, if I feel like getting away, I can always go visit Ingrid."

"Are you there a lot?"

"Probably more than Cheryl likes. I go up some weekends, often staying over on Saturday night. I miss the space, you know. They've got nearly an acre lot, on the edge of the redwood forest. It's quite beautiful."

"I'm glad you haven't turned into a city girl, Jackie. Look at you, still so comfortable in your jeans."

"I tried for a long time to forget that, you know. I wanted to fit in. Ingrid and I are friends. Good friends, really. But she didn't even know about my past. I never told them about where I'd come from, and they didn't ask."

"Why wouldn't they ask?"

Jacqueline shrugged. "I could say that maybe they didn't care enough to ask. But that's not it. I think they accepted that if I wanted to tell them, I would. Neither of them are close to their families. They don't really talk about that, either, so it wasn't hard."

"And in your mind, you really had no family?"

"Exactly. It wasn't like they were in my thoughts, you know?"

"Did we never cross your mind, Jackie?"

"*You* crossed my mind, Kay. I thought about you a lot. I never forgot you."

"I'm glad." Kay smiled across the table. "Because I never forgot you, either."

CHAPTER EIGHTEEN

Jacqueline smoothed the one pair of dress slacks she'd brought with her, then slammed the door on her Lexus. Kay thought she looked nice, even though she was wearing the same blouse she'd worn to the funeral. She hadn't exactly packed for a week's stay and, after today, she was officially out of clothes.

Mr. Lawrence's secretary greeted her with a curt nod. "Ms. Keys."

Jacqueline smiled politely. "Am I early?"

"No, they've been waiting," the older woman said disapprovingly.

"Good." Jacqueline strolled confidently to the door, knocking once before entering. Five men, all in suits, stood immediately.

"Jacqueline, come in," John said, motioning to the only empty chair. "You know your uncle, of course. This is Matthew Drake, his attorney."

Jacqueline politely shook his hand, sliding her glance to her uncle. "Uncle Walter, how are you?"

"Fine, Jacqueline. You're looking well."

"Thanks."

"And this is Tim and Jim Gentry."

Jacqueline raised an eyebrow. The Gentry twins. What had their mother been thinking? *Tim and Jim?*

"Ms. Keys, nice to meet you," Tim or Jim said.

"They will represent your mother," Lawrence said. "Have a seat, and we'll get started."

Jacqueline sat and addressed Tim or Jim. "How is my mother, anyway?"

"Well, she's in the hospital, as you know."

"Yes. Are we doing a live video feed to her or something?"

"Excuse me?"

"I just can't imagine my mother missing this," she said, noticing that Walter covered his mouth to hide a smile. Yes, even as a kid, she could feel the tension between Uncle Walter and her mother. No love lost there, for sure.

"We will be acting on her behalf and of course—"

"Reporting back to her immediately."

"Yes."

Jacqueline looked at John and raised both eyebrows. He nodded.

"Shall we begin?"

Jacqueline let Mr. Lawrence's voice fade into the background, instead, watching the reactions of the others. To her Uncle Walter's credit, he gave no visible reaction to learn that Jacqueline had inherited her father's share of Pine Springs Lumber. It occurred to her then that perhaps her father had already told him of his intentions. His only visible sign of surprise was when he raised his eyebrows at the mention of the bank. Her father's share in that, too, was left to Jacqueline. Tim and Jim were frantically writing notes, no doubt on orders from her mother. The will was rather straightforward, leaving most of his liquid assets to his wife, except some stock that he'd put in Jacqueline's name years ago, and a house on South Padre Island.

Jacqueline hid her surprise well, she thought. *South Padre?* Good Lord. What would she do with a house on the island?

"Lastly, he is leaving one million dollars to the city of Pine Springs, Texas to be used only for improvements to the existing City Park and the building of a new library for public use." Lawrence closed the folder and looked up. "Any questions?"

"Excuse me," Tim or Jim said. He looked at his notes. "There was no mention of Keys Industries."

"No. Keys Industries is not a part of his estate. The company, upon Nicolas Keys's death, reverted in full to the co-owner."

"Co-owner? Walter Keys?"

"No. Jacqueline Keys."

"I don't understand."

Lawrence passed a copy of the affidavit across the table.

"Co-owner?" Uncle Walter asked.

"Yes."

"But . . ."

Mr. Lawrence passed a copy to him as well, and Jacqueline watched as they read, wondering if any would question it. Walter passed the paper to his attorney, obviously confused by the legal document.

"So this is not part of his estate?" Tim or Jim asked.

"No."

"I'm . . . I'm surprised, Jacqueline. I had no idea you and your father reconciled," Walter said. "Does your mother know?"

Jacqueline smiled. "What do you think?"

"I think you're in for a fight."

"There will be no fight, Walter. The affidavit is perfectly legal," John Lawrence said.

Walter looked to his attorney.

"Yes. It's quite explicit regarding ownership."

Walter nodded. "I see. Well, Jacqueline, I guess we have some business to discuss."

"I suppose we do."

"I assume you want to sell. I'm willing to listen."

"Sell? Why do you assume that?"

Uncle Walter sat up straighter. "Well, you don't live here, for one thing. For another, I'm certain you have no idea how to run a lumber business."

"You're right about that. I'm hoping my father hired capable managers, Walter." Jacqueline stood. "Actually, I was hoping to get a tour of the plants later today. If you have the time, that is."

He nodded. "Do you even remember where the mill is?"

"About two?" Jacqueline asked, ignoring his question.

"Very well."

"Good." She turned to the twins. "Give Madeline my regards." She shook hands with Mr. Lawrence. "Thank you," she said quietly. "I'll be in touch."

"Of course."

Jacqueline walked out into the sunshine, finally releasing a sigh. It had gone better than she'd expected. Of course, once her mother heard the news, she was certain she'd get a call from one of the twins. Well, she'd let Mr. Lawrence handle that. Right now, she wanted to get into her jeans.

It was only eleven. She had plenty of time to change and surprise Kay with lunch. She smiled—just the thought of the other woman brightened her day.

"Friends, just friends," she murmured as she drove to Kay's house. Regardless, she was glad to have Kay in her life again. And if it was as friends, that was still better than not at all.

She pulled on the same jeans she'd worn yesterday, throwing the rest into a pile. She needed to remember to do laundry tonight or she'd be walking around town in her sweat pants. She decided a greasy hamburger for lunch would hit the spot and drove to the Dairy Mart, waiting in line at the drive-thru, impatiently tapping her fingers on her leg. Ten minutes later, she was on her way to the new strip center, the smell of burgers and fries making her stomach growl.

Thankfully, Kay's car was parked out front, and she walked in, glancing around the store for a familiar face.

"Hi. May I help you?"

Jacqueline met who she assumed was Mrs. Cartwright. She smiled and held up the bag. "Looking for Kay."

"Oh? Is she expecting you?"

Jacqueline shifted the bag to her left hand and extended her right. "I'm Jacqueline Keys, an old friend. I'm staying with her."

"*You're* Jacqueline Keys? Oh my. Well, I was sorry to hear about your father. You probably don't remember me. Gladys Cartwright. My husband worked at the mill for years."

"I'm sorry, no."

"Well, I didn't imagine you would. I heard that you were in town, but I had no idea you were staying with Kay."

And no doubt the news will be all over town by nightfall, Jacqueline guessed.

"Where is she? I brought lunch."

"Oh, Kay's in the back working on an order."

Jacqueline nodded. "And the back would be . . . where?"

"I'm sorry. Here, I'll show you."

Jacqueline followed the older woman, trying not to be annoyed. Small towns and all, they couldn't help it.

"Kay? You have a visitor."

"Okay. I'll be right there," Kay said without looking up.

"Actually, I thought I'd join you back here," Jacqueline said.

Kay's head jerked up, a smile lighting up her features. "Jackie! What are you doing here?"

She held up the bag. "Lunch."

"Oh, you didn't have to do that." She put her pen down and walked over, one arm circling Jacqueline's shoulder. "Mrs. Cartwright, do you mind holding down the fort for awhile longer?"

"Of course not, dear." She walked away, then stopped. "I'll be right outside if you need me."

Kay's eyes collided with Jacqueline's, both twinkling with amusement. "I'll be fine, Mrs. Cartwright. But thank you." When the older woman left, Kay apologized. "I'm sorry."

"It's okay. She's just looking out for you. Maybe later you could

140

scream or something, give her something to worry about," Jacqueline teased.

"You're just awful. I will not. She loves to gossip, and it would be all over town that you *tried* something with me."

"Well, I'll let you slap me. That should put me in my place."

Kay pointed to a chair. "Sit down and quit causing trouble."

Jacqueline did. "I guess I should have called first. You don't have plans, do you?"

Kay smiled. "Plans? No, Jackie. I have no lunch plans. In fact, I'm glad you came. I want to know what happened." Then she reached for the bag. "What'd you get?"

"Burgers."

"Great." Kay pulled out one. "Oh, and fries. You get extra points for fries."

"Maybe we should keep a tally then."

"Well, you got extra points for last night's dinner." She bit down on a crunchy fry. "What's for dinner tonight?"

"How can you think of dinner when you're eating lunch?"

"I have a very high metabolism," she stated.

"Uh-huh. That's how you've stayed so skinny?"

"Well, that and, you know, I can't cook."

Jacqueline pulled her own burger out, spreading out the paper and pouring her fries out, dousing them with ketchup.

Kay took a bite and grinned. "You remembered how I like them. No tomatoes."

"Who could forget? You threw enough of them at me over the years."

Kay reached over and grabbed Jacqueline's hand. "It was nice of you to do this. Thank you."

"My pleasure. And I also knew that you'd be curious about the reading and all."

"Yes. So spill it."

Jacqueline laughed. "Nothing to spill. No fireworks."

"None? How boring. Your Uncle Walter didn't grab you by the throat, demanding answers?"

"Nope. Although he assumed I wanted to sell."

141

"And do you?"

"No."

Kay smiled. "Good. So, what are you going to do with it?"

"Well, I don't rightly know," Jacqueline drawled in her best southern accent.

Kay laughed. "Who was there for your mother?"

"Tim and Jim Gentry."

"Both of them?"

"Yeah. Although only one spoke."

Kay nodded. "That would be Tim. Jim's a little shy. Always has been."

"How do you tell them apart?"

Kay smiled. "Well, obviously, the one who talks is Tim."

"Very funny."

"So, you don't know your mother's reaction, huh?"

"No. But I can't wait." Jacqueline took a bite of her burger. "I'm actually going out to the mill this afternoon. Uncle Walter is going to give me a tour."

"No kidding? Well, I guess you should see what you own, right?"

"Right. But Kay, what the hell am I going to do with a lumber company? Not to mention the bank. Keys Industries controls eighty percent of the goddamned bank!"

Kay stared. "I wonder if Rene knows. She walks around like she owns the town, ever since Jonathan became vice president."

Jacqueline laughed. "Well, if she doesn't know, I want to be the first to tell her."

"But really, Jackie, you only have two choices. Keep it or sell it. Simple."

"Simple, huh?"

"Although I doubt your Uncle Walter could afford to buy Keys Industries."

"No. He couldn't. It's worth ten times what the sawmill is worth. If I sold, it would be to a large corporation."

"But you don't want to do that?"

"I don't know enough about it, really. Hell, I don't know anything about it. I need to meet with the managers, the accountants, see how organized everything is. If my father did indeed make all the decisions, the managers may be just as lost as I am."

"You know, maybe Greg could help you. He'd at least know who the managers are and maybe give you some insight. That is, if you trust him."

"At this point, he might be the only one I do trust. At least I know him."

Kay grinned. "And you also know that Rose would kill him if he did anything to go against you."

"You think so?"

"Of course. Rose cares about you. She also wears the pants in the family."

"Why am I not surprised?"

CHAPTER NINETEEN

The old road to the mill was paved now, but other than that, not much had changed. The road cut right into the forest and she thought it ironic. All these huge trees growing so close to the mill, standing sentinels, watching as the logging trucks brought in their fallen brethren to meet their fate. Not much had changed, no. That is, not until she saw the mammoth gates blocking her path. Beyond the ten-foot wire fence stood a multitude of buildings. Most, she assumed, were the plants Greg had been describing, as smoke billowed out through massive chimneys. She frowned, imagining the pollutants being sent into the once clean air of Pine Springs.

She stopped at the gate and waited until the guard walked over.

"May I help you, ma'am?"

"I'm Jacqueline Keys. I have an appointment with Walter Keys."

The man studied her for a moment then glanced at his clipboard. "You don't remember me, do you?" he asked as he flipped through the pages.

"Excuse me?"

"I'm Paul Buchanan. I was a few years behind you in school."

Jacqueline searched her memory, but she couldn't recall this name or face. "I'm sorry, no. But, it's been a lot of years."

"Yeah, it has."

He stood looking at her, and Jacqueline finally raised an eyebrow. "You going to let me in or what?"

"Oh, sorry. Actually, no, you're not on the list."

"I see. But Walter is here?"

"Oh, yeah, he's here. Came in a couple of hours ago."

"Good. So, Paul, you want to give him a call or what?"

"Sure. I'll see if I can find him."

Jacqueline tried not to be annoyed, either at Uncle Walter or this Paul person. He was just doing his job. But make no mistake, by the time she left today, they would all know who she was.

Jacqueline waited, somewhat patiently, until Paul came back.

"He said for you to go straight to the offices and wait for him there."

"He said that, huh?"

"Yes, he did."

"I see. And where might I find Greg Kubiac?"

"Greg? Oh, he's in the office. Just ask someone, they'll find him."

"Thank you, Paul."

She waited while the electronic gates swung open, then followed the signs to the office. It was a two-story brick structure that looked completely out of place among the other buildings. She saw her father's parking spot and very nearly used it, but instead, pulled into a visitor's slot. No need in pissing everybody off the first day. As soon as she opened the car door, noise from the machinery filled the air. Every building seemed to be creaking at the seams and she stood, looking around, seeing men moving from building to building, forklifts carrying unfinished lumber, trucks hauling debris from one plant to the other. Massive. Again, what the *hell* was she going to do with this?

"Jackie?"

Jacqueline turned, smiling at the friendly face who greeted her. "Greg! How did you know I was here?"

He walked down the steps to meet her. "Paul called ahead. Said you'd asked about me. You're supposed to meet Walter?"

"Yes. But I wanted to talk to you about a few things. Maybe here is not a good place."

"Of course. Come into my office," he offered.

"No. Maybe here at the mill is not a good place," she clarified.

"What do you mean?"

"Greg, with my father's death, I now own Keys Industries, not Walter and not my mother."

Greg's eyes widened. "Oh, wow."

Jacqueline smiled. "Yeah, understatement. So, I'd like to discuss some things with you. In private."

"Okay, sure."

They both looked up and saw Walter approaching. "And I'd like to keep it between us, if you know what I mean."

"I worked for your father, Jackie. Not Walter."

"Good. Maybe tonight, Kay and I could come over?"

"Oh, Rose would love that. I'll call her later," he promised, turning to leave just as Walter walked up.

"Jacqueline, I see you found it."

"Yes. It's gotten a lot bigger," she said as she looked around her.

"Your father's doing, not mine." He looked up the steps as the door closed on Greg's retreating back. "I wasn't aware you knew Greg."

"He married Rose Garland."

"Oh, yes. I'd forgotten how close you and Kay were. Rumor has it you're actually staying with her."

"No rumor. I am."

He nodded. "Well, you want to see the office first or just head on out to the plants?"

"Let's do the plants. I hate offices."

"Very well. Be right back. I just need to fetch something for you."

She shrugged, shielding her eyes against the sun as she looked around. Jesus, what the hell was she going to do? Maybe she should just sell it and be done with it. Whoever bought it surely wouldn't lay off workers. If they could afford to buy it, they would be financially sound. Then it hit her. For the first time, it really hit her. She was now a very wealthy woman. And money always brought problems. She'd learned that from her childhood. People treated you differently. Hell, she'd learned that after her first novel was made into a movie. People she hardly knew were suddenly best friends and the friends she did have acted like she was now a different person.

"Here we go." Walter handed her a hardhat. At her raised eyebrow, he said, "Regulations."

"Uh-huh," she murmured but dutifully put it on. She followed him along the sidewalk and got into the opposite side of a golf cart.

"Your father bought four of these a few years ago. Said he was getting too old to visit the plants on foot."

Jackie nodded. "Good idea."

As they neared the first building, Walter pointed. "This is the plywood plant," he said loudly.

He stopped the golf cart and they both got out, Jackie following him inside. Most of the men ignored them as they moved about, trying to stay out of the way. "I can go over how it all works," he yelled. "Or just show you around."

She shook her head, motioning for him to walk on. They walked to the back of the plant, where the finished product was being cut and stacked on pallets, waiting for a forklift to move it. Once outside, the noise subsided somewhat.

"Noisy as hell," she said.

"Yes. They all are. Everyone wears earplugs inside." He pointed. "Fiberboard is over there. And the creosote plant is in the back."

"Where the black smoke is coming from?"

"Yes."

"What kind of environmental safeguards are in place?"

"We meet the minimum standards on all the plants," he said.

She nodded, then pointed to the old mill that she remembered. "The sawmill is practically surrounded."

"Yeah. But it's convenient. All of the by-products from the mill go immediately to the plants. In the old days, we'd have to store it and wait on the trucks to pick it up."

Jacqueline nodded, remembering the huge mounds of sawdust and chips that were piled high around the mill. She was about to ask another question when Walter's cell phone rang.

"Excuse me," he said politely, then answered. Jacqueline watched his face, noting the frown. "Yes, she's here now." He looked over at her. "I understand, but it appeared to be perfectly legal."

Ahh. Her mother, no doubt. Jacqueline crossed her arms, not ashamed at all to be listening in on the conversation.

"There's nothing I can do, Madeline. Talk to your lawyers." With that, he disconnected and shrugged. "Sorry."

"She's heard?"

"Oh, yes. I've been avoiding her calls all day."

"You two never really got along, did you?"

"Not really, no. But now, I don't have to see her again, do I?"

Jacqueline lowered her head, then looked back up. "Uncle Walter, how do you really feel about all this?"

"Well, the way I look at it, I haven't lost anything. And honestly, I never expected anything from Nicolas, unless perhaps his share of the sawmill." Then he smiled. "Thank God Madeline didn't get it, is all I can say. No offense, Jacqueline. I know she's still your mother."

"Well, that's where you're wrong. She's just a stranger to me."

He shifted nervously. "Me and Joan, well, we couldn't believe what she did. No one could. Especially Nicolas. It devastated him that he couldn't stand up to her. You may not know this, but he changed a lot after that. Became a different person, really. More likable, more down to earth. The old Nicolas Keys would never have left one million dollars to the city for a park and library."

"Well, then perhaps some good came of it all, huh?"

"You know, I'm sure Joan would love for you to come by and visit. Maybe have dinner with us one night."

"No offense, Uncle Walter, but it's been a long time. I've changed, too. Perhaps for now, we should just stick to business."

"I understand. Of course." He walked back toward the golf cart and Jacqueline followed. "About that, have you decided what you're going to do?"

"Do?"

"I mean, with all this. It can run itself for awhile. You were right, Nicolas hired good men. Some are local, but most not. But, bottom line, it's going to need direction. There has to be someone to defer to when questions arise. And they will, trust me."

"The sensible part of me says to sell it and be on my way. But the stubborn part says to stay and piss my mother off."

He laughed heartily, bending over at the waist. She finally joined in, not really intending it to be so funny. It was simply the truth.

"Oh, can you imagine the talk in town? It would kill her, I think."

"Well, that's not my intention."

"Paybacks?"

She grinned. "Perhaps." Despite her earlier apprehension, she was actually enjoying her time with Walter. He'd mellowed quite a bit. She wondered if he was all that upset that she was here. All these years, he hadn't had to change a thing, just keep running the sawmill like he always had, only suddenly, he was making a lot more money doing it. Why should he want the headache of Keys Industries? "Listen, let's can the rest of the tour. I think I'd like to meet with the managers and see what's going on and who's in charge. Or are they deferring questions to you now?"

"No. Nicolas made it clear that I was no part of Keys Industries."

"I'm sorry. I know you worked closely together."

"Again, no offense, but he did his thing and I did mine. And I'd have been crazy to buck it, even if I could."

"What do you mean?"

"He had controlling interests in the sawmill. So, whatever decisions were made, we discussed it, but if it was something he really wanted to do, he didn't need my approval."

"But?"

"But, we usually agreed, so there were few problems. When he first got the idea for the plants, I thought he was crazy. But, he used his own money to finance them so I didn't really have a say. When he wanted to build them here, on sawmill land, I couldn't say no. He was majority owner."

"But you were compensated?"

"Yes. Keys Industries paid Pine Springs Lumber, which in turn, paid me."

Jacqueline shook her head. Uncle Walter, bless his heart, really didn't have a clue. Because her father owned sixty percent of the sawmill, Keys Industries only paid out forty percent of the normal cost, yet yielded one hundred percent of the profit. Her father was actually a very smart man. Even she, with little business sense, could see that.

"Since you already know Greg, I'll let him introduce you around. I can't promise that everyone is here, though. Their schedules vary and some work from home at times. Greg will know."

"What exactly is Greg's position?"

"Started out running the computers. Not that I know a whole lot about that. I mean, I've got one in my office, and I know how to check my e-mail, that's about it. But your father liked him, and Greg's pretty smart. But exactly what he does? I don't know. I only know he's got his nose in a computer all day long."

Jacqueline paused as she walked around the golf cart, sticking out her hand to shake her uncle's. "Thank you for the tour. I appreciate it."

"No problem. And I'm sorry about the thing at the gate. I completely forgot to tell Paul you'd be coming by."

Jacqueline stared at him, trying to see if he was lying or not. What better way to put her in her place than to have the gates closed to her? But no, he seemed completely sincere. "It's okay. I'll be in touch. We will, no doubt, have a lot to discuss."

"You know where to find me."

She watched him drive off, dirty jeans, work hat and all. No, he wasn't a businessman or entrepreneur. He was just a man who loved his work. And, if she sold to a large corporation, he would be very easy to take advantage of. They would have him for lunch.

She sighed, finally taking off the hardhat and running her fingers through her hair. She couldn't worry about Walter now. She had her own problems. With that, she climbed the steps to the offices, pausing only briefly before opening the door. It was cool and quiet inside. A young woman sat at the reception desk and smiled politely at her.

"Good afternoon. How can I help you?"

Jacqueline moved forward, smiling slightly. "Is Greg around?"

"Yes, ma'am. Do you have an appointment?"

Jacqueline raised an eyebrow. For a small town, they were awfully concerned with appointments. "No. But please get him for me, would you?"

"And your name?"

Jacqueline grinned. "Jackie."

"Jackie?"

"Just Jackie."

She nodded slowly, pointing to one of the visitor chairs. "Stay here."

"Right here?"

"Yes."

"Okay."

Jacqueline rolled her eyes. God, she'd rather be anywhere than going through all this. Well, actually, she'd rather be sitting on the floor with Kay, talking. It occurred to her that Kay was still as affectionate as ever. Kay was always touching her when they were kids and that hadn't changed. Jacqueline liked it. In fact, she—

"Jackie?"

151

Jacqueline blinked, putting thoughts of Kay from her mind. "Greg."

"Trying to scare the hired help?" he whispered.

She laughed. "Sorry. Couldn't resist."

"Come on back."

His office was a mess, littered with computers and cables and papers and, God, a thousand pictures of Rose and the kids.

"Excuse the clutter, but I swear, I know where everything is."

Jacqueline picked up a picture, smiling. It was from years ago. Rose was still thin, and there was only one kid in the photo. Lee Ann, no doubt. "Cute."

He blushed, but straightened the picture when Jacqueline put it back. Then he sat down in his chair, waiting for Jacqueline to start.

Instead Jacqueline looked around, counting monitors. "You have four computers in here?"

He grinned. "Actually, I have nine. Each monitor can be hooked up to several at once."

"So, you really are a computer geek," she said as she took a seat. "Yep."

She smiled. "In my day, that was considered an insult."

"Quite a compliment today, thank you."

She nodded. "So, what exactly do you do here?"

"My title? I'm the network—"

"Not your title. What do you do?"

He shrugged. "A little of everything, actually. I run the network, of course. And the security cameras are all online. I manage all the servers—we have five of them. And most recently, I've been doing the purchasing online, and sales."

"Purchasing and sales? What do the managers do?"

"Each plant has a manager. They keep track of inventory, mainly. They let me know what we've got to sell. If the demand is more than we can produce using only the sawmill for by-products, we'll purchase waste from another mill and ship it in."

"Doesn't that cut into the profit?"

"Yes. But your father didn't want to lose business."

"What about maintenance?"

"Maintenance? On the equipment?"

"Yes."

"There's a crew. We're round the clock now. Have been for the last six years or so. Maintenance has a regular shift, just like everyone else. Why?"

"Just wondering if that was outsourced or not."

"No, no. Keys Industries is pretty self-sufficient."

"How many managers are there?"

"Well, let's see." He counted silently, marking off names on his fingers. "Counting Walter?"

"Yes."

"Five managers over the plants. Then, maintenance has one, but they're not really involved in the operations, you know."

"Are they all here today?"

"No. Peterson lives all the way over in Jasper, and he only comes in once a week. He works from home. Mark Edwards is traveling this week."

"Traveling?"

"He's creosote plant. The regional office for the phone company is taking bids on poles."

"So, there's not like a sales group?"

"No. Your father was it. But, everything is pretty much set. We've got contracts for most of the home building suppliers in the entire state, not just East Texas. And we ship to six surrounding states. There is one thing that he was working on that someone's going to have to take over, though."

"What's that?"

"Cattle feed."

"Cattle feed?"

"There's a place in Canada that buys most of our sawdust and wood chips. They make wood molasses—it's used in cattle feed."

"And?"

"And your father didn't want to sell the sawdust for pennies and let some company in Canada turn around and sell the feed for a huge profit. We're making next to nothing on the deal."

"So, make it yourself?"

"Yeah."

"He obviously had too much time on his hands."

"Well, like I said the other night, he had a vision."

She closed her eyes. *A vision? Great.* "Okay, accountants? Did he have a CPA firm in town or what?"

"No, they're all here. Four in that department, plus a secretary."

"They handled all finances?"

"Yes."

"And who, you know, audited them?"

"Your father has a firm out of Houston that audits and does the taxes."

"That's smart."

"Yeah. We haven't had any problems since I've been here. No one's lost their job, anyway."

"Okay, you know what? I'm on overload right now. I wanted to meet with some of them, but not now. Right now, I think I need a drink."

Greg laughed. "I know what you mean. You want me to tell them you'll come back, what? Tomorrow?"

"How about you send out an e-mail to everyone that we're going to have a staff meeting? I'd like everyone to attend, even this Peterson person in Jasper. And the accounting staff, of course. I'll see if Mr. Lawrence can make it, too."

"I'll get right on it. What time?"

"Let's do it Friday morning. That'll give everyone notice. What about the traveling guy? Edwards?"

"I'll get in touch with him. He's in the Dallas area."

"Thanks, Greg."

"So? Are we still on for tonight? Rose wanted to know if she needed to do dinner or if you'd come after?"

"Tell you what. I think Kay gets cranky if she doesn't get her pizza fix at least once a week. How about we pick up a couple to bring over?"

"That sounds great."

"What about the kids? Anything special?"

"Kay will know."

Jacqueline stood, extending her hand to Greg. "Thanks Greg. We'll talk more tonight, okay?"

"Sure. Look forward to it."

Jackie paused at the door. "One more thing. Where was my father's office?"

"Second floor. You want to go up? I'm sure Mrs. Willis would show you around."

"Mrs. Willis? That was his secretary's name way back then."

"She's still here."

Jacqueline nodded. "Tell you what. Why don't you call her, tell her I'm on my way up. I just want to look around some."

"Of course."

Jacqueline took the stairs next to Greg's office, wondering how many times a day he used them. At the top, she paused only slightly before opening the door. She entered at the edge of a large lobby. A vase of a dozen roses sat on one of the two tables, which were both littered with magazines.

"You must be Jacqueline. Come in, dear."

Jacqueline saw the tiny woman move gracefully into the lobby, beckoning her closer.

"I'm Mrs. Willis, you probably don't remember me."

"Yes, I do, actually. You're looking well."

The older woman blushed. "As charming as your father. I swear, no one took the news harder than I did. That man was a saint, as far as I'm concerned."

Jacqueline nodded, then looked around. "Nice. Did he occupy the entire floor?"

"Half." She pointed. "Through the double doors down there, the managers all have offices. And Mr. Lawrence, of course."

"He has an office here?"

"I assume John only told you as much as he thought you needed to know."

Jacqueline shoved her hands in her pockets, walking slowly

toward the office that bore her father's name. She turned. "My father obviously trusted you, you've been with him forever."

The old woman just smiled. "How do you like living by the bay? I understand it's beautiful there."

Jackie hid her surprise, or thought she did. "It's quite lovely, Mrs. Willis. Very different from East Texas."

"Oh, I imagine."

Jackie nodded. "I assume then, that you are aware of my position?"

"Of course, Jacqueline. May I call you Jacqueline?"

Jacqueline grinned. "I doubt I'll answer to Ms. Keys."

"Speaking of her, rumor has it that you've been banned from the hospital."

Jacqueline's eyes twinkled. "Who controls the hospital, Mrs. Willis?"

"Why, Keys Industries, of course."

Jackie smiled. "Shall we have her discharged?"

The old woman bent over in laughter, then drew Jacqueline into her father's office.

"Come, look at where he spent his time. He was very happy here, Jacqueline. He spent much more time here than he did at home. Were you aware that your parents had separate wings in their home? Tragedy, what she drove him to."

Jacqueline ran her hands across the shiny, wooden desk. Everything was neat, tidy. Her mouth fell open when she saw the picture. It was of her. She was walking along Monterey Bay. Her eyes flew to Mrs. Willis.

"He kept up with you, yes."

"You knew about the will in advance? About Keys Industries?"

"Oh, yes."

"Yet Madeline never knew?"

Mrs. Willis stood up straight. "I never gossip, Jacqueline. Whatever is spoken inside this room, never leaves this room."

Jacqueline moved to the windows, looking out at the plants. "Who did my father trust the most?"

"What do you mean?"

She turned back to the room. "Of the managers, of the staff, who did he trust the most?"

"What exactly is it you're asking?"

"Who was his right hand?"

Mrs. Willis smiled. "Oh, that's easy. Greg Kubiak. He's one smart young man. Your father relied on him for nearly everything."

Jacqueline frowned. "Yet he wasn't one of the managers."

"Well, no, he knew too much about the whole operation to be one of the managers."

"What's his salary?"

"Oh, I don't have access to payroll records."

Jacqueline cocked her head, eyebrow raised.

"But I could find out, of course."

Jacqueline pointed at the phone. "Now?"

CHAPTER TWENTY

It was after four when Jacqueline finally drove into Kay's neighborhood. She was on overload. Mrs. Willis had been very talkative, reminding Jacqueline again that what was spoken in her father's office went no farther. But still, she had been appalled by Greg's low salary, especially when compared to what the managers received.

But she didn't have time to think about it all now. She was out of clothes. The first thing she did when she walked in the house was start laundry. She stripped and stood naked, shoving her clothes into the washer. She was hesitant about adding Kay's clothes to her own, but she thought it would be rude not to. She sorted through Kay's hamper, pulling out darks that she added to her load. The whites, well, maybe they could wait. She thought Kay might kill her if she knew Jacqueline had been sorting through her underwear.

She took time to read her e-mail, pleased that Ingrid *loved* the first draft she'd sent.

"Great. Maybe she'll leave me alone for awhile," she murmured.

She replied, telling Ingrid that she wouldn't be leaving until next week at the earliest. She didn't elaborate. Ingrid would be pacified now that she had the draft.

After a quick shower, she pulled on sweats and waited patiently for the dryer to finish. Jeans took forever to dry and she wondered if she'd be reduced to wearing her sweats to Rose's house. Not a great way to talk business with Greg.

She was still pacing in the laundry room when Kay arrived home. She stuck her head out just as Kay stepped in the kitchen.

"Hey."

"Hey, yourself." Kay looked her over, then looked into the kitchen. "What's that I don't smell?"

Jacqueline smiled. "Pizza."

"Pizza? I thought you were working on your points."

"I thought you loved pizza?"

"I do. I'm just teasing. Rose called me. I understand we have a date tonight."

"You don't mind, do you?"

"Of course not."

"I did laundry, too."

"Turning into a housewife, huh?"

"Very funny. Don't think I didn't consider stealing some of your jeans."

"Good thing I'm shorter than you." Kay put her purse on the counter, then turned back to Jacqueline. "Did you at least do mine, too? I hate doing laundry."

"Yes, I did. I was worried about that little sweater thing you wore the other day. It wasn't supposed to be dry cleaned, was it?"

"Not dry cleaned, no. But it doesn't need to be in the dryer."

"Oh shit." Jacqueline rushed back into the laundry room, opening the dryer and shuffling through the jeans to find the sweater. She pulled it out. "Damn," she murmured. She held it behind her back. "Was it one of your favorites?" she called.

Kay stepped behind her. "Why? What's wrong?"

Jacqueline held it up. "It might fit Lee Ann now."

Kay smiled, then laughed. "Oh, Jackie. Some things never change, do they?"

"I don't know what you're talking about."

"Of course you do. I doubt my mother has forgiven you yet."

"That was not my fault. She said to do all the whites. That sweater was white."

"That sweater was . . ."

"I know, I know. Hand knitted by your great-great-grand-mother a hundred years ago."

Kay leaned forward. "I hated that sweater," she said quietly. "And I wasn't really fond of this one, either."

"I'm really sorry."

"No problem. And you're right. Lee Ann will love it." Kay took it with her as she retreated to her bedroom.

Jacqueline was sprawled on the sofa, eyes closed when Kay came back, dressed in faded jeans and a long-sleeved T-shirt. Kay stared at her for the longest time, her eyes moving over her long legs to her waist, finally resting on her face. She looked so relaxed, so comfortable. And tired. Kay wondered if she'd been having trouble sleeping. Jackie had not said.

"What are you looking at?" Jacqueline murmured. She hadn't opened her eyes, but she felt Kay's presence.

"I was looking at you, of course."

Jacqueline turned her head, smiling. "And?"

"And? I was wondering if you'd been sleeping okay. You look tired."

Jacqueline sat up. "No, I'm sleeping fine. I was just thinking, not sleeping."

"Oh? Want to talk?"

"Yeah, I do. But we don't have time. Maybe after I've had a chance to talk to Greg and sort some of this out, I'll feel better about it. Right now, I'm overwhelmed by it all."

"How was your Uncle Walter?"

"He was okay, really. And I think he was sincere. If I'd been in his shoes, I'd be a little bitter, I think. But he seems content the way things are."

"So, no alliance with your mother?"

"No. Actually, she called while I was there. He wasn't very pleasant to her."

"What's next then?"

"I'm going to meet with the office staff on Friday. Greg was going to set it up for me. I want to see how everyone feels about me being there, for one thing." She buried her hands in her hair. "Oh, Kay, my gut tells me to sell this thing and get on with my life. But, something is telling me not to. And I don't know what it is."

Kay sat down beside her, circling her shoulders with one arm. "Maybe you're just genuinely concerned with the welfare of the workers. You suddenly feel responsible for them."

"Yeah. That's part of it. Did I tell you that my father left one million dollars to the fair city of Pine Springs?"

"No! You're joking?"

"No. It's supposed to go to the city park and for a new library."

Kay smiled. "So, some good did come out of it."

"Yeah, it did. I'm sure that threw my mother. But, knowing her, she'll take credit for it."

"And we both know she would never have done that."

"Exactly."

"Well, maybe you just need to give it time, Jackie. Sleep on it. Let it sink in."

"You're probably right." Jacqueline sat up, feeling Kay's arm slip away from her. "We should get going. I'm sure my jeans are dry by now."

"Go check on them. I'll call in a pizza order."

"Don't forget the kids," Jacqueline reminded her.

"No. They like the cheese sticks." Kay stood and pulled Jacqueline to her feet. "Go check your laundry."

Thirty minutes later, they were pulling up to the pizza place, and Kay watched as Jacqueline walked inside, tall and straight.

Again, she thought what an attractive woman she was. Her blond hair was a little shorter and darker than it'd been in high school, but not by much. Just styled differently. But she was still athletic looking, fit. And tan. Kay assumed living in California, one wouldn't have to worry about losing a tan during the winter months.

She was only slightly aware that she was picturing Jackie with an all-over tan. *What are you doing?* She had no idea. She only knew that she loved being in Jackie's presence. She always had. Being around Jackie made her *feel* good. She couldn't explain it. Actually, she didn't *want* to explain it. She didn't want to analyze anything. She just wanted to enjoy her time with Jackie, for however long she had. After that, well—

Her eyes were again drawn to the woman as Jackie walked back to the car, three pizza boxes piled high in her arms. Jackie stopped, her head tilted to the side as she met Kay's eyes through the window. Kay realized she had stopped breathing.

Then Jackie gave a subtle wink, breaking the spell. Kay reached over and opened the door for her.

"This smells good. We may have to sample some before we get there."

"Rose will kill you," Kay said as she took the boxes from Jackie.

"Rose has too many rules."

"Yes, she does." Kay turned to Jackie, looking at her profile in the darkness. "You'll want to talk to Greg alone, I guess."

Jacqueline turned her head quickly and met Kay's eyes. "Yeah, I mean, that's okay, right? I'm not trying to keep anything from you guys, it's just . . ."

"I know, Jackie. I was just wondering if I need to keep Rose and the kids occupied. You know how nosy she is."

"Well, unlike most of the men I've met recently, I think Greg will share whatever I have to say with Rose anyway. It's just, I'd like to talk to him without interruptions."

"I understand. I'll get a board game out so Rose and I can play with the kids."

"Thanks, Kay." Without thinking, Jacqueline reached across the seats and found Kay's hand. She squeezed, feeling the light pressure as Kay returned the gesture.

Jacqueline relaxed as she drove through the deserted streets, turning off the main road only a few minutes later. They parked in the driveway next to Greg's truck and the motion light came on immediately.

"No sneaking up, huh? What's with everyone and motion lights?"

"Don't know if you've noticed, but street lights are few and far between."

Jackie nodded. "You're right. I hadn't noticed."

"Besides, I'm sure there is some sort of alarm attached to the lights. Lee Ann will no doubt be waiting at the door."

And she was, holding it open as Rose yelled at her from the kitchen to shut the door, bugs were getting in!

Jacqueline and Kay smiled at each other. "I really do love your sister, you know."

"How could you not?"

Rose met them at the door, trying to keep Lee Ann and Denny inside. "Thank God. They were driving me crazy. Not only were they waiting for pizza, but they were waiting for Aunt Kay and that pretty woman," Rose said.

Kay laughed and turned to Jackie. "You have a fan club already."

"Great," she drawled.

Jacqueline watched as Kay lifted Lee Ann into her arms for a hug, then quickly repeated the gesture with Denny. The twins, barely two, were already at the table, tucked into highchairs. The boy was . . . Harrison? Hell, she couldn't remember. But the girl was Emily. Right? She tugged on Kay's arm.

"What?"

"Harrison and Emily?" she asked, pointing.

Kay smiled. "Emma."

"Emma. Right."

"Relax."

"I am."

"You don't have to know their names. They don't really talk much, you know."

"I don't want Rose getting on me for not knowing their names."

"What are you two whispering about?" Rose demanded.

"Nothing," they said in unison.

"Uh-huh. Up to no good, probably."

"Hey guys," Greg said. "I didn't hear you come in." He looked like he'd just gotten out of the shower.

"Just got here."

"Good. You want a beer?" he asked.

"I've got tea," Rose called.

Kay rolled her eyes. "I'll have a beer."

"Me, too."

The pizza boxes were spread out on the table, and they all helped themselves, the two older kids reaching immediately for the cheese sticks. Jacqueline sat back, watching. Everyone looked so happy, so content. It was wonderful how Rose had managed to duplicate her parents' household. Her kids were very lucky.

Kay watched Jackie, noting the thoughtful expression on her face. Without warning, Jackie turned and captured her eyes. Kay was caught off guard by the intimacy she glimpsed there. The crystal blue of Jackie's eyes held her, and once again, Kay realized she had stopped breathing.

The room receded, and Jacqueline was aware of her heartbeat as it drummed in her ears. Now, just like all those years ago, she had a nearly overwhelming desire to close the distance between them. An ache . . . a need . . . that was so profound, it was physically painful. But now, like then, she pulled her eyes from Kay, thankful her hand didn't tremble as she reached for a slice of pizza. Amazing how one look into those blue eyes could bring back the intense cravings she'd had as a teen.

❧

Jacqueline settled into the lawn chair next to Greg, the muted voices of Kay, Rose and the kids fading in the darkness.

"Sorry that we don't have a study or somewhere to talk," Greg apologized.

"I happen to think sitting outside on such a pleasant evening as this beats any study, Greg." She cleared her throat. "I also know my father was grossly underpaying you, so I don't expect a study."

Greg looked away. "I've only been with the company eight years. I can't complain."

Jacqueline leaned forward. "Mrs. Willis tells me that my father trusted you completely."

"I tried not to disappoint him. He was actually a fairly easy man to work for."

"As you know, I am completely in over my head with this business," she said. "And whether I keep it or sell it depends on the people my father hired to run it. You've told me, and Mrs. Willis has told me, that the managers are all top-notch. But they need direction. I hardly think I'm the one to give it." Jackie crossed her legs, her gaze resting on Greg until he finally met her eyes. "I think . . . I think you're the best one to give it, Greg."

"*Me?*"

"Yes. For one thing, you're the only one there I even remotely trust. Hell, you're the only one I know."

"But, Jackie, I've only been there eight years. They're not going to take direction from me. Some of the managers have been with your father for years and years. They think . . . well . . . never mind."

"They've already decided among themselves who is taking over?" Jacqueline guessed.

"They have been speculating. They assume Mr. Lawrence will appoint someone as interim."

"I've not actually discussed this with Mr. Lawrence." She shifted in the chair, wondering why she just didn't sell the damn thing and be on her way. "You said yourself, the managers were each experts in their own plants, yet none were knowledgeable of

165

the whole operation. Mrs. Willis tells me you were his right-hand man. Is that not true?"

"The last year or so, he had me more involved, yes. Like I said, purchasing and sales, both. He allowed me to see the big picture and what his goals were." He leaned forward. "But Jackie, I hardly think he was grooming me for anything."

"Why not? You're young, bright. You've not been entrenched as a manager in one of the plants, which obviously limits your knowledge of the company."

"I'm barely thirty, Jackie. Most of the managers are in their fifties. Mr. Peterson is sixty-one. He's worked with your father in some capacity for over twenty years."

Jacqueline smiled. "Which is exactly why I don't trust him." She watched Greg for a moment, then continued. "How many of them are aware of this cattle feed thing you were telling me about?"

Greg shook his head. "Probably none. Whenever your father wanted to venture into something new, he didn't announce it until he was ready to launch. I would assume Mr. Lawrence knew about it."

"I'm guessing, Greg, that you actually helped him put his ideas together. Am I right?"

"I worked with him on it, yes."

"So, if we wanted to implement this latest idea of his, you think you'd be able to do it?"

Their eyes met.

"I think so. I mean, if I had—"

"The authority to make decisions, the clout to enforce them?" Jacqueline stood, pacing on the tiny patio. "Greg, if you tell me you don't want to do this, I'll understand. But right now, you're all I have. I don't want to entrust this business to anyone else. I think you can do a good job."

Greg stood, too, and walked out into the yard, facing Jackie. "I'd like to say that I'll give it a shot, but the others, they'll balk. I know them."

"How can they balk? They're not the boss."

"Maybe you should run this by Mr. Lawrence first. He may already have some things lined up."

Jackie smiled slightly. "He's not the boss, either."

Greg shoved his hands in his pockets. "I see you have your mind made up."

"This whole situation is rather overwhelming to me, Greg. And I don't want to let it control me." She walked off the patio to join him in the yard. "So, in order to keep things running until I can sort it all out and decide what I'm going to do, I want you to take over. And I'm not stupid, Greg. I know this is a good old boy network here, and I know it won't be easy for you. But I'll have John make it plain to the others that everything goes through you, just like everything went through my father."

"Okay. If you think we can do this, I'll give it my best."

"Good. Now, what are the chances of me gaining access to the company's computer system?"

"Considering that I control the network, I'd say pretty good." Greg said with a smile.

"Tomorrow morning, I'd like to log in and poke around a bit. Personnel files, payroll, that sort of thing."

"From off site?"

"Yes. Can you call me in the morning and give me a quick tutorial?"

"Of course."

Jackie grasped his shoulder and squeezed. "This is a good opportunity for you, Greg. I think you'll do just fine."

"Why do you think my husband is pacing?" Rose whispered to Kay.

Kay reached around Lee Ann to toss the dice, glancing out the window to watch the two shadows on the lawn.

"They're talking business, I guess."

"Yeah, but what? He was very evasive when he got home."

"Mommy, it's your turn," Lee Ann said, nudging her.

"Sorry." She looked at Kay. "You know something, don't you?"

Kay shrugged. "Not my place, Rosie."

"What do you mean, not your place? I'm your sister!"

Kay just stared at her.

"Oh, yeah. I forgot. Jackie *always* outranked me."

"It's not that," Kay said. "It's just, I don't know how much she wants out in public yet. And I'm sure Greg will fill you in."

"Public? I'm hardly public," Rose insisted.

Kay raised both eyebrows. "You gossip worse than an old hen, Rose!"

"What's gossip, Mommy?"

Kay grinned, waiting for Rose's response. Rose stuck her tongue out at Kay before answering.

"Gossip is something you'll learn all about when you get into high school. Until then, you don't need to worry your little britches about it."

Kay shook her head. "Lame, Rose."

"What's lame, Aunt Kay?"

"You really think Greg can handle it?" Kay asked as they drove home.

"I don't know. What do you think?"

"He's super smart, I know that. And I know from talking to Rose, at least in the last year or so, your father was getting him more involved. But Jackie, run the whole *thing*?"

"From what everyone has told me, the operation is set and runs smoothly on its own. There are just some decisions to be made regarding purchasing and sales, decisions that my father made. And from what I understand, Greg has been monitoring that for him. So yeah, I think Greg probably knows better than any of the managers what's going on." Jackie let out a heavy breath. "Kay, I don't mind saying, I'm way over my head here."

"I'm sure it's a bit frightening."

"It's fucking frightening!" Jacqueline said with a laugh. "I came back for a funeral I didn't want to go to. I never would have imagined he'd leave me his business. I mean, Kay, what was he thinking?"

"Well, judging from the letter he left you, he was trying to make amends."

"You know, if he hadn't left me that damn letter—hadn't said that he didn't want Madeline to get the business—I'd just sell the thing and be on my way. Hell, I'd give it to somebody. I don't want his money! I don't *need* his money!"

Kay reached over and squeezed Jackie's thigh. "Jackie, don't let this make you crazy. It's overwhelming, I know. But just take it one day at a time."

"I feel like I'm in a dream or something, you know?" Jacqueline reached down and covered Kay's hand, pressing it harder into her thigh. "I'm just kinda making it up as I go."

Kay's eyes lighted on their hands, and she had the strangest sensation travel through her body. Jackie's hand was warm on her own, and Kay spread her fingers, squeezing lightly on Jackie's thigh, feeling the gentle tremble of Jackie's leg. She looked up, watching Jackie's profile as she drove. Then Jackie turned, meeting her eyes. In the brief instant that their gazes locked, Kay stopped breathing entirely.

"I'm sorry," Jacqueline murmured, releasing Kay's hand. *What are you doing?*

Kay cleared her throat. "Sorry for what?"

Jacqueline shook her head, cursing the silly teenage crush that she couldn't seem to shake. But it wasn't all her fault. Kay was just too affectionate, too physical. And Jacqueline was not immune to her touch. She never had been.

Kay realized her hand was still resting gently on Jackie's thigh. She moved it, but only far enough to wrap her fingers around Jackie's forearm.

"Do you think I'm afraid of you, Jackie? Because you touch me? Is that it?"

Jacqueline shrugged. "Straight women, sometimes, get uncomfortable when—"

"We've always touched, Jackie."

Yes, always. And at the end, it had been pure torture. Jacqueline remembered one night in particular. A Friday night. The football game had been out of town, and Kay decided she didn't want to go. Billy Ray was taking a bunch of his friends, and Kay didn't want to ride with them. So, Jacqueline stayed behind, too. They made popcorn and watched TV and fended off Rose as she tried to crash their party.

"It's not like I can't smell the popcorn," Rose yelled through the door. "Let me in!"

"Go away, squirt!" Jackie yelled back. "We're talking."

"I'm nearly thirteen! Quit calling me squirt!"

Kay laughed and bumped Jackie's shoulder. "You know, she only yells when you're here."

"Probably because that's the only time you lock her out of your room."

Pounding on the door finally brought Kay off the bed. She jerked it open, staring down her sister.

"Rose! Stop already. Jackie hasn't been over in nearly a month. We would like some privacy, if you don't mind."

"Rosie? Leave them alone," Mrs. Garland yelled down the hall.

"Now you've done it," Kay said. "Mama heard you."

"Can I at least have some popcorn?"

Kay looked at Jackie, waiting. Jackie took one more handful from her bowl, then offered it to Rose.

"Here you go, squirt. You can have the rest of mine."

Rose snatched the bowl, grinning. "Thanks, Jackie."

Kay shut the door and locked it, then joined Jackie on the bed, moving her bowl of popcorn between them so they could share.

"She's crazy about you, you know," Kay said.

Jackie grinned. "Well, what's not to be crazy about, huh?"

Jackie shut her eyes for a moment as Kay leaned back against the pillows, their shoulders brushing. Common sense told her to move away, away from her touch, but she couldn't make herself move. It felt too good.

"I'm glad you decided not to go to the game, Jackie. You haven't stayed over in ages." Kay moved her hand, lightly resting it on Jackie's hip. *"I've missed this."*

Jackie managed to stifle her moan, but the hand on her hip was hot, burning her skin. She cleared her throat, but her voice was still husky when she spoke.

"I've missed this, too, Kay."

Kay moved the popcorn and turned on her side, facing Jackie. Jackie felt as if her heart would explode at any moment. She was certain Kay could hear it as it pounded out of control. She kept her eyes glued firmly on the TV, so afraid to even look at Kay as she lay next to her.

"Do you think we're too old for this?"

Jackie dared to look at her then. "Too old for what?"

"Sleepovers. We're seventeen."

Jackie swallowed nervously. "Like maybe we shouldn't share a bed? Does it bother you?"

"No! Of course not. I love sleeping with you, Jackie. Especially like now, when it's cold."

"Why when it's cold?" Jackie asked hesitantly.

" 'Cause of the way you snuggle."

"Snuggle? I don't snuggle," Jackie insisted.

"Yeah, you do. You're like my own personal heater when you wrap your arms around me and hold me."

This time Jackie couldn't stop the groan that escaped and she lay her head back, eyes looking at the ceiling. Oh my God, she thought to herself, you hold her when you sleep!

"What's wrong?"

Jackie turned, meeting the blue eyes that were so close to her own. Blue eyes that were filled with trust and love. And Jackie knew the night couldn't come fast enough.

"I love sleeping with you too."

"Are you okay?"

Jacqueline turned, bringing her mind back to the present. "Yes. I'm sorry."

Kay grinned. "You missed our turn."

"Oh, shit. Sorry." Jacqueline turned at the next block. "I was—"

"Lost in thought?"

"Yeah."

"About?"

Jacqueline shook her head. "Just thinking back to when we were kids."

Kay again rubbed Jackie's arm. "Jackie, is something bothering you? I mean, something other than the will and all?"

"No. Why?"

"Just . . . just in case you needed to talk. You know, we can talk about anything."

"What brought that on?"

"You have that same look on your face as you used to get when we were in high school. But back then, you didn't share, did you? You were afraid to talk to me. I'm just telling you, if there's something you want to talk about, please don't be afraid."

Oh, Kay. If you only knew. But Jacqueline shook her head, slowing the car as they approached Kay's driveway.

"I'm fine, Kay. Really."

But later, as Jacqueline lay in bed, eyes still wide open, she wondered if maybe it wouldn't be better to just tell Kay the truth.

"Tell her what?" she whispered out loud. *Tell her you still have a stupid teenage crush on her?*

She rolled over, punching the pillow. She didn't need this now. She didn't need to have these . . . *feelings*. She needed to get the business straightened out, she needed to decide what she was going to do with it, then she needed to get the hell out of Pine Springs, Texas!

172

CHAPTER TWENTY-ONE

When Kay walked out of her bedroom Friday morning, Jackie was in the same place she'd left her Thursday night—sitting at the table, poring over reports that Greg had printed out for her, her little computer within arms reach.

She walked behind her, lightly resting her hand on Jackie's shoulder. Jackie looked up and flashed a smile.

"Good morning."

"Been up long?"

"Hour or so. Couldn't sleep," Jacqueline confessed.

Kay reached for the nearly empty coffee cup. "How about a refill?"

"That'd be great. But you don't have to wait on me."

"This is hardly waiting on you." Kay laughed. "Breakfast in bed, now that would be waiting on you!"

Jacqueline watched her walk away, her mind picturing herself lying naked in bed, waiting for Kay. And it wouldn't be a breakfast tray she'd be waiting for. She closed her eyes and chased the image away. For the last few days, the direction of her thoughts had taken a decidedly intimate track. And she wasn't sure how to stop them.

"You're not nervous, are you?" Kay called from the kitchen.

"A little," Jacqueline admitted.

Kay placed the coffee cup within reach, then sat across from Jackie. "Need to talk it out?"

Jacqueline took off her glasses and rubbed her eyes, then smiled shyly at Kay. Yes, she needed to talk it out. Unfortunately, she didn't know where to start.

"Did you know that Greg was only making forty thousand?"

Kay raised her eyebrows. "Around here, that's excellent."

"Peterson, one of the managers, is making well over a hundred thousand. Close to two, if you count all this extra crap he gets." Jacqueline found the list of employees and their salaries. "It's very top heavy. I'm sure some of them got raises as the company prospered, just because they'd been with my father so long." She found another printout. "Greg gave me a breakdown of how much time everyone is logged into the network. Peterson averages about ten hours a week. His assistant averages over forty. His assistant gets paid less than Greg."

"Surely you can't judge time logged into the network as time worked, can you? I mean, don't they travel?"

"Yes, they travel. They also have laptops. Peterson's assistant travels too. My point is, it appears Peterson gets the pay while his assistant does the work." Jacqueline handed Kay the report. "All of the managers average at least thirty hours a week, about what their assistants do. All except Peterson."

Kay leaned forward. "I'm just guessing here, but you're not real impressed with this Peterson guy?"

"No, I'm not. And Greg seems to think that Mr. Lawrence is going to recommend I appoint Peterson to run the place while we transition."

"You've not talked to Mr. Lawrence about any of this?"

"No. He's going to be at the plant this morning. We're going to meet first, then have the staff meeting."

"And you're really looking forward to that?"

Jackie laughed. "I'm not exactly boardroom material. I just want to lay down some ground rules and hope everything runs smoothly while I'm gone."

"Gone?" Their eyes met. "You're leaving?"

"Kay, you're going to eventually get tired of having a roommate." Before she could stop herself, Jacqueline reached for Kay's hand. "Besides, I can't stay here forever. Ingrid will be hounding me before too long for edits."

"But what about everything here?"

"If my mother contests the will, it could be awhile before everything is settled. But Keys Industries, that's a done deal, I guess." Jacqueline released Kay's hand and picked up her coffee cup instead. "If Mr. Lawrence agrees with me having Greg run things, then that'll be smoother, and I can trust John to keep everything in order. And I'll probably have David fly down here to go over everything, just to be safe."

"David?"

"He's my attorney. Not that I don't trust Mr. Lawrence, but I don't know where his true loyalty lies. I've known David since college."

Kay looked away. "You're going to sell it, aren't you?"

"If I had any sense, I would."

Kay stood. "Well, I guess I can't blame you. It's an awful lot to be saddled with."

Jacqueline let her walk away. She didn't know what to say to her. Sell it? Yes, it was the sensible thing to do. But there was the matter of her father's letter and the nagging guilt that she couldn't shake. And Kay obviously didn't want her to sell it. But Jackie knew the reason for that and it had nothing to do with the business. It was an excuse to keep her here. And who could blame her. For all Kay knew, Jacqueline would leave again and they would drift apart.

Yes, it would be the sensible thing to do. Fade from Kay's life, before Jacqueline screwed it up completely by doing something totally inappropriate. But the thought of leaving here, without

Kay, was painful to think about. Jacqueline rested her chin in her palm, her eyes sliding closed. Yes, too painful to think about being alone again.

Jacqueline was impressed when Paul waved her through the gates with a smile. She drove the winding road to the offices, feeling confident as she pulled into her father's parking spot. She owned the damn thing. Might as well start acting like it.

However, when she got out and slammed the door, preparing for a staff meeting, she felt extremely underdressed. Oh, she'd struggled with Kay's iron that morning, pressing the lone cotton shirt she'd brought along. However, she'd already abused the funeral suit twice, so she'd dutifully pressed her jeans, tucked the shirt inside, and stole one of Kay's belts. And no matter that her soft, leather boots were chic, or that she'd taken extra time with her makeup. She still felt underdressed.

But what the hell. She was the boss. She could dress however she pleased.

"Yeah. Who cares?"

She laughed, then walked up the steps. She was a little amused at her nervousness. She had nothing to lose here today. Because if anybody pissed her off, she'd just sell the damn thing and be on her way. She simply didn't need—or want—the headaches.

"Yes, may I help you?"

Jacqueline arched an eyebrow. It was the same woman who'd taken her to Greg the other day. She obviously had a short memory.

"No, thank you."

Jacqueline walked past, only to be grabbed by the arm.

"I'm sorry, ma'am, but you can't just go back there. Do you have an appointment?"

Jacqueline decided to take pity on the woman. She obviously didn't have a clue as to who Jacqueline was. And why would she? They hadn't been introduced. So, Jacqueline held out her hand.

"I'm Jacqueline Keys. I don't believe I need an appointment," she said as pleasantly as she could.

The woman blushed crimson. "I'm so sorry."

Jacqueline gave a firm handshake, then dropped her hand. "Nothing to apologize for. We had not been formally introduced." Jacqueline pointed to the stairs. "Mr. Lawrence is in?"

"Oh, yes, ma'am. And the managers are gathered for a staff meeting. I guess I know why now."

Jacqueline smiled slightly. "So, it's okay if I go up?"

"Oh, yes! I'm sorry. Would you like me to take you up?"

Jacqueline shook her head. "No, thanks. I can find my way."

She paused at Greg's door. Three monitors were filled with data, and he was running his finger across one of them, studying the figures. She knocked lightly.

"Come on in," he murmured without turning around.

"It's me."

He swung around then. "Jackie!" He looked at his watch. "Is it that time already?"

"Going up to see John first." She moved farther into the office, her voice low. "You still okay with everything?"

He nodded. "If you are."

She gave a relieved smile. "Absolutely." She watched as his eyes traveled over her body. "What?"

He grinned. "I like casual."

Jacqueline felt a slight blush creep across her face. "I didn't exactly come packed for boardroom meetings."

Greg straightened his own tie. "Your father had a dress code," he stated. "Ties for the men, dresses for the women."

Jacqueline's eyes widened. "You're joking? *Dresses? Always?*"

"Yes."

"How many women work here?"

"Besides Arlene out front and Mrs. Willis upstairs, Ms. Scott is director of personnel, and there are two women in accounting. And then each of the managers has a secretary."

177

"I see." Jacqueline smiled sheepishly. "Well, the first executive decision I'm making is to do away with the damn dress code."

"It's been that way forever, they tell me."

Jacqueline was still shaking her head when she opened the door to the third floor. Mrs. Willis greeted her immediately.

"Welcome back, Miss Keys." If she was surprised by Jacqueline's attire, she made no mention. "They've all been whispering among themselves," she said with a smile.

"Got them thinking, do we?"

"I'd say." She pulled Jacqueline toward her father's office. "You want some coffee before you meet with Mr. Lawrence?"

"What flavor?"

"Flavor?"

"Of coffee?"

"Well . . . coffee flavor. What do you mean?"

Jacqueline placed her laptop and briefcase on her father's desk. "Bottled water?"

"We have some, yes."

"Perfect."

"Shall I bring it to you in Mr. Lawrence's office?"

Jacqueline raised her eyebrows, then looked around. "Actually, I thought we could meet in here."

Mrs. Willis grinned. "Excellent idea. I'll call him."

Jacqueline was admittedly snooping in the drawers of her father's desk when John Lawrence walked in. She quickly closed the drawer she had been nosing into and rested her arms on the desk.

"Good morning, John. I hope you don't mind meeting in here."

"Of course not. It'll be more private. I can't remember the last time all of the managers have been here at once." He sat down, placing a stack of folders on the desk. "I put together some information on the four managers," he said. "I assumed you'd want to discuss them before you decided who to place in charge."

Jacqueline took the folders, then leaned back in the chair and crossed her arms. "Who would you place in charge, John?"

"Well, based on seniority, Ron Peterson."

Jacqueline nodded. "Okay. If not based on seniority, who?"

"I'd probably still recommend Ron. He's been with your father for over twenty years, long before Keys Industries was created. He would have the most experience, for one thing."

"How do you think everyone else feels about it?"

"I think they probably all anticipate Ron getting the nod."

Jacqueline leaned forward again. "Particleboard?"

"I beg your pardon?"

"Particleboard plant. That's his area?" If John was surprised that she knew this, he didn't show it.

"Yes. At the beginning, there was only plywood and particleboard being produced, both in the same plant. Ron managed the plant while your father continued with his aspirations to build more. The demand was more than the one plant could produce, so your father built another plant, one specifically for particleboard, leaving the original for plywood."

"So, all these years, he's been in particleboard?"

John nodded. "Yes. As each new plant was operational, your father hired a new manager. Ron felt comfortable in particleboard. Obviously, he knew it well."

"I understand each manager was responsible for setting the salary for their staff, from their assistants on down the line to the workers in the plants."

"That's correct."

Jacqueline was about to mention Greg's name when something told her not to. As she suspected, John Lawrence was all set to hand over the control of Keys Industries to Ron Peterson. And Jacqueline had no intention of ever letting that happen. So, let John be as surprised as everyone else when she named Greg.

"Well, let's get this show on the road," she said as she stood. It was only then that he stared at her, much like Greg had done. "Oh, I forgot to tell you, I did away with that silly dress code."

He smiled slightly. "It was Madeline's idea."

"Why am I not surprised?"

CHAPTER TWENTY-TWO

Jacqueline waited patiently in the conference room for the managers and their assistants to file in. She sipped nervously from the water bottle Mrs. Willis supplied, then smiled gently at the other woman. Mrs. Willis was perched next to her, pad and pen ready to take notes as Jacqueline had instructed. She booted up her laptop, glad there was wireless network access.

She had not physically met everyone, but Greg had given her a password, allowing her to log onto the network. She had no restrictions, so she was able to get into everything, including personnel files. Some of the photos were obviously outdated, but she had no problem naming the faces that walked into the room now. She watched as Ron Peterson and his assistant, David Jimenez, walked in. She nodded slightly at Greg as he sat across the room from her.

She leaned over and whispered to Mrs. Willis. "Is everyone here?"

"There are only two from accounting. Were you expecting the whole staff?"

"No." Jacqueline looked at John. When the attorney would have spoken, Jacqueline stood. "Thank you all for coming." She looked around the room, meeting the curious stares from the others. "My name is Jacqueline Keys. As I'm sure you've all heard by now, upon my father's death, I am now sole owner of Keys Industries." A few people nodded, but the others simply stared without emotion.

She walked slowly behind the chairs, wondering how to begin this. Blurting out that Greg was in charge would hardly be appropriate. Easier, but not appropriate. No, she needed to prove a point.

"Obviously, I have no experience with a lumber company." She nervously shoved her hands in her pockets. "And I'm told that my father made all of the decisions concerning the company. Therefore, we're going to need—"

"Excuse me, Miss Keys. Allow me to perhaps save some time here. I'm Ron Peterson, senior manager."

Jacqueline was pleased with herself for managing to keep the smile off her face, but it had been too easy. She nodded at him, silently giving him the floor.

"We've been discussing the situation among ourselves, and I've already met with John about this."

Jacqueline glanced quickly at John Lawrence, wondering why he had not shared this with her.

"I've been with your father for over twenty years. Why, I remember you when you were barely a teenager," he said with a chuckle. "I think we all feel that I'm the only one here qualified to take over the management of the company."

"Is that right?" She paced again behind the chairs. "You're over particleboard, is that correct?"

"Yes, ma'am. Have been since the beginning."

"But you feel like you're qualified to manage *all* the plants?"

"Well, obviously being here twenty years, you pick up some knowledge of them all."

"I see. So, for example, if I ask you how many contracts we have pending for creosote posts, you'd know that?"

He looked at Mark Edwards. "Well, I'd have to check with Mark."

"Greg? How many contracts are pending?"

"Two."

"They are?"

"The regional phone headquarters in Dallas is taking bids for creosote poles, and we've put a bid in to Home Warehouse for posts to supply a six-state area."

"Thank you." She walked back to her chair and sat down. "Mrs. Willis tells me that my father was planning to bring a new plant into production. Mr. Peterson, you want to fill everyone in on it?"

He cleared his throat and glanced nervously at the others. "Well, Miss Keys, none of us were aware . . . we didn't know of a new plant."

"You mean he didn't share this with you?"

"No."

"You've been here twenty years, and you want to take over the management of the company, yet you know nothing of these future plans?"

"I'm sure, if only Mrs. Willis knew, then it must have been in the preliminary stages."

"Greg, why don't you share with everyone the idea that my father had for the new plant?"

"He wanted to produce cattle feed," Greg said as laughter erupted around the table.

"Cattle feed? Come on, Greg. We're a lumber company," Peterson said. "I'm sure Nicolas wasn't planning to diversify the company that much."

"Well, Ron, we already sell to a company in Canada that makes cattle feed," David Jimenez, his assistant, said.

"Sell what?"

"Sawdust. Woodchips," Greg supplied.

Jacqueline was pleasantly surprised that David Jimenez not only knew they sold it, but was willing to contradict his boss.

"Since when do cows eat woodchips?" Peterson asked, again eliciting chuckles from those around him.

Greg and Jacqueline exchanged glances, and Jacqueline nodded.

"Ron, they make molasses out of it," Greg said.

Jacqueline raised her hand. "Let's table the cattle feed for a bit, shall we?" She stared at the monitor of her laptop, wondering which item to bring up first. Might as well start with the most sensitive one.

"I'd like to talk about budgets. It's my understanding that each plant is given an operating budget and each manager controls it. Right down to salaries. Is that correct?"

She looked up, seeing several nods, but little else.

"Mr. Peterson, since you have emerged as the spokesman for the group, explain to me how salaries are set."

"What do you mean?"

"Is there a sliding scale, based on seniority? Is there a merit system in place? I guess what I'm really asking is how are raises determined?"

"Well, there's not really a sliding scale. Each shift has supervisors. In my area, I rely on my supervisors' input to determine any raises. I assume the other areas are the same."

"Particleboard, plywood, fiberboard, creosote and the sawmill. Five plants. Walter's area, the sawmill, has the highest salaries. Particleboard, Mr. Peterson, has the lowest. When I say lowest, I'm not talking management, only your hourly shifts." She pulled out one of Greg's reports. "For example, Jesus Hernandez. He's been with the company nearly ten years. He's had exactly three raises in that time. Yet, in checking his personnel file, there are no complaints, and he's never been written up for anything. In fact, in ten years, he's missed only six days of work." She locked glances with Ron Peterson. "Mr. Peterson, can you tell me why this employee is still making below ten dollars an hour?"

"No, not without checking his file, and checking with his shift supervisor. Maybe he's just never been recommended for a raise."

"You have another employee under you, Steven Yates. He's been here four years. He's had three raises. He's also been promoted to day shift. I see in the file here that Mr. Hernandez has requested the day shift for the past five years, yet he still works nights. Can you explain that?"

"Again, Miss Keys, without speaking with the supervisors, I couldn't say."

"So, are you telling me that the supervisors set the salaries and not you?"

"No, of course not. I set the salaries."

"David Jimenez, your assistant? You also set his salary?"

"Of course."

Jacqueline took a deep breath, then shrugged. "Perhaps this is not the place to bring this up, but since I have no management skills, what the hell." She looked at John before continuing. "My problem here, Mr. Peterson, is that this company is very top heavy. You, for example, approach two hundred thousand, with your salary and perks. Whereas your assistant makes below forty." She looked across the room. "Mr. Edwards, by comparison, makes half what you do. His assistant makes over fifty."

"I've been with the company twenty years. Mark's only been here ten or so."

"Twelve, Mr. Peterson." She pulled out another report. "I hope you don't think I'm singling you out, Mr. Peterson—I'm just using you as an example—but I have a problem with your time."

"My time?" Ron Peterson nervously loosened the tie around his neck and unbuttoned the top button of his shirt.

"You see, we're able to monitor how long each employee is logged onto the network. That gives us an idea of who is working and, well, who is not. You average about ten hours . . . a *week*, Mr. Peterson. David averages nearly fifty. I also show that your e-mail is forwarded to David, which indicates to me, that, basically he's doing your job."

It was one of those moments that Jacqueline had heard of so often, but never experienced. She could have literally heard a pin drop.

"But we can discuss that later, Mr. Peterson, in private."

"Wait just a minute here, lady. What makes you think you can come in here and speak to us like this?"

Jacqueline stared across the table. "Excuse me? *Lady?*" She stood slowly. "Mr. Peterson, in case you missed the beginning of this meeting, I own this company. I am your *boss*. I suggest you sit down . . . and shut up."

Again, she looked around the room, surprised that no one noticed her shaking hands. She quickly shoved them into her pockets. "Anyone else like to voice an opinion before we continue?" The only ones who dared to meet her eyes were David Jimenez, Greg and her uncle. She saw a glimmer of respect in all three. "Very well." She fingered the wireless mouse, quickly bringing up another screen. Her wish list, she'd called it last night. Perhaps too ambitious, but she'd toss it out there.

"I have some changes I would like implemented as soon as possible. Ms. Scott, I'd like you to set up some kind of a sliding pay scale, based on seniority. I'd like to have in place a yearly cost of living raise across the board. I'd also like some money set aside for merit raises. Merit raises will be the only thing determined by supervisors." She looked over at the director of personnel. "Questions?"

"No, ma'am."

"Good. Once this is in place, and we've agreed on it, I'd like to have salaries adjusted to reflect it. I'd also like to have someone take care of Jesus Hernandez, because, quite frankly, I'm appalled."

"Of course."

"I also want to adjust management salaries. There is no reason for one manager to be making twice as much as another, especially when we're talking six figures." She looked pointedly at Ron Peterson. "Some of you can expect to see a decrease."

His palm slammed down on the table, startling those around him. "You can't do this! John, tell her. I have a contract."

"Mr. Peterson, my father has not signed a contract with you in six years, according to your personnel records."

"You listen to me. You can't come in here and do this. We'll walk out. Then what'll you have? This company will fold without us."

This time, she allowed the smile to reach her face. "Mr. Peterson, Mr. Edwards, anyone else who feels like you can't work for me," she pointed at the door. "Please, now is your chance."

Peterson stood up and looked at the others. "Well? Come on."

"I'm not going anywhere, Ron."

He leaned forward. "Don't you see? She can't run this place without us."

Jacqueline turned to Mrs. Willis. "Do we have security?" she whispered.

The older woman nodded.

"Mr. Peterson, sit down."

"No! You can kiss my ass! I quit!"

Jacqueline let out her breath. Yes, it was just too easy.

"Very well." She turned again to Mrs. Willis. "Please call security and have them escort Mr. Peterson from the premises. You may go with him to his office, in case he has some personal things to take."

"I don't need a goddamned escort."

"Trust me, it is for the company's benefit, not yours." She dismissed him with a flick of her eyes. "Mr. Jimenez, I seem to have a manager's position open. Interested?"

"You'll be sorry," Ron Peterson said loudly as tiny Mrs. Willis grasped his arm and led him from the room. "You have *no one* here that can run this company."

When the door finally shut, she looked at the others, waiting until they all looked at her. "I detest dead weight. Ron Peterson collected a salary, but offered little to the company in return. No one here is indispensable," she said, sparing a glance at John Lawrence. She looked again at her wish list, suddenly very tired. "I have some other things I'd like to see changed, but I'll wait and discuss them with the new president." She cleared her throat. "There is one change I want implemented immediately, so please pass it along. Ms. Scott, you'll send an e-mail? I hate dress codes. Throw it out."

Nervous laughter followed, and she grinned. "Guys? Lighten up. Nobody is getting fired." She was rewarded with more relaxed smiles.

"Ms. Keys, if I may be so bold," John Lawrence said. "But you mentioned a new president. We've never had an old president."

"Well, president just seemed like the right word. We've got directors over personnel and accounting. We've got managers over the plants. I thought we needed a president over the whole bunch." She stood. "And, speaking of that, I'll let you get on with business." She closed her laptop and stood. "Greg Kubiak is the new president of Keys Industries. If anyone has questions or concerns, I have an e-mail address now that Greg will share with you. Please give him your support." She looked across the table at John. "Mr. Lawrence, may I have a word?"

Jacqueline carefully placed her laptop on her father's desk, then turned to John Lawrence.

"Well?"

"Your father would be very proud the way you came in and took control."

"John, why didn't you tell me that you'd already discussed the leadership role with Ron Peterson?"

"I'm sorry. I just assumed from your earlier comments that you weren't prepared to make decisions regarding the company."

"When did you meet with Peterson?"

John shifted nervously, then stood behind one of the visitor's chairs, grasping the back as if for support.

"Jacqueline, if you think I have some ulterior motive, I assure you, I do not. Ron Peterson spoke with me on the day of your father's accident. He had no way of knowing about you. He was simply offering his services. I spoke with him again yesterday about this. I told him that I would recommend to you that he take over."

"Why Peterson? Just because he's been here twenty years?"

"Namely, yes."

Jacqueline sat down, motioning for John to do the same. "Were you aware of the salary discrepancies, John?"

"I know the salaries of all the managers, if that's what you're asking."

"Did my father set their salaries?"

"Initially, yes."

Jacqueline leaned forward. "You're not saying that they gave themselves raises based on their budgets, are you?"

"To some extent, yes. Your father still had to approve them. It wasn't like they were given free reign."

"Were you also aware that Ron Peterson did very little actual work?"

"I knew that he put a lot of responsibility on David."

"Yet David was never compensated financially." Jacqueline rested her elbows on the desk, staring at John. "Ron Peterson threatened to resign because he thought I would never accept. He assumed you would make certain of that. Isn't that right, John?"

"Yes, I suppose so."

"In my opinion, David Jimenez is much more valuable to this company than Ron Peterson. Under no circumstances will he be brought back in. Do you agree?"

"I'm only your legal counsel, Jacqueline. As I said, your father made all the decisions and rarely consulted me."

"So you didn't know about his plans for a new plant either?"

"No."

"You're telling me Mrs. Willis and Greg Kubiak were the only ones he confided in?"

"He relied on Greg for a lot of things."

"So I'm told." Jacqueline stood and stared out over the plants. "How do you think Greg will be treated?"

"Greg is well-liked. He's smart. He's also only been here a handful of years."

Jacqueline turned back around. "I trust Greg. He'll make the right decisions. I'd like for you to make it clear to everyone that he is in charge." She paused. "And if I came across as a royal bitch this morning, I apologize. I'll blame it on nervousness as much as anything."

John smiled. "Yes, I'm sure the B-word has been tossed around. You also put the fear of God into them. I've no doubt they'll listen to Greg. It's no secret you're friends with the Garlands."

"Yes. That's why I trust him."

CHAPTER TWENTY-THREE

Kay laughed as Eric lifted Jackie off her feet and pulled her into his arms. Jackie was tall, but Eric towered over her, and Jackie had no choice but to hold on to him.

"Put me down, you big lug," Jacqueline teased.

"I will not! I haven't seen you in twenty years."

"It's fifteen, and I can still kick your ass."

"Oh yeah, I see *that* happening!" But he put her back down, this time pulling her into a more subtle hug. "You look great."

"Thanks, Eric. And man, did you grow up."

He playfully flexed his biceps. "I work for a living." Then his smile faded. "Sorry about your father, Jackie."

She shrugged, not knowing what to say.

"Is Rhonda coming?" Kay asked. "Rhonda is his fiancée," she explained to Jackie.

"She'll be along."

"Fiancée? First time around, Eric?"

"I've been working offshore for so long, it's hard to have a normal relationship."

Jacqueline grinned. "Is that a yes or a no?"

Eric blushed. "Second time around. First one didn't make a year."

"Not that I'm taking up for her, Eric, but being twenty-three and a newlywed, and having your husband gone for a month at a time can't possibly be a lot of fun."

"I know you're still friendly with her, Kay. You don't have to explain."

Kay turned to Jackie. "You may remember her, Linda Browning. She was just a year ahead of us in school."

"The name sounds familiar."

"I'm leaving now. I refuse to stand here and talk about Linda. Please don't mention her to Rhonda. You know they can't stand each other."

"My God. You've been divorced twelve years, Eric."

"It's got nothing to do with that and you know it."

"Are you serious? Rhonda is still mad about *that*?"

"About what?" Jacqueline asked.

"At the county fair a few years ago, Linda accidentally dropped Rhonda's pecan pie during the judging at the bake-off."

"*Accidentally*? Is that what she told you?" Eric turned to Jackie. "Rhonda and Linda were the two finalists. How could she accidentally drop a pie? She did it because we had just started dating, I know it."

Jackie and Kay exchanged amused glances.

"She did and you know it, Kay!"

"There you two are," Rose called. "I didn't even know you were here."

"Just got here," Jacqueline said. "Have been catching up with Eric a little."

"Well, I don't know what you did to my husband today, but he had a dozen roses delivered to me at the café this afternoon. The only other time he's done that was when I told him I was pregnant

191

with Lee Ann." Rose leaned closer. "And I pray to God *that* ain't the case! I already had two extras to make up for Kay."

"Rose!"

"Where's Rhonda?" Rose asked, ignoring Kay.

"She's coming," Eric said.

"Yeah, I was just hearing about Linda and Rhonda and the pie thing," Jacqueline said.

"*Linda*," Rose hissed. "I swear, she ain't got the sense God gave a goose. Do you know she kept Eric's last name? They were married ten months!"

"I see you're quite fond of her as well," Jacqueline teased.

"Please. Can you imagine if Eric was still married to her? She's as fat as a tub of lard."

"Rose!"

"Well, it's the truth, Kay. I'm not lying."

"Girls? Who are you gossiping about?"

Rose rolled her eyes. "I swear, Mama can hear me two counties over." Rose linked arms with her sister. "Come on, Kay. Help me with the burgers."

Kay looked at Jackie and smiled apologetically.

"I'll be fine."

"Come on, let's get something to drink," Eric offered.

Rose and Greg's backyard was bursting with activity. Besides Rose's four kids, Sammy and Tess's son tagged along behind Denny, and the five of them were making enough noise to rouse the neighbor's dog.

Eric laughed at the look on Jackie's face. "You get used to it after awhile."

"I suppose."

"Can you believe how tall Sammy got?"

"No, but fifteen years is a long time. Everyone's changed."

"That's for sure." He fished in the ice and pulled out two beers. "This okay?"

"Got anything light in there?"

"Light beer? Geez, Jackie, I figured you for the dark stuff."

"Sorry."

192

"I guess you heard about Kay and Billy Ray," he said, his voice lowered, as he handed her a beer.

"Yeah, Kay told me."

"Kay? I figured Rosie would be the one to fill you in. Kay doesn't talk about it."

Jacqueline just shrugged.

"So, it was all true, huh?"

"What?"

"You. The reason you left."

"True in that my mother sent me away? Or true in that I'm gay?"

"I guess both."

Jacqueline stood up straighter. "Yes, both are true." She raised her eyebrows. "Problem?"

"Well, no. I guess if Kay doesn't have a problem, then I don't."

"Kay? What do you mean?"

"Well, you're staying with her. You know how people talk in this town."

"Eric, are you being a big brother and looking out for her, or are you genuinely concerned about me?"

He laughed. "Oh, Jackie, hell, I know how close you and Kay were." He pointed across the patio. "Brother-in-law looks beat. You wouldn't think playing with computers all day would stress him out so."

Greg did indeed look tired. He met Jacqueline's eyes and gave a weary smile.

"Excuse me, Eric, but I need to visit with Greg for a bit."

"Sure, Jackie."

"Look me up when your fiancée gets here."

"Don't you worry."

"You look nice tonight."

"Rose, I'm in jeans," Kay said dryly. "How many tomatoes should I slice?"

"All four. And I just mean, they look nice on you. I wish you'd have some kids so you could spread out like me."

"I doubt the sole reason is having kids, Rosie."

"And what do you mean by that?"

"You work at the café and eat Mama's cooking. You come home and cook. And I know you've not forgotten that I can't cook to save my life."

Rose pointed the knife at her. "Never too old to learn. And trust me, I will not let Lee Ann fall into the same trap as you did. She's already got that little tomboy attitude, thinking she needs to be outside playing ball or something."

"Same trap as me? I was not a tomboy, Rose."

Rose laughed. "Of course you were. You spent more time on your bike chasing after Jackie than you ever spent in the house, not to mention climbing that old oak tree."

"That doesn't make me a tomboy. Jackie, she was the tomboy."

"Yeah, talk about stereotype."

"*Rose!*"

"Well, it's the truth. And don't get me wrong, I love Jackie to death. But think back, Kay. She was playing sports with the boys, beating *up* the boys, and she *never* wore dresses."

"And what's your point, Rose."

"I'm just saying, we should have known."

Kay spread her hands. "And if we'd known, what would we have done? Stayed away from her? Forbid her to come to our house?"

Rose lowered her voice. "Does it bother you? I mean, you guys used to sleep together all the time. Even when you were in high school."

Kay stared. "Rose, what's up? Are you *worried* about me?"

"Don't be ridiculous. Jackie would never hurt you."

"Then drop it." Kay rinsed the head of lettuce, surprised at Rose. Apparently, her sister was worried that Jackie might . . . try something. *Geez.*

"By the way, I have a little surprise for you."

"Oh, yeah?" Then Kay whipped around. "God, you're not pregnant, are you?"

"Good Lord, no. I'd shoot myself." Rose looked over her

shoulder into the empty living room before speaking. "Eric invited a friend."

Kay went back to her lettuce. "That's nice."

"A guy friend. A guy he works with."

Kay slowly turned around. "And?"

"And, he's single. And Eric says he's cute."

"And?"

"Kay! Give me a break here. At least act a little excited."

"Excited? You're trying to set me up with a guy who works off-shore with Eric? Now that would make for an interesting relationship."

"Well, Eric says he's a really nice guy. He's going to stay here the whole month."

"*What?*"

"He's from Mississippi. Doesn't have a whole lot going on there, so Eric invited him to stay here with him for the month."

"Eric invited? With no encouragement from you?"

"Well, he's been mentioning this guy for months now." Rose shrugged. "I may have dropped a hint or two."

"Sure you did. Well, you can forget it."

"Kay, what would it hurt to go out with him?"

"And when would I do that?"

"This weekend, or next week, or make plans for next weekend."

Kay shook her head. "I have company."

"Oh, please. Jackie wouldn't mind being scarce if you had a guy over."

"No, but I mind. She won't be here much longer, and I don't intend to sacrifice any of that time."

"Wait before you pass judgment. This guy might knock your socks off."

"How did everything go?" Jacqueline asked.

Greg smiled. "Better than I thought, really. Having Peterson gone helped. Jackie, I never thought he'd do that."

"No. And I assume he never thought I'd take him up on his res-ignation."

"You were right. David has been doing his job for the last several years. It's no secret."

"Any other situations like that?"

"Fiberboard. Carl Hybeck has been pushing more and more on Gene."

"And you took care of it?"

"I talked to him about it today, yes."

Jacqueline smiled. "Good."

"I didn't have to threaten much, not after what happened with Peterson."

"I was a bitch, I know."

"You were great."

Jacqueline grinned. "Rose got flowers."

"Yeah, well, I got a raise." Greg lowered his voice. "And it's too much, Jackie. I don't know what to do with that kind of money."

"We can't have the president making less than the managers, now can we?"

Their eyes met. "I won't let you down."

"I'm not worried about that, Greg."

"I talked to Jesus Hernandez today."

"Oh yeah?"

"Moved him to days. I've never seen a man more excited."

"And his raise?"

Greg laughed. "He almost shit his pants!"

"Are there others like him? I didn't have time to check them all."

"I've got Ms. Scott going over everything. I spent most of the afternoon building her a database so she could dump all the records in there and we could sort through them."

"I know this has all happened so fast, but we've got to find someone to replace you, don't we?"

"Replace me? On the network?" He shook his head. "No, no, no."

"Ah, I forgot. Computer geek. The network is your baby."

"Well, I could probably use an assistant, but I wouldn't want to give up control of the network. I mean, there are way too many things you can do when you control the network."

"So we're looking for someone trustworthy? Like you?"

"Thank you."

"Hire who you need, Greg. Did John Lawrence hang around after I left?"

"For awhile. We went over everything. Your father was never one to share information with everyone. He told them what he thought they needed to know. I think that's why none of the plants mixed. I think if we are more of a team, and we all know what each other is doing and how much profit each plant is bringing in, we could be more competitive. But before I went too far, I wanted to check with you."

Jacqueline laughed. "Greg, you do it how you want to do it. I told you, I don't have a clue about this business."

"Mr. Lawrence seemed to think I was overstepping."

"How so?"

"He said there was a fine line between enough information and too much."

"Greg, do you have any idea how much Keys Industries is worth?"

He shook his head. "But I can imagine."

"And it's not a corporation. It's a privately owned business. So if you have all these employees making x number of dollars and they are suddenly privy to the enormous wealth of the business, aren't they going to want a salary increase?"

"But they're all making good salaries now. For around here, they're making exceptional salaries."

"But if you found out the business was bringing in *millions* each year, aren't you going to want to be compensated more?"

"So, Peterson's salary wasn't exactly breaking the company."

"It was a drop in the bucket. Peterson, however, was like a tick, feeding off the company but giving nothing back. If you take a look at the contracts for particleboard for the last two years, David Jimenez negotiated most of them. And I think David is a good example of promoting hard work. Make it clear to the others if they do the job, they'll be compensated."

"I thought you had no management skills."

Jacqueline grinned. "As I told Kay, I'm making this up as I go."

"Your father would be proud, you know."

Jacqueline shrugged. "I think he'd just be thankful I haven't sold out to my mother."

Greg lowered his voice. "Speaking of that, Mr. Lawrence got a call late this afternoon from one of the Gentry twins. From what I gathered, I think your mother is trying to get a judge to block your ownership of Keys Industries. He didn't seem overly worried about it though."

"What do you mean, from what you gathered? He didn't tell you?"

"No. I was in his office when he took the call. I only overheard his side of the conversation."

"Greg, I know this is difficult for you, but technically, you're Mr. Lawrence's boss. He works for Keys Industries."

"Yeah, but this had to do with you."

"If it had to do with me, then why hasn't he called me?"

Kay spied Jackie and Greg deep in conversation, and she hung back, quietly watching. Rose had her occupied for nearly the last hour, but she should have known not to worry that Jackie would be alone. And judging by the looks on their faces, they were talking business. So, she took the opportunity to watch without being seen. Jackie had been here over a week and Kay still couldn't believe she was back. Couldn't believe that they'd picked up right where they left off. Jackie had changed in so many ways, yet she hadn't changed a bit. And Kay was as drawn to her today as she had been all those years ago.

Without notice, Jacqueline turned, her eyes finding Kay immediately. It startled her, but then Kay didn't know why she should be surprised. They'd always been aware of each other's presence. It was eerie, almost. But Jackie smiled and motioned her over, so Kay complied.

"You lurking in the bushes?" Jacqueline teased.

Kay nearly blushed. "I didn't want to interrupt. I knew you were talking business."

Jacqueline shrugged. "Nothing that's a secret, Kay."

Kay looked at Greg. "So, how did it go?"

"I survived, and they didn't all quit on us, so I guess we'll be okay."

"Good. Rose said you hardly slept last night."

It was Greg's turn to blush. "Yes, I was nervous as hell. But you should have seen Jackie. She came in and took over."

Jacqueline laughed, meeting Kay's eyes. "I was a bitch."

"And your Peterson guy?"

Jacqueline grinned. "He resigned. Imagine that."

"Did you push him?"

"Maybe a little."

Greg stepped away. "I see Rose waving frantically for me. I better go see what's up."

When they were alone, Kay affectionately squeezed Jackie's hand. "Greg did okay?"

"Yes. Greg will be fine. I'm not worried about him. I'm more worried about John Lawrence not trusting him. Greg said he overheard a conversation with one of the Gentry twins and John. Apparently, Madeline is trying to get a court order to block my ownership of Keys Industries. John didn't bother sharing this with Greg, nor did he call me."

"Can she do that? I mean, block it?"

Jacqueline shrugged. "I don't know. John doesn't seem to think so. Maybe that's why he's not mentioned it to me."

"Are you worried?"

Jacqueline shook her head. "It's not like it would break my heart if I lost it. I mean, it's going to have to go along on its own, anyway."

"What do you mean?"

"My father worked sixty hours a week, sometimes more." Jacqueline met Kay's eyes. "I've got another career, one that takes up a lot of my time. I can't devote a whole lot of time and energy to this if I want to keep writing."

Kay lowered her head. "I keep forgetting sometimes that you're only here temporarily."

This time it was Jacqueline who reached out, Jacqueline whose fingers entwined with Kay's. "No matter what, Kay, we'll always be close. I promise, I won't disappear again."

Before Kay could speak, Rose was leading a handsome young man toward them. "Oh, God," she murmured.

"What?"

Their eyes met. "Rose is trying to fix me up."

Jacqueline looked at the man approaching, and yes, he was attractive, rugged looking. She felt the tightening in her chest immediately.

"I'll get out of your way then," she murmured, intending to escape. Kay wouldn't let go of her hand. Their eyes met again.

"Stay."

"Should have known you two would be holed up somewhere," Rose said as she walked up. "I want you to meet Josh, a friend of Eric's who is visiting Pine Springs. Josh, this is Jackie, an old family friend. And this beautiful gal is my sister, Kay."

Kay and Jackie exchanged amused glances, and Kay just barely kept herself from groaning out loud at Rose's introduction. *Beautiful gal?* But she found her manners, politely offering her hand.

"Nice to meet you."

"Good to finally meet you, Kay. Eric and Rose have told me so much about you."

Kay smiled. "Oh? Eric and *Rose?*" She turned to her sister, her eyes sparking. "Unfortunately, today was the first I've heard of you."

He winked at her. "They wanted to surprise you."

Kay plastered a smile on her face. "Well, they did that."

"Jackie, why don't you help me with the burgers," Rose said, linking arms with Jackie and pulling her away.

"I thought Kay helped you."

"Just preliminary, not with the meat."

Jacqueline looked back at Kay and their eyes met for a second before Kay turned back to Josh.

"Well, what do you think?" Rose asked quietly.

"About what?"

"Josh! What else?"

Jacqueline shrugged. "He's okay."

"*Okay?* He's cute as can be!"

Jacqueline shrugged again. "I suppose. If you like that sort of thing."

Rose laughed out loud. "I sometimes forget, Jackie, that you *don't* like that sort of thing! But Kay does. And it's been forever since she's been out on a date."

"Well, maybe they'll hit it off."

"I hope so. I hate seeing her alone."

"Wouldn't she still be alone? This guy works with Eric."

"You know what I mean. I just wish she *had* someone. She's so attractive, lots of men have asked her out, but she refuses."

"She had a very bad experience, Rose. You can't blame her for hesitating."

Rose pulled Jackie into the kitchen, motioning at the sink. "Wash your hands. We've got about thirty patties to make." Rose took the bowl of ground meat from the fridge that she had seasoned earlier. "And I know what an asshole Billy Ray was to her, but that doesn't mean all men are like that. Look at Greg, for instance. He's the gentlest man I've ever met in my life. He never raises his voice, he's great with the kids. I just want her to find someone like that."

Jacqueline took a handful of the ground meat and formed a ball, lightly squeezing it between her palms. "Greg's a great guy, yeah. But for you. Maybe Kay's not attracted to the same kind of men you are."

"You're saying she's attracted to jerks like Billy Ray?" She pointed at the patty Jackie had made. "Poke a hole in the middle."

Jacqueline stared. "What?"

Rose held hers open-faced, then stuck her index finger in the center of the patty. "Poke a hole."

Jacqueline still stared. "You're serious?"

"It keeps it from shrinking."

"*What?*"

"Geez, Jackie, it's so simple. It won't shrink up when you cook it."

"Because there's a *hole* in it?"

"Of course."

Jacqueline laughed. "So, restaurants all across the nation haven't caught on to this trick?"

"Very funny. Maybe they just haven't figured it out yet."

"How about we do half and half, and then we'll measure shrinkage?"

"Will you stop being a smart-ass and poke a damn hole in it!"

Kay stared at Josh, struggling to find a topic for conversation. But all that would pop into her head were visions of her beating the holy crap out of Rose. So she smiled politely and cleared her throat, finally pointing to his empty beer bottle.

"Need another?"

"Well, if you're buying," he said with a laugh.

"I'll get this round," she said, barely able to avoid rolling her eyes as they walked toward the coolers. "So, Josh, how old are you?"

"Twenty-seven. You?"

"Older than that," she said dryly. *Twenty-seven?* Yes, she would beat Rose to a pulp.

❦

Jacqueline avoided the coolers of assorted beer, instead, filling a glass with iced tea. It was good and sweet, just like she remembered Mrs. Garland making it. Sweet tea was not exactly a staple in Monterey. She faded into the shadows, watching the activity around her. Almost like old times, yes. But fifteen years still separated them. And she didn't doubt that if she should disappear again, they wouldn't cry over her being gone. Well, except Kay. Jacqueline knew Kay wouldn't let her escape again.

With just the thought of Kay, Jacqueline's eyes slid across the backyard, finding her immediately. Her body language was much like Jacqueline remembered from high school. Tall, aloof, arms crossed protectively along her waist. Jacqueline could see it now—the distance—but back then, she only saw Billy Ray and his nearness to Kay. She tumbled back fifteen years.

At the edge of the bleachers she peered through the shadows, watching as Billy Ray clutched Kay's arms, holding her tightly against the metal as he moved forward.

She felt her heart catch painfully, and she had to force herself to remain hidden. All instincts told her to run, run to them and pull Billy Ray to the ground, away from Kay. She moaned with pain as Billy Ray leaned forward, capturing Kay's mouth forcefully.

She made herself turn away before Kay caught her again. She was running out of excuses as to why she was following them. Instead, she moved silently in the shadows, away from Kay . . . away from Kay and the boy who was kissing her.

Jacqueline let out her breath as her vision cleared, finally admitting that it was not Billy Ray who held Kay's attention this night. No, that honor went to a handsome young man named Josh. And as she stared, Kay's eyes slid away from Josh, meeting her own, holding them captive.

Kay's breath caught as she locked glances with Jackie. In an instant, she was taken back fifteen years, and she remembered that same haunted, wounded look . . . and the longing in Jackie's eyes.

She never understood it before, could never put words to describe it. But now, now that she was older, now that she *understood*, oh God, now the realization of that look hit with such clarity—such certainty—it simply took her breath away.

The longing in Jackie's eyes was—it was for her. It always had been.

Oh my God.

Kay pulled her eyes from Jackie, blinking several times as she tried to focus on what Josh was saying. She finally shook her head. It didn't matter.

"Excuse me," she said, holding up her hand. "I hate to be rude, but . . . excuse me."

With that, she turned and walked purposefully toward Jackie, blue eyes locked on blue.

They stood close, eyes questioning. Finally, Jacqueline motioned with her head toward Josh.

"You like him?"

Kay shrugged. "Seems like a nice guy."

Jacqueline nodded. "Good."

"Good?"

Jacqueline cocked her head. "He's kinda cute."

Kay shrugged again. "You think so?"

Jacqueline forced a smile. "Sure."

Kay lowered her head for a moment, then raised it, meeting Jackie's eyes again.

"When I looked up and saw you watching, it reminded me of some other times, in high school," Kay said quietly. "With Billy Ray."

"Kay, I . . . I never—"

"No." Kay reached out and clutched Jackie's arms, silencing her. "Tell me, were you jealous of Billy Ray?" she asked softly. "Jealous when he kissed me?"

Jacqueline wanted to pull her eyes away, tried to pull her eyes away, but Kay held them. What could she say?

"Jackie? Were you?"

Jacqueline let out a heavy breath and closed her eyes. "Yes," she finally whispered. She felt Kay's hands squeeze her arms tightly.

"And I was so very jealous of Danny."

Jacqueline raised her eyebrows. "*What?*"

Before Kay could answer, Eric appeared with who Jacqueline assumed was his Rhonda. A small woman—nearly a foot shorter than Eric—with *big* teased hair, she smiled brightly as she looked at Jacqueline.

"Now I remember her," she said to Eric. She stuck out her hand. "Rhonda Jones, nice to see you again."

"Hi Rhonda. We've met?"

"I was two years behind you in school. Of course, I don't expect you to remember me. I didn't play sports. I was president of Future Homemakers for three years."

Jacqueline smiled. Oh, yes, the club that taught you how to be a good little wife. Eric needn't worry about having a well-kept home, at least.

"I apologize. I don't remember you."

"Don't apologize. That was years and years ago." Then she leaned closer. "What do you think of Josh for our Kay?"

"Rhonda—" Kay started, but Rhonda cut her off.

"He's so nice, Kay. He's sweet as sugar. Why, he'd make bees leave a honeycomb, for sure."

"He is a nice guy," Eric agreed. "He's going to stay with me for the month."

Kay nodded. "Yes, I know. Rose filled me in."

"Good. We were hoping maybe the four of us could drive over to Jasper one evening and catch a movie," Rhonda suggested.

"Dinner, too," Eric added.

"We'll see," Kay said. Then she pointed at Jackie. "As I told Rose, I have company right now, and I want to spend time with Jackie."

"I'm sure Jackie wouldn't mind if you had a date," Eric said.

Jacqueline was about to answer when she felt Kay squeeze her arm.

"She may not, but I mind, Eric. I haven't seen Jackie in forever. And nothing against Josh, but I'd rather be with Jackie."

So there, it was all decided, and Jacqueline had yet to open her mouth. But she felt she should at least offer a night off for Kay, in case she really wanted to go on a *date* with this Josh person. The thought appalled her, but she offered anyway.

"I, er . . . I could manage on my own for a night if you wanted to go to a movie, Kay."

Kay turned her head, ignoring the others as her blue eyes locked on Jackie's. She tilted her head slightly. "Is that right?"

Jacqueline swallowed down the lump in her throat and simply nodded.

Then Kay smiled, her eyes softening. "Thanks, but I don't really want to go to a movie."

"Just dinner then," Rhonda offered.

"Guys, please. I appreciate what you're trying to do, and I know Rosie is behind this, but I'm just not interested in going out right now. Not with Josh or anyone else."

"I swear, Kay, you've got to get over what that bastard did to you," Eric said loudly. "You can't carry that with you forever."

"I know, Eric. But it really has nothing to do with Billy Ray."

"There you guys are," Rose called. "I found Josh wandering around by himself. How rude of you," she said to the group, but her eyes were on Kay.

Kay smiled apologetically. "I'm sorry, Josh. I kinda ran out on you."

"That's okay. I found the beer," he said, holding up a can. "Can I get you one?"

"No, thanks. I think I'll have tea with dinner." Kay looked at Rose. "Speaking of that, do you need some help?"

"No. Greg's putting the patties on the grill now. Everything else is ready."

Jacqueline laughed. "The famous patties with the hole in the middle!"

Rose shook her finger at Jackie. "Kay, tell her about the shrinkage."

Kay laughed, too. "Rose has done a very scientific study on shrinkage, and has concluded that hamburger patties without a hole in the middle shrink more than those with a hole. Therefore, all of her patties have holes in them!"

Josh frowned. "I don't understand."

Rose patted his hand. "Kay will explain to you over dinner."

Kay and Jackie exchanged glances, then were pulled in opposite directions as Rose took Josh and Kay with her, and Eric and Rhonda drew Jackie over to the grill where Greg looked every bit the chef, apron and all.

He waved the spatula at them, then looked at Rhonda. "Do you mind checking with Rose about the wieners? She said she wanted to do a handful of hotdogs, too."

"Sure, Greg."

"I'd love a beer, Eric."

"Coming right up. Jackie?"

"Sure. Light."

Once alone, Greg smiled at her. "I've been watching. They're all playing matchmaker with Kay and Josh, and she'd rather be with you."

Jacqueline hoped the shadows hid her blush. "We just haven't seen each other in so long, I think Kay's afraid to miss any time."

"I keep telling Rose to leave her alone, but Rose won't rest until she has her married off again."

"Kay can be stubborn."

Greg laughed. "That's true." Then his expression turned serious. "Her eyes have been so lifeless for so many years, we hardly notice it any more. But the last week or so, since you've been back"—he looked directly at Jacqueline—"she's got a spark again. Rose seems to think it's because she got to talk to you about what happened, that maybe she's finally put Billy Ray to rest. She thinks Kay might be receptive to dating now."

Jacqueline shrugged. "Maybe so."

❦

During dinner, Jacqueline found herself squeezed on one of the picnic tables with Rose and Greg, Sammy and Tess, and Mr. and Mrs. Garland, and the grandkids. She tried to keep her eyes from straying to the other table, where Kay was sitting next to Josh, but invariably, she glanced there often. Eric and Rhonda were both talking at once, drawing Kay into conversation. And more often than not, Kay would look away from them, only to lock glances with Jacqueline.

"You know you're babysitting tomorrow, right?"

Jacqueline looked at Rose with a blank stare. "Excuse me? Babysitting? *Kids?*"

"Just the two older ones. Mama keeps the twins." At Jacqueline's raised eyebrows, Rose shook her head. "Kay didn't tell you?"

"Tell me what?"

"Third Saturday of every month, Greg and I go over to Crockett. He's got some friends there from college. We spend the weekend with them. It's the only time we have to get away. We've been doing it for the last couple of years."

"Once a month? *Every* month?"

"We've skipped a couple of times, but not often." Rose looked at Greg. "But Greg tells me that this may be our last time for awhile."

Jacqueline looked at Greg. "Why's that?"

"I'll probably be at the plant most Saturdays. At least until I feel comfortable with it all."

Jacqueline nodded. She didn't doubt Greg would be there most Sundays, too. And she knew, no matter how strong their marriage was, it would take its toll. She would talk privately with him later. "Don't overdo it," was all she said now.

"He wanted to cancel this weekend," Rose said.

"It'll still be there Monday, Greg," Jacqueline said. "I'm going to meet with John tomorrow, clear up a few things."

"What's that?" Rose asked.

"Just chain of command type thing, Rose," Jacqueline said.

"Enough shop talk," Mrs. Garland said. "I want to know about this Josh person. Is he trustworthy?"

"Mama, of course. Do you think I'd set her up with someone who's not?"

"You? I thought it was Eric's doing."

Rose laughed. "Eric couldn't play matchmaker to save his life!"

"He seems young," Mr. Garland said.

"He's a few years younger than Kay, but so what?" Rose leaned forward. "He's *cute*."

Mrs. Garland shook her head. "I'm not so certain Kay wants to be set up. In fact, I bet right now she's wishing she was sitting over here with us."

"Mama, she's afraid to date, that's all. And Eric has already put the fear of God in Josh if he touches her!"

Jacqueline's eyes slid across the backyard to the other table. Kay looked lost in thought as the conversation went on around her. Then she lifted her head, eyes colliding with Jacqueline's. Jacqueline's breath left her at what she saw there . . . at what she *imagined* she saw. But Kay's eyes were open to her, and she saw an understanding in them, an awareness that frightened Jacqueline a little. The voices around her faded, and she was suddenly afraid to go home with Kay tonight.

But in the end, it didn't matter. Lee Ann had begged to spend the night with Aunt Kay and Kay had agreed. Jacqueline wondered if perhaps Kay was a little afraid to be alone with her as well.

CHAPTER TWENTY-FOUR

Jacqueline waited patiently in John's study, absently looking at the pictures displayed on nearly every available space. John was apparently very fond of his grandchildren. She turned around, moved to the leather sofa and sat. She had called earlier, promising to be brief. John had an eleven o'clock tee time. Mary ushered her into his study, saying John was just getting out of the shower.

She leaned her head back against the cool leather, her mind on Kay, wondering what thoughts were going through her head this morning. They'd not had another second alone to talk. Jacqueline went to her room and closed the door while Kay and Lee Ann bickered over which story to read before bed. And this morning, when Jacqueline had finally ventured from her room, Kay and Lee Ann were on the sofa, watching cartoons. Kay had locked glances with her, saying that coffee was already made. Jacqueline brought her coffee to the table and booted up her laptop, needing to return e-mails and check in with Ingrid. In between, she watched Kay. Even when she wasn't looking, she was aware of Kay's eyes on her.

They would have no time alone to talk, even later in the evening. Rose was dropping off Denny at noon, and they would have both kids until tomorrow afternoon. And perhaps it was just as well. What would she say if they were alone? What questions would Kay ask? No, it was best. Jacqueline wasn't prepared to have a heart-to-heart talk with Kay.

She looked up as the door opened, smiling at John Lawrence in his golfing attire, knickers and all.

"Nice."

He looked down. "Too much?"

"No. Very dapper."

"Thank you. Mary thinks I look sexy." He moved to his desk, offering her one of the visitor's chairs. "Sorry to keep you waiting."

"No problem. I just wanted to go over a couple of things, John." She settled down, casually crossing her legs. "First off, I'm probably going to be leaving next week."

"So soon?"

Jacqueline nodded. "I have deadlines . . . obligations there. I thought I'd only be away a few days, and it's going on two weeks." She stared at John. "Greg tells me you got a call from Madeline's attorney."

John nodded. "Yes, I did."

"Were you not planning to tell me?"

He waved his hand. "It's nothing. Frankly, I didn't want to bother you with it."

"It's no bother. I'd rather be advised of things, John. That way, they won't sneak up and bite me on the ass later on."

He nodded. "Of course. And your father was the same way, but I was trying not to overwhelm you. And there's nothing to worry about. Your mother has filed with the district court to block your ownership of Keys Industries."

"And there is nothing to worry about? John, you and I both know that I did not knowingly and willingly sign that affidavit."

"Yes, but we are the only ones who know. And Judge Crawford will rule in our favor."

Jacqueline leaned forward. "How can you be sure?"

211

John smiled. "Hank Crawford and your father go back a lot of years, Jacqueline."

Jacqueline's eyes widened. "He bought a *judge*?"

"Don't be so surprised. Your father was very powerful. Most of the local politicians were at his beck and call, not to mention several in Austin. They relied on his contributions for their campaigns. In return, they voted in his favor, whether it was for more logging in the state forests or a lower tax rate for the company or anything in between."

"But my father is dead."

"He was a very shrewd businessman, very smart. Long before now, Judge Crawford knew of your existence and your connection with Keys Industries. Your father made sure of it. They all knew. As they know that one false step and their funding stops. They know I'll see to that."

Jacqueline stood, pacing across the room. "Jesus, John, it's like the Mafia or something."

John laughed. "I can assure you, your father had no one killed. It's all about money, Jacqueline. Money brings power, and your father had a lot of power."

"So, my mother files against me. It'll be heard by the district judge who will rule in our favor. Then what? Can she appeal?"

John nodded. "She can. But it won't go anywhere."

"So, it goes to an appellate court? You're saying that even then, they'll rule in our favor?"

"Jacqueline, it can go out of state to an appellate court, and they would still rule in our favor."

"So I shouldn't worry about this?"

"I would have told you if it was something for you to worry about."

"Okay. I trust you." She ran her fingers across the leather on the visitor's chair, wondering how to bring up Greg's position. Directly, she supposed. "John, don't keep things from Greg, okay?"

"What do you mean?"

"I just mean he's in charge of the company right now. Keep him informed, John. Especially after I leave. I don't want secrets."

John nodded. "Okay, of course."

Jacqueline rested her hands on John's desk and leaned forward. "I know you think of him as just a computer geek and that I shouldn't have appointed him president. But John, I trust him. He's not looking out for himself right now. He's looking out for me, and he's looking out for the company. And you know why? Because he genuinely cares about this company, John. And if we're not careful, he's going to be up there seven days a week, trying to make it better."

"He got a very healthy raise, Jacqueline. Don't think Ms. Scott hasn't spread the word around. The others might be a bit surprised by his increase."

"And don't think Greg doesn't know that she's spread the word around. That's why I know he'll be up there seven days a week, trying to earn that salary."

John nodded. "Very good. So he'll work longer and harder than everyone else, and they'll grow to trust and respect him. And you said you had no management skills. Very good."

"Thank you. But I don't doubt that if I'd given him half as much, he'd do the same thing." She sat down again. "Is there anything I need to know about the bank or is that situation going to run on its own?"

"That is secure. Your father allowed Mr. Spencer free reign."

"And he's trustworthy?"

"Absolutely. Like myself, your father compensated him nicely. There was no alternative *but* to be trustworthy. He did indicate that Mr. Wells, the current president, would like to meet with you. Just a formality, I'm sure."

"Not this time around, John. Like I said, I'll be leaving next week. I don't know when I'll be able to return, but if anything comes up, you know how to reach me. I've also got company e-mail now. I'd like you to keep me informed, John."

"Of course."

Jacqueline nodded and stood. "Well, I guess everything is under control. I don't want you to miss your tee time."

"Thank you. It's a beautiful day for golfing. They say it's supposed to rain most of next week."

"Well, I'll let you get to it."

"One more thing, Jacqueline. We've not discussed finances."

"Finances?"

"Your father's personal accounts that were in the company's name. We need to transfer them to you. Do you have a CPA at your disposal? Perhaps I could recommend one."

"I have someone, yes."

"Good. Have them give me a call."

Jacqueline paused. "Shouldn't we wait on the judge's ruling? Just to be safe?"

John shook his head. "He's not issued a stay, and he won't. We're free to operate as if you are the owner. There are no worries, Jacqueline."

CHAPTER TWENTY-FIVE

Kay stood quietly beside the microwave, aimlessly watching the popcorn bag turn, wondering for the hundredth time what Jackie had been up to today. She'd left before ten with barely a good-bye. Kay flicked a glance to the clock and tried not to worry. Nearly four. Surely, if Jackie was in some sort of trouble, she would have called.

But she wasn't in trouble, Kay knew. Jackie was most likely avoiding her, avoiding the situation. Avoiding any sort of conflict, just like she'd done in high school.

"Damn stubborn woman," she muttered. Kay wished she'd kept her mouth shut last night. But the look in Jackie's eyes, the *longing* she saw there, very nearly broke her heart. And she wanted to talk to Jackie about it, find out what was going through her mind.

And yet, she was afraid of what was going through Jackie's mind. It was one thing to realize that the attraction she had for

Jackie back then was more than friendship, that it bordered on sexual attraction. *Bordered?* But it was quite another, as an adult, to put words to those feelings, to put action to those feelings. Kay gripped the counter and closed her eyes. And if Jackie was of the same mindset, what would happen? Would something that should have been discussed fifteen years ago suddenly be brought to light? Would something that should have happened fifteen years ago suddenly happen now?

The bell on the microwave pulled her out of her thoughts, and she opened the door, carefully grasping the edge of the bag. She poured the hot popcorn into two bowls and took them into the living room. Lee Ann and Denny were on the floor, eyes glued to the TV. It was an indulgence Kay allowed because Rose rarely let the kids near one. And with Lee Ann nearly seven and Denny just thirteen months younger, their tastes overlapped. She glanced at the stack of Disney movies she'd rented, hoping they'd last the night.

"Here you go. Popcorn."

She got a "thanks, Aunt Kay," from Lee Ann. Denny took his bowl without a word, his eyes never moving from the screen.

Normally, she would sit on the sofa and read during their movies, but she couldn't seem to relax. And if Jackie didn't show up soon, Kay would be forced to call her cell, something she didn't want to do.

Jacqueline drove slowly down the streets, meandering through town, reluctantly making her way back to Kay. She'd stayed away as long as she could.

She'd gone by the lumber mill, just to see the activity on a Saturday. She'd driven all the way to Blue Hole on a whim, reminiscing about the times she and Kay had ventured to the forbidden swimming hole. An old limestone quarry, it was completely fenced off now. In the old days, the blue, blue water beckoned on hot summer nights. No one dared try to sneak on the property during the day. But at night, kids would park along the old dirt road and hike in the half-mile to the pit. The water was clear and cold. And deep. Rarely a summer went by when someone didn't drown out at Blue Hole.

Now, she made her way back through Pine Springs, the late spring day abnormally warm. But she was enjoying the weather. April in Monterey was still damp, cold and foggy. And she admitted she'd miss the flowers, the greenness of East Texas once she left.

Kay's house came into view, and she felt an adolescent nervousness settle over her. Fifteen years ago she wasn't prepared to talk to Kay about this, she certainly wasn't prepared now. But after last night, when she admitted she'd been jealous of Billy Ray, jealous of him *kissing* Kay . . . of Kay's admission that she'd been jealous of Danny, there was no alternative *but* to talk about it. And Jacqueline was determined to be adult about it. No more hiding.

"Yeah, adult like driving around East Texas for the last five hours," she murmured.

But no, she would tell Kay about her silly crush when they were teenagers. She would tell her how . . . how her feelings for Kay made her realize she was gay. And hopefully it wouldn't send Kay off the deep end. Hopefully they could talk about it—laugh about it—and then go on.

Kay looked up when she heard the kitchen door open. With the movie on, she'd not heard the garage door go up. Jackie rounded the bar, stopping when their eyes met.

Kay gave a hesitant smile.

"Everything okay?"

"Yeah. Sure." Jacqueline looked away. "I was just . . . driving around a little."

Kay folded the magazine she'd been holding, not reading. She stood and walked toward Jackie. The kids had not looked away from their movie, but Kay kept her voice low.

"Have you eaten?"

Jacqueline shook her head.

"Pizza is the normal fare with the kids."

"That's fine."

Kay looked back at the kids, then lightly grasped Jackie's arm. "I thought maybe, once we get them settled, we could talk." She shrugged. "We could go into my room and pretend to watch a movie."

With their eyes locked together, Jacqueline felt all of the nervousness she swore she'd left outside. She nodded, trying to ignore the warm hand touching her skin. Yes, they needed to talk.

"Good. Let me call in the pizza."

"I'm going to take a quick shower," Jacqueline said and escaped into her room. She leaned against the door for several minutes, trying to calm her racing heart. She couldn't even be near Kay without wanting to touch her . . . *kiss* her.

Jesus, get a grip.

"Lee Ann, you know how to work the remote," Kay said from her doorway. "We want to watch a movie too. And you're too young to see it," she said with a grin, trying to pacify the kids. They had begged Aunt Kay to stay out there with them.

"Can we have more pizza?"

"Have as much as you want." Oh, Rose would kill her.

Jackie was standing hesitantly beside the bed, her eyes wide. Kay just barely kept from laughing at Jackie's nervousness. Geez, you'd think the woman was afraid of her or something.

"Grab a side," Kay said. She held up two DVDs. "Any preference?"

"No. It doesn't matter."

Kay blindly picked one. No, it didn't matter. They weren't going to watch it. They were going to talk and Kay wanted some background noise. She went into her closet and pulled two extra pillows from the top shelf, tossing them onto the bed.

"We used to have at least six pillows when we were kids," Kay said. She took the wineglasses and bottle of wine to the bed. "Of course back then, we didn't share wine."

"Dr. Pepper," Jacqueline said.

Kay laughed. "Yes, you'd get very cranky if we tried to serve you anything *but* that."

Jacqueline fluffed the pillows behind her, trying to relax. She kicked her shoes off and tucked her sock-clad feet under her jeans. She was pleased that her hand didn't tremble when Kay poured wine into her glass.

"By the way, Rose hasn't talked to you about Josh, has she?"

"What do you mean?"

"When she was dropping Denny off, she was asking a lot of questions about my plans for the next few weeks. I think she's got something up her sleeve."

"She's convinced Josh is perfect for you."

"Perfect? He's twenty-seven. He lives in Mississippi. What is she *thinking*?"

"She's just worried about you, Kay. She told me she hates the thought of you being alone."

"And she can't come to terms with the fact that it's by choice and not design," Kay said.

"Is it?"

Kay nodded. "I've been asked out. And if I was interested in any of them, I'd have said yes. But none of them stir even the *slightest* interest."

"And Josh?"

"And Josh is no different," Kay said. She turned, facing Jackie. She waited until Jackie met her eyes before speaking. "Why didn't you tell me?"

Jacqueline swallowed. Well, so much for small talk. "And what would I have said, Kay?"

"I swear, Jackie, nothing's changed. You *still* can't talk to me about this."

Jacqueline watched the wine swirl as she tipped her glass from side to side. She took a deep breath and closed her eyes. "Okay, I had a ridiculous teenage crush on you in high school. Is that what you want to hear?" She opened her eyes when she felt warm fingers entwine with her own.

"Why do you say it was ridiculous?"

"Because at first, I didn't know what to do about it. I didn't know what it meant. We were friends. I wasn't supposed to feel like that about you. When I . . . when I finally accepted that I was gay, I was afraid to be around you."

"Afraid of what you might do?"

"No! Kay, I told you, I would never have touched you." Jacqueline looked away. "I was afraid you'd find out, is all. And that you would be afraid of *me*. And I couldn't stand the thought of us not being friends."

"I would have never let that come between us, Jackie."

"You don't know that. You can say it now, but we were kids. You don't know what you would have done had I come to you and told you I was gay, told you I *liked* you," Jacqueline finished in a whisper.

"Oh, Jackie." Kay rested her hand on Jackie's knee, rubbing lightly. "You're right. I don't know what I would have done. But maybe more things would have made sense to me then." Kay squeezed Jackie's knee, waiting until blue eyes found hers. "Last night, when I saw you looking at me, you had the same look in your eyes that I saw so many times back then."

"I'm sorry."

"Sorry for what, Jackie? You said you were jealous of Billy Ray. I couldn't see it back then, but I see it now. And I *was* jealous of Danny." It was Kay's turn to look away, and she fidgeted with her own wineglass. "I thought I was jealous because he was taking time away from my best friend." Kay looked up, daring to meet Jackie's eyes. "But that wasn't really why I was jealous," she admitted quietly. "I was jealous because he was *with* you."

Jacqueline didn't know what to say, so she said nothing at all.

Kay cleared her throat and wet her suddenly dry lips. "Why . . . why didn't you ever try to kiss me?" Kay asked in a whisper.

When their blue eyes locked together, Jacqueline had a difficult time breathing. Her heart was pounding so loudly, she was certain Kay could hear it. She slid her eyes lower, resting on the lips that, as a teenager, she'd imagined kissing thousands of times. And now, here they were, fifteen years older, sitting on Kay's bed, and those lips that she'd wanted so badly were but a breath away. Jacqueline's desire was at war, and she struggled to maintain a grasp on her senses. Her mistake was letting Kay's blue eyes capture her own. Something she couldn't see as a kid, she saw now. Her desire was mirrored in Kay's eyes.

"*Yes*," Kay whispered.

Jacqueline moaned at just the thought of kissing Kay. Without another word, she leaned toward her, aware of Kay's ragged breathing, of the pulse pounding rapidly in Kay's throat. Her eyes slid closed as she—

"Aunt Kay?"

They pulled apart guiltily, both breathing as if they'd run a race. Kay closed her eyes for a moment as her hand rested against her chest.

Oh my God.

Before Kay could speak, Lee Ann was crawling in bed between them, oblivious to what she'd interrupted.

"Movie's over, and Denny fell asleep."

"He did?" Kay finally looked up, daring to meet Jackie's eyes. The desire she'd seen earlier was nearly gone, replaced with apprehension. And perhaps regret.

Jacqueline stood up and collected her shoes. "I'm actually kinda tired myself. I think I'll call it a night."

Kay nodded, afraid to speak. She couldn't very well beg Jackie to stay up until the kids were asleep, beg her to finish the kiss they'd barely started.

CHAPTER TWENTY-SIX

Jacqueline showered before venturing into the kitchen. She'd heard them earlier, heard the kids' laughter, heard Kay's teasing voice. She slept in later than normal, but she was afraid to be alone with Kay. With the kids there as a buffer, there would be no time for talking, for . . . *kissing*.

She leaned against the counter to steady herself, finally daring to meet her own eyes in the mirror. She had purposefully avoided thinking about what happened last night, what *almost* happened. She still couldn't believe she had been so close to kissing Kay after all these years. And the whispered word Kay had breathed was still fresh in her mind.

Yes.

But what did it mean? Was Kay suddenly curious? Or was she giving voice to suppressed feelings after all this time?

Whatever the answer, Jacqueline wasn't sure she could handle it.

Kay looked up when Jackie walked into the kitchen, heading straight to the coffee without so much as a glance. This she was expecting. Jackie was no doubt embarrassed over what had *almost* happened. And Kay was too. After all, she'd started it, she'd wanted to talk, and then she'd practically begged Jackie to kiss her.

But in the light of day, she wasn't so sure anymore. Maybe she'd simply imagined the look in Jackie's eyes. Maybe the attraction she had for Jackie—still had for her after all these years—had absolutely nothing to do with sex. Maybe it was just that, an attraction. An extension of their friendship. Maybe Kay was reading too much into it.

"Are you okay this morning?" Jacqueline asked quietly, hesitantly.

Kay met her eyes, drowning in the blue depths like she'd done hundreds of times before. Only now, she accepted what she saw in Jackie's eyes, she accepted what she felt for Jackie. And it had everything to do with their friendship, yet it had nothing whatsoever to do with friendship.

"I'm okay. You?"

Jacqueline glanced at the kids who were busy eating pancakes, then looked back at Kay. "Last night . . . Kay, I'm sorry," she whispered.

Kay nodded. "Yes, I'm sorry too. If Lee Ann had only waited five more minutes, then I'd already know what it's like to kiss you."

Jacqueline's eyebrows shot up.

"You want pancakes?"

"*What?* Kay?"

"Hmm?"

"You're making me crazy," Jacqueline whispered.

"Good. It's about time. Now, do you want any pancakes?"

Jacqueline shook her head. "No. I don't think I can eat," she murmured. She took her coffee cup, intending to go back to her room—and think. But a tiny hand touched her arm.

"Aren't you going to eat? Aunt Kay made pancakes just for you."

"For me? She did?" Jacqueline looked up at Kay, seeing the slight blush on the other woman's face.

"She said you used to eat ten at a time."

"Ah, but that was when your grandma was cooking. I'm scared to eat Aunt Kay's cooking." She was rewarded with a wet dishcloth to the face.

CHAPTER TWENTY-SEVEN

"Rose said she'd feed us leftover burgers, but I have a sneaky suspicion that she invited Josh, too."

"Mommy says Josh is cute," Lee Ann said.

"Josh is also young," Kay said, sparing a glance at Jackie in the rearview mirror.

"But he *is* cute," Jacqueline teased.

"Hush."

"Aunt Kay, is Josh going to be your boyfriend?"

"No, Lee Ann, he's not."

"But Mommy says ya'll are going to have a date."

"Is that what Mommy says?" Kay asked through clenched teeth. "I think I need to have a talk with your mommy."

"What time did they get back?" Jacqueline asked.

"She called at two."

"They weren't gone long."

"No. They usually don't get back until six most weekends. I'm sure Greg was anxious to return."

"Yeah. I just hope he doesn't—" She stopped, aware of Lee Ann listening to their conversation. She met Kay's eyes in the mirror, seeing her nod slightly.

When they pulled into the driveway, Kay let out a heavy sigh. "As I suspected."

"What?"

She motioned to the street with a quick toss of her head. "Eric's truck."

"Ahh. So, another round with Josh," Jacqueline said as she got out, helping Denny with his backpack. She stopped when warm fingers wrapped around her forearm.

"I have zero interest in Josh," Kay said quietly as their eyes locked together. "And you know it."

Jacqueline nodded, the look in Kay's eyes frightening her a little. Jacqueline realized that whatever was going to happen between them, she wasn't in control any longer. Kay was in control. And the look in her eyes told Jacqueline that Kay *knew* she was in control. Jacqueline was simply at her mercy. The thought made her weak.

They found them in the backyard, enjoying the last of the sunshine. Spring rains were forecast for tomorrow.

"Hey guys," Rose called, then she bent over, pulling Lee Ann into a hug. "How's my big girl?"

"Guess what we had?"

"What?"

"Pancakes!"

"Pancakes? Aunt Kay *cooked*?" Rose asked, surprised.

"Look, I can open up a box with the best of them."

Rose turned to Jackie. "Did you eat?" she asked quietly.

"She forced me," she said with just a hint of a smile.

"You both are so funny." Kay slugged Jackie in the arm. "And see if I *ever* cook for you again!"

Jacqueline rubbed her arm. "They were good. Maybe not as fluffy as your mother's, but they were still good."

Rose leaned closer to them, her voice low. "Don't let Josh know you can't cook. Cooking is very important to men."

"Rose, listen to me. You can play matchmaker all you want, but I am not attracted to Josh. In the least. So quit pushing it."

"How can you not be attracted to him?"

Kay raised her hands in exasperation. "I'm just not Rose. So drop it."

Rose looked at Jackie. "Can you talk some sense into her? He's practically an Adonis, for pity's sake!"

Jacqueline shrugged. "If she doesn't like him, she doesn't like him."

Kay laughed, linking arms with Jackie. "Thank you, Miss Keys. I couldn't have said it better myself."

Rose stared at them. "You're acting strange."

Kay released Jackie, smiling as she noticed the slight blush on Jackie's face. Damn, Jackie could still be so vulnerable. And try as she may, Jackie couldn't hide her feelings from Kay any longer. Kay could read through every disguise, and right now, she knew if she should touch Jackie, she would feel her tremble. And why, oh why, couldn't she have seen that fifteen years ago? So much time wasted.

"I'm not acting strange, Rose."

Rose put her hands on her hips. "Give me one good reason why you don't like Josh."

Kay glanced quickly at Jackie, seeing the slight twitch of her lips. *Well, let's see, Rose. He's a man, for one thing. And he's not Jackie, for another.* She closed her eyes. Perhaps too much for Rose to handle. So, she went to something safer.

"He's twenty-seven."

"So?"

"I'm almost thirty-four."

"And?"

Kay shrugged. "He drinks too much."

"*What?*"

Kay motioned with her head. "Have you ever seen him without a beer in his hand?"

"That doesn't mean anything. Do you ever see Eric without a beer?"

Kay nodded. "Exactly my point. Eric drinks too much."

"Kay, you can't judge everyone by Billy Ray. He was practically a drunk."

"He *was* a drunk, Rose."

"And what does that have to do with Josh?"

"Girls," Jacqueline said, stepping between them. "Now is probably not the right time or place for this discussion."

"I'm sorry. You're right," Rose said. "I just wish you'd keep an open mind, Kay."

"I will, but Rosie, please quit worrying about me."

Jacqueline cleared her throat. "Here comes . . . your date."

"There you are! Rose said you guys were coming over." Josh looked them over. "You're Jackie, right?"

Jacqueline smiled, glancing quickly at Kay. "Yes. And you're . . . Justin?"

"Josh," he corrected, then linked arms with Kay. "Come on over. I'll get you a beer."

Rose elbowed Jackie. "*Justin?*"

Jacqueline shrugged. "Just messing with the kid," she said as she watched Kay walk away from her.

Kay hated to be rude, but if Josh didn't take his hands off of her soon, she was likely to slug him.

"I was thinking, maybe one day this week, we could go out to dinner," Josh suggested. "Eric says the Mexican food place in town is pretty good."

Kay took a step back, causing Josh's arm to slide away from her back. "Yes, very good food. However, I'm not having dinner with you."

"Why not?"

"Josh, you seem like a nice guy. Really." Kay smiled gently. "But I'm just not interested."

"What do you mean?"

"I mean, I'm not interested in you. In dating you," she clarified. She didn't want to be a total bitch.

"But Rose said—"

"You'll find that Rose says a lot of things." She quickly scanned the backyard, finding Jackie sitting alone in a lawn chair. She shook her head, wondering why Rose had left Jackie by herself. "Excuse me."

She didn't wait for Josh to comment. She walked purposefully toward Jackie, smiling when Jackie looked up.

"What are you doing?"

Jacqueline shrugged. "Sitting. Watching."

Kay squatted down beside Jackie's chair, shyly resting a hand on Jackie's thigh. She felt the other woman tense, felt the tremor that traveled through Jackie's body. She found it amazing that her touch had such power. And she found it amazing that Jackie's eyes could possibly turn bluer than they already were.

"Kay—" Jacqueline whispered, covering Kay's hand with her own, pressing it tightly against her thigh. "You don't know what you're doing."

"No, I don't suppose I do," Kay murmured. She was aware of the warmth under her fingers, and she spread them, grasping Jackie's thigh. Such a simple touch, yet it caused her heart to race, caused her breath to catch.

"Can't leave you alone for a minute."

Kay jerked her hand away guiltily as Rose walked over. She stood, aware that her legs were shaking. "You talking to me or Jackie?"

"Both of you. I swear! There's a handsome man dying for your attention over there, and what do you do? Migrate back to Jackie. Jeez. Some things never change."

Kay and Jackie exchanged smiles. "We have fifteen years of catching up to do, Rose. Why can't you understand that?"

"Because there's a cute *guy* over there, that's why." Rose took her hand. "And it's not like he fell out of the ugly tree, Kay. Have you *seen* his biceps?"

"Rose, I love you, but you're getting on my nerves," Kay said.

"I'm sorry, Kay, but I just have a feeling about Josh. I think he might be the one."

"The one?"

"Yeah, the *one*."

"Rose, trust me, he's not *the one*."

Rose shook her finger at her sister. "Your problem, Kay, is that you're too picky!"

"And your problem, Rose, is that you're in my damn business!"

"Girls," Jacqueline warned. "Play nice."

"Jackie, she's just so damn stubborn," Rose said loudly.

"If you like him so much, *you* go out with him!" Kay countered.

They both turned as Greg cleared his throat behind them. "You might want to yell just a little bit louder. I'm not certain they heard you two doors down."

Kay covered her cheeks with both hands. "I'm sorry," she said quietly. Her eyes slid to Jackie, and there was nothing there but understanding.

"I'm sorry too," Rose said. "I'm pushing, I know." She grasped Kay's arm. "I just want you to have someone, Kay. I hate that you're alone."

"Rose, you've got to understand, I'm *fine*. You're the only one worried about me being single."

"I'm not the only one, Kay. I'm just the only one voicing my opinion."

Jacqueline finally stood. "Rose, give her a break, will you?"

"Easy for you to say, Jackie. You're here, then gone again. You don't have to see her alone, day after day."

"Rose, you're out of line," Kay said quietly. She looked at Greg. "Please?"

"Come on, Rose. Let's get the burgers out."

"I'm sorry, sis. I just—"

"I know, Rose. It's okay." Kay let out a weary sigh when they walked away. "I know she means well, but she just wears me out sometimes."

"Has she always been this adamant about you dating?"

"No, not really. She's suggested blind dates before, she's just never gone through with them."

"I think she's . . ." Jacqueline stopped. "Never mind."

Kay wrapped warm fingers around Jackie's hand. "She's what?"

Jacqueline locked glances with Kay. "I think she's worried about . . . me."

"Worried about you?" Kay moved closer. "Worried about *me* with you?" she asked quietly.

Jacqueline looked away. "Yes."

Kay smiled. "That may be true, but that's not why she's pushing Josh."

Jacqueline looked back at Kay. "If I wasn't here, would you want to go out with Josh?"

"You mean, if you hadn't come back into my life?"

Jacqueline nodded.

"Honestly, no. I wouldn't want to go out with him. There's no interest there, Jackie. There's never been for anyone. But you," she added quietly.

Jacqueline nodded. She didn't know what to say.

"Does that make you feel better?"

Jacqueline tilted her head. "I'm not sure. But then, I'm not sure of a lot of things right now."

Kay smiled gently. "That makes two of us."

CHAPTER TWENTY-EIGHT

They drove home in complete silence. Jacqueline pretended to watch the sunset. Kay pretended to watch the road.

They left Rose's early, certainly earlier than anyone else. But Kay found her eyes searching out Jackie's, and all she really wanted was to be alone with her. To talk, maybe. Or maybe not. She felt a nervousness settle over her, unlike anything she could equate it to. If anything came of this, this thing between them, she would have to be the one to bring it out. Jackie never would. Just like Jackie couldn't bring herself to tell Kay way back when that she had feelings for her, feelings that went beyond friendship.

As she slowed, waiting for the garage door to open, Kay felt the tension build in the car and knew that Jackie felt it as well. She wondered if Jackie was afraid, knowing that they were alone, knowing that no one was here to interrupt. She thought it funny that they'd not discussed the kiss they'd almost shared last night. Funny, but not unexpected. Jackie would *never* bring it up.

They both got out, slamming the doors in unison. Jacqueline waited politely for Kay to walk into the kitchen, her eyes landing everywhere—anywhere—to avoid eye contact with her.

Jacqueline walked into the living room, intending to escape into the spare bedroom. She would close the door, she would boot up her laptop, she would check e-mail, work—anything to avoid thinking about the other woman in the house.

"Jackie?"

Jacqueline paused in the hall, the shadows hiding the fear on her face. She didn't turn around. "Yes?" She felt Kay move close behind her.

"We're not seventeen anymore."

Jacqueline swallowed hard, finally turning. "I know," she whispered.

Kay took another step closer. "Jackie, did you ever . . . did you ever fantasize about me?"

Jacqueline met Kay's eyes in the shadows, but she couldn't speak.

"Did you fantasize about . . . kissing me?"

Jacqueline closed her eyes, her heart pounding so loudly, she could hear it echoing in the hallway.

"Did you?" Kay asked in a whisper.

"Yes," Jacqueline breathed. She felt Kay's hand touch her stomach, felt it travel higher.

"Did you fantasize about touching me?"

Jacqueline felt Kay's thumb move between her breasts and she barely managed to swallow back her moan.

"Jackie, did you?"

"*Yes.*"

Kay moved closer still, their thighs brushing. Kay's hand trembled as she moved it higher, between Jackie's breasts, then higher. She lightly rubbed her thumb over the pulse pounding so in Jackie's neck.

"Did you think about me touching you?" Kay whispered.

"*Kay—*"

"Tell me. Did you, Jackie?"

Jacqueline could stand it no more. She grasped Kay's arms, moving her against the wall, pressing her body flush against Kay, holding her there. Their eyes locked together, fire on fire. She felt Kay trembling in her arms.

"I fantasized about you, too, Jackie."

Jacqueline couldn't wait. Without another word, she took the lips that were so close, the lips that she'd dreamed of as a teenager, the lips that had haunted her as an adult. Her moan mingled with Kay's as their mouths mated for the first time. Her tongue shyly traced Kay's lower lip, finally slipping inside at Kay's beckoning. Frantic hands pulled her closer, and Jacqueline grasped Kay's hips, molding their bodies together.

It was a sensation unlike anything Kay had ever experienced. Her body simply *melted* into Jackie. All of her senses came alive at once, and she knew she had never really been kissed before. Not like this. Not with such passion, such desire that had her feeling faint. She finally pulled away, breathing hard.

"Oh, good God, Jackie," she gasped. "I'm going to fall down."

"I've got you."

"Please, Jackie," Kay whispered. She moved her hands to Jackie's waist, urgently pulling the T-shirt from Jackie's jeans. "Don't make us wait any longer."

It was Jacqueline who thought she was going to fall down when she let Kay's bra slip from her fingers to the floor. The shadows did nothing to hide the rise and fall of Kay's chest, nothing to hide the small breasts from Jacqueline's greedy eyes. It was a body she used to know so well, a body she'd watched change from adolescent to teen. A body that had matured into the lovely woman standing naked before her now.

Then it hit her. She and Kay were about to make love.

"I'm scared, Kay," she whispered.

Kay smiled. She should have known. So, she took one of

Jackie's hands and drew it to her, surprised that it trembled when she placed it over her breast. She couldn't contain the quiet moan that escaped at Jackie's tentative touch. She closed her eyes as her own hands moved across Jackie's naked flesh.

"Make love to me, Jackie," she breathed.

It was then, when she felt Jackie's body cover her own, that the rightness of it all hit her. She'd only had one sexual partner before, and Jackie's gentle touch upon her body was so different from the brutal hands she remembered. She opened her eyes when she felt Jackie's warm mouth cover her breast, and she arched into her as Jackie's tongue swirled over her nipple. Her body came alive, sensations that were foreign to her traveled through her system—vibrating from every nerve ending—and she moaned from the pleasure of it all. *Yes*, it was so right to have Jackie loving her.

Jacqueline was trembling as her hand moved along Kay's waist to her hip—warm, soft skin greeting her at every turn. Kay's quiet moans aroused her even more, and she had to force herself to go slow when all she wanted was to be inside Kay, to feel her wetness, to *taste* her wetness.

She groaned, moving from Kay's breast back to her mouth, finding soft lips that opened to her, for her. Kay's arms pulled her close, hands moving lightly across her back, sliding to her hips. She felt Kay's thighs part, felt Kay arch to reach her. Jacqueline lowered her hips, meeting Kay forcefully as their tongues dueled. Their hips danced in an ancient rhythm, then Jacqueline could stand it no longer. With her knees, she urged Kay's thighs farther apart, moving her hand between them.

Kay felt delirious as she waited for Jackie's hand to touch her, to take her, to *claim* her finally after all these years. She never knew her body could be so aroused by another's touch, never knew she could be transported to another level of ecstasy just by Jackie's hands, her mouth. But, *God*, she was about to explode, and Jackie's hand had yet to reach her, had yet to move into her wetness, move into *her*.

"*Jackie* . . . oh, Jackie," she murmured, eyes sliding closed again as she felt Jackie's hand move over her hips, across her thigh, achingly close to her throbbing center.

Jacqueline's restraint faded at Kay's whispered words. Without another thought, her fingers slid into wetness, disappearing deep inside Kay. She felt Kay close around her, felt Kay arch against her, heard the moans—not knowing if they were Kay's or her own. Her eyes closed as her fingers moved with Kay, bringing her close to orgasm. Incoherent sounds came from Kay as her hips jerked against Jacqueline's hand. Jacqueline's breathing was labored, and she opened her eyes, seeing the glistening wetness on her hand. She licked her lips, moaning loudly, knowing she *had* to have her mouth there.

Kay was only slightly aware of the mouth that covered her intimately, of the tongue that raked only once against her swollen clit. That was all it took to send her over the edge. She screamed out immediately, her body no longer hers to control. Her orgasm shook her head to toe and she trembled fervently as the convulsions slowly subsided. She blindly pulled Jackie to her, needing her closeness, needing her strength.

"I have no words, Jackie," she whispered against her neck.

Jacqueline had no coherent thoughts as she wound her naked body around Kay. *Oh my God . . . you just made love to her*. Panic was about to set in. A part of her was afraid that Kay would regret this, that Kay would pull away from her. She rolled to her back, pulling Kay with her, holding her close. Her lips moved softly across Kay's face. Then she gasped as she felt Kay's hand caress her breast.

"You have such beautiful breasts," Kay murmured. "I used to love looking at your body." She looked up, meeting Jackie's eyes in the shadows. "I just never knew why."

"Kay, you're not . . . you're not sorry, are you?"

"Oh, God, *no*. Not sorry, Jackie. It was . . . it was so beautiful." She looked away, her hand again moving between Jackie's breasts, touching first one, then the other, watching in fascination as the nipples hardened. "I want to make love to you. I want . . . I want to touch you that way." She looked up again. "You want that, don't you?"

"Kay, I've wanted that forever."

She watched as Kay's eyes darkened before pulling away from her own. Then her heart nearly stopped before drumming back to life again as her teenage dreams began to come true, beginning with Kay's mouth covering her breast.

CHAPTER TWENTY-NINE

Kay woke first, the unfamiliar weight of another's arm across her waist. Unfamiliar, yet so *very* familiar. Even if the events of last night weren't still fresh in her mind, she'd know it was Jackie holding her. She would know Jackie's touch, her scent, anywhere.

She slowly closed her eyes, trying to ward off the panic attack that she knew was about to hit. Last night, she'd not had time to think. All she wanted was Jackie's hands on her, and her own hands on Jackie's skin. Nothing else mattered. But now, now as the sunlight crept through the blinds, reality hit. She was lying naked with another woman. A woman who had made love to her—a woman she had made love *to*—for hours on end.

Oh God.

She had to escape. She just couldn't face Jackie now. What would she say? Was it a mistake? No, it had felt too right for it to be a mistake. Too right and too perfect. But now what?

Oh my God. I'm a lesbian.

Am I?

She shook her head. She wasn't ready to deal with it now. She wasn't ready to *talk* about it. So she did the only sensible thing she could think of.

She ran.

Jacqueline rolled over, her body pleasantly sore. She knew she was alone before she opened her eyes. Disappointed at first, she realized how late it must be. Kay would already be at work. So she tossed the covers off and stretched, a satisfied moan escaping as visions of last night flooded her mind.

Made love.

Damn, but did she ever think this day would come? She smiled. Only in her dreams. But last night, Kay, with her inexperience, had taken her places no woman had before. Kay knew exactly how to touch her. It was as if . . . as if Kay had dreamed it a thousand times.

She showered and pulled on yesterday's jeans, reminding herself that she needed to do laundry again. There was no coffee . . . and no note. In fact, little evidence Kay had been there.

As she spooned coffee from the can, she looked around thoughtfully, wondering what Kay was thinking, how she was feeling. She wished Kay had woken her so they could talk. Kay would, no doubt, need to talk.

While the coffee made, she dug through drawers in Kay's desk, looking for the phonebook. She found *Kay's Hallmark*, and dialed. An involuntary smile lit up her face when she heard Kay's voice.

"Good morning," she murmured.

Silence. Then, "Hello."

Jacqueline raised her eyebrows. "If you'd hung around a bit, we could have talked about it, Kay," she said quietly. "Are you all right?" She heard a long sigh and the slight clearing of Kay's throat.

"I'm not sure, Jackie."

Jacqueline closed her eyes. "Should I say I'm sorry?"

"Sorry? I think last night was my doing," Kay whispered. Then she cleared her throat again. "Now's not a good time to talk."

"I understand." *Damn.*

"I'll . . . I'll see you later."

Jacqueline nodded, listening to the dial tone for a few seconds before hanging up. "I guess she freaked out," she murmured. *Damn.*

CHAPTER THIRTY

Kay hung up the phone, angry with herself for being so short with Jackie. It wasn't Jackie's fault. She had done nothing wrong. Kay was the one who had practically attacked her in the hallway last night. Kay went to her first. Kay was the one who had pulled Jackie into her bedroom. No, if left up to Jackie, they would never have crossed over that line from friends to lovers.

Lovers.

Just the thought of it made Kay weak, and she grabbed the countertop for support as every kiss, every touch, came flooding back. She closed her eyes, still able to feel Jackie's mouth on her skin, still taste and smell Jackie as her own mouth moved across Jackie's body.

Lovers. Yes.

"Kay? Are you all right?"

Kay blinked several times, finding herself face to face with Rene Wells. Why in the world would Rene Wells stoop so low as to enter her little store? It wasn't even Christmas.

"Hello, Rene." Kay stood up straight. "I'm fine. What brings you here?"

"Why, can't I shop at your lovely little store?"

Kay shook her head. "You normally don't."

Rene had the good grace to blush, but she covered it nicely with a charming smile.

"We were talking about you yesterday," she said. "The in-laws always have us over for brunch after Sunday service. John and Mary Lawrence were there, too," Rene said.

"How nice," Kay murmured politely.

"They mentioned that Jackie Keys was staying with you. We knew, of course, that she was in town, what with the funeral and all," Rene said with a toss of her hand. "Rumor has it that she was mentioned in her father's will. Can you believe the nerve of some people? Crawling back into town to lay claim to the family fortune? And after all the shame she brought to her poor mother."

Kay opened her mouth to defend Jackie, then decided against it. She owed Rene no explanation. Rene would find out soon enough.

"And Kay, do you think it's safe for her to stay with you?"

"Safe?"

"Rumors are already spreading across town."

"What rumors?"

"That the two of you are more than friends, if you know what I mean."

Kay laughed. "I know what you mean, Rene. What I'm wondering is why you felt the need to come down here to tell me this?"

"I'm just looking out for your well-being, Kay."

"We both know that's bullshit, Rene," Kay said with the best smile she could muster. "We're not friends, and we don't socialize. If fact, you seldom patronize my store." Kay moved around the counter and faced Rene. "My guess is, you want to be first in line at the gossip mill. But you know what, Rene, none of this is your business. So why don't you go on back to the country club and tell them you struck out with me."

Rene took a step backward, hand at her chest. "Why Kay Garland, I can't believe you speak to me like this." Her voice lowered. "I do believe it was a loan from our bank that set you up in this . . . *business*, wasn't it?"

Kay smiled. Oh, she couldn't *wait* for Rene to find out Jackie controlled the bank now. "Yes, it was. Although I don't recall *your* name being anywhere on my loan application."

"I doubt they would have approved you for the loan had we not gone to school together, Kay. You might want to keep that in mind." She turned quickly and fled from the store.

Kay's smile turned into an outright laugh. God, Rene had no idea how the real world functioned. But then her smile faded as her thoughts went back to Jackie. She had been so short with her, so distant. All because she was . . . what? Embarrassed? Embarrassed that they'd made love so thoroughly?

She was no longer certain why she ran from Jackie this morning. Guilt? She could think of a hundred excuses, and one of them would be what the town would think, her family, her friends. It was the thing she hated most about living in a small town. Everyone knew your business. And this would be a secret she doubted they could keep. Why, even now, Rene Wells was probably on her cell phone, relaying her visit to her country club friends.

Jacqueline snatched up her cell when it rang, hoping it would be Kay. But Greg's voice greeted her.

"You busy?"

"No." Jacqueline looked at her laptop, the screen saver flashing across. "Just working on some edits," she lied. "What's up?"

"Well, Mr. Lawrence came by. He said you were leaving soon. Is that true?"

Jacqueline twirled her glasses in her hand, nodding. "Yes, soon, Greg. I'm just not certain of the date. I was actually going to call you today and see if there's anything you want to go over before I leave."

Greg laughed. "There are a thousand things I could go over. But I was looking at your wish list you forwarded to me. Mostly employee benefits and the like. If you're serious about implementing these, I can get with Ms. Scott and get you a timeline."

"Yes, I think we're sorely lacking in the benefits we provide to our employees. Some are simple and inexpensive, others I realize will cut into profit. It's just something I think needs to be done. We may be more productive in the long run."

"I agree. I'll get on it right away."

Jacqueline paused, remembering the way Kay had left that morning. Perhaps it would be better all the way around if Jacqueline left now. No sense in prolonging the inevitable.

"Greg, why don't you work something up today. Perhaps we can go over it tonight. If I feel like we're on the same page, I may head on out tomorrow, then."

"Okay. Sure." Greg cleared his throat, then paused. "Does Kay know you're planning on leaving?"

"No." She paused too. "But it won't be a surprise, Greg." She tossed her glasses on the table. "I'll come over to your place. Meet you there after work?"

"Sure."

Jacqueline spent the rest of the day doing laundry and making arrangements for a flight out. She figured if she left early enough, she could be in Dallas by noon, so she booked a two o'clock flight to San Francisco. A quick e-mail to Ingrid ensured her that someone would pick her up. She even promised to go back with Ingrid and visit for a few days. That would be better than going alone to her condo, where there would be nothing to distract her.

CHAPTER THIRTY-ONE

Kay was disappointed that Jackie's car wasn't in her driveway when she got home. Disappointed, but not necessarily surprised. Jackie was most likely avoiding the confrontation that she assumed would occur when Kay got home. Confrontation? No. But they needed to talk. *She* needed to talk.

Kay admitted she was over the initial shock that she'd actually made love with Jackie. Yesterday, last night, it had all been so clear to her. But in the light of day, she'd panicked. Now, well, now she'd had a day to get used to it, to accept it. And what she and Jackie had done last night was simply express—physically—what they felt for one another, what they felt years ago, and certainly what they feel now, as adults.

When Jackie touched her, when Jackie made love to her, everything she'd ever felt for Jackie suddenly made sense. How, as a kid, she'd been willing to follow Jackie anywhere, just to be with her. And later, as a teen, how she'd craved Jackie's touch. The two of them had been so affectionate with each other, it was nearly second nature for them to touch when they talked. And now, as adults, that need to touch—and be touched—was as strong as ever.

And last night, they didn't fight it any longer. They *couldn't* fight it. What happens next, however, Kay had no clue. Which is why she wished Jackie was home.

She found a note instead. Apparently, Rose was making spaghetti for the group.

"Please don't let Josh be there," she murmured.

But she needn't have worried. Jackie's car was the only one in the driveway. Kay pulled in behind her, walking quickly through the light drizzle that had been falling all afternoon. The spring storms that had been forecast stayed to the north. She didn't bother with the doorbell. After two quick knocks, she walked in.

"In the kitchen," Rose called.

Lee Ann and Denny were at the table, coloring. Lee Ann looked up long enough to smile at her. Rose met her with a spoon extended.

"Taste."

Kay obliged, nodding. "Good. Needs more basil."

Rose laughed. "As if I'd take cooking advice from you!" She covered the pot, adjusting the temperature to simmer.

"Where is everyone?"

"I put the twins down for a nap a couple of hours ago."

Kay waited patiently. "And?"

Rose smiled. "And you mean Jackie?"

"I assume she and Greg are holed up somewhere?"

"They're playing on the computer. Greg has some graphs or something," she said with a flick of her hand.

Before Kay could go look for them, Jacqueline stuck her head in.

"Rose, got any more of that iced tea?" Jacqueline stopped when she saw Kay. "I didn't hear you come in."

Kay fell into Jacqueline's eyes, and she leaned against the counter for support. Everything she felt last night seemed to hit her at once. "Hey."

Jacqueline gave a hesitant smile. "Hey, yourself. Everything okay?"

Kay nodded. "Yes, everything is fine now."

"Good."

"Sorry."

Jacqueline shrugged. "It's okay."

"My fault."

"We should have talked," Jacqueline said quietly.

Rose finally cleared her throat. "Hello," she drawled in four syllables. "I obviously missed part of the conversation because you are making *no* sense." She grabbed Jacqueline's glass. "Where's my husband?"

Jacqueline pulled her eyes away from Kay. "He's finishing up some flow charts for me."

Rose handed Jackie a full glass of tea. "Well, it needs to stop. He works all day, then comes home and gets on the computer. He hasn't hit a lick at a snake around here in two weeks!"

Jacqueline laughed. "In English, that means what, Rose?"

Rose filled another glass and handed it to Kay. "It means I have chores for him to do around the house and he's not done them, smart-ass."

"Well, he'll have plenty of time once I'm gone."

Kay turned, searching, finally finding Jackie's blue eyes. "You're leaving?" she asked quietly.

Jacqueline nodded.

"When?"

Jacqueline looked briefly at Rose, then back at Kay. "I have a flight out of Dallas at two tomorrow."

"I see." Kay cleared her throat. "And when did you decide this?"

Jacqueline hesitated. "This morning."

Kay nodded, looking away. "I see," she said again.

Jacqueline looked at Rose, seeing the questions flying through her mind. Now was *not* the time to have this discussion with Kay, even though she could see the hurt in Kay's eyes. All she wanted was to go to her, to hold her.

"Hey, Jackie? Come look at this," Greg called from the back of the house.

Jacqueline paused, one more look at Kay, then slipped quietly away.

"What the hell was that about?" Rose asked the minute Jackie was out of earshot.

Kay squared her shoulders, refusing to let Rose see how upset she was. Tears, she could never explain. So, she played dumb.

"What was what about?"

"I felt like I was eavesdropping on a private conversation, that's what. Although I don't know why I'm surprised. You two were always in your own world." Rose lifted the lid on the spaghetti sauce, stirring slowly. "Just thought I'd let you know, but the rumor mill has been overactive."

"What do you mean?"

"You and Jackie. I heard whispers all day today."

"What about me and Jackie?"

"Oh, Kay, surely you're not *that* naive. She's been staying with you for two weeks. Although no one talks about it, *everyone* remembers the reason she left. And even if they didn't, she's practically a celebrity. And she's *out*, as they say."

"Rene Wells, the bitch," Kay hissed, then looked quickly at Lee Ann. The girl was no doubt listening to every word.

"What are you talking about?"

"She came by the shop today, fishing for info about Jackie. I swear, just like in high school."

Rose closed the lid, then walked closer. "You know, Kay, if something *was* going on with you and Jackie . . . I mean, not that I think it ever would . . . but if there was, you could tell me, you know. I wouldn't freak out."

Kay laughed nervously. "Oh, Rose, of course nothing's going on. Don't be silly. I've known Jackie forever. We're just friends, and we'll never be anything but that." Kay cleared her throat. "And yes, you would freak out."

Jacqueline stood in the hallway, her heart breaking as Kay's words washed over her. What had she expected? Did she think Kay would confess to Rose that they'd made love last night? Did she think Kay was ready to embrace this change? She shook herself, finally moving into the kitchen. Kay's eyes flew to her own.

"Forgot my tea," she murmured.

"Jackie—"

Jacqueline stared into Kay's eyes, acknowledging that she'd overheard. She gave a slight nod, then walked away.

Oh God. Kay closed her eyes, moving away from Rose, knowing the hurt she saw in Jackie's eyes was because of her. What a hypocrite she was. In private, to herself—to Jackie—she could admit what she felt . . . what she *was*. But to *Rose*? To any of her family? Could she? Could she say out loud that she and Jackie were now . . . lovers?

No. Not ever.

She couldn't. Despite Rose's words, she would never understand. Mama would never understand. And not just that. She owned a business, for God's sake! Would people still patronize her store? No, most likely, they would stay away in droves, and she would become the joke of Pine Springs.

"Kay? What's wrong?"

Kay shook her head, reaching blindly for her glass of tea. "Nothing. Just . . . hate that Jackie is leaving already," she murmured. She took a deep breath, finally facing Rose, hoping the smile on her face looked genuine. "I'm going to miss her."

"I know. But at least this time, you know she'll be back."

Kay wished she could be sure of that.

"But I'm tired of her taking all of Greg's time. Now go tell them dinner is ready." Rose turned to the kids. "Lee Ann, clean up the colors. Time for dinner." Rose stuck her head into the hall. "Kay, tell Greg to get the twins," she yelled.

Kay nodded, knowing very well that Greg, as well as the neighbors, had heard her. She found Jackie bent over Greg's shoulder, the computer squeezed into a corner of Rose and Greg's bedroom. They were both pointing at the monitor, and Kay allowed her eyes to travel the length of Jackie. In the short time it took, memories from last night flashed through her mind, causing Kay's breath to catch, her heart to pound. As usual, Jackie felt her presence. She stood slowly, back straightening. She turned her head, meeting Kay's eyes. Kay saw Jackie's eyes darken, and she wondered what Jackie had seen in her own.

Desire? Could Jackie possibly know what thoughts were running through her mind right now?

"Greg, Rose wants you to get the twins," Kay said quietly, her eyes never leaving Jackie.

"Yeah, I heard," but he continued tapping away on the keyboard.

"I think she meant now. She's a little cranky."

"I've seen enough, Greg," Jacqueline said. "You can e-mail me the rest."

"Are you sure?"

"Sure," Jacqueline said.

As soon as Greg left them alone, Kay moved closer, her eyes still locked on Jackie's blue ones.

"I'm sorry," she whispered.

"For?"

"For this morning. For what you overheard with Rose." Her eyes slid shut. "For your leaving me again," she whispered.

"Oh, Kay, I'm not leaving you. I'm leaving . . . *us*. It'll be better for you if I'm gone."

"No, Jackie. You're leaving because I freaked out this morning and ran from you. You're leaving because I couldn't talk to you about it. And you're leaving because of what I told Rose."

Their eyes held.

"Yes," Jacqueline admitted quietly. "Yes to all of those."

"God, Jackie, I don't want you to go. The thought of you leaving breaks my heart."

Jacqueline took Kay's hand and drew it to her, placing it above her left breast, holding it close. "It breaks my heart too."

"Don't go," Kay whispered.

"I will never forget last night, Kay. You don't know how special it was."

"Yes I do."

"You're not ready to live this life, Kay. You know you're not. You may never be. But I'm too old, I've been out too long. I can't go into the closet and hide this, Kay."

"I've got my family to think about," Kay said. "My business." Kay shook her head. "Jackie, I could never be . . . be open about this."

"I know. And that's why I'm leaving."

"Jackie, please, maybe give me some time—"

"*Girls? Dinner!*" Rose yelled.

Jacqueline squeezed Kay's hand. "We'll talk tonight."

"I don't want to talk tonight. I want to make love with you again," Kay whispered.

Jacqueline's eyes closed briefly. "God, Kay. You don't know what those words do to me."

Kay moved closer. "Just the thought of you touching me makes me weak, Jackie."

Their eyes were locked together, their lips only inches apart when Rose yelled for them again.

"*Goddamn,*" Jacqueline murmured.

Kay squeezed her hand. "Come on, sweetie."

Jacqueline felt her heart breaking once again as Kay released her hand. She knew they would make love again tonight. And she also knew that she would still leave tomorrow.

I'm in love with her.

The truth didn't shock her. She admitted to herself she'd always been in love with Kay. Always. That's why, year after year, she could never find anyone to chase Kay from her heart, could never find anyone to replace her. *And I'm leaving her again.* Because this time, Kay was choosing her family over Jacqueline.

"Jackie?"

Jacqueline nodded sadly. "Coming."

CHAPTER THIRTY-TWO

Kay drove through town, having to force herself to mind the speed limit. Dinner had been endless, and she wondered what Rose thought of her and Jackie's silence. Silent, yes, but they couldn't keep their eyes from one another. She looked in the mirror briefly, seeing Jackie following close behind. She couldn't wait to be alone with her.

Jacqueline had a tight grip on the steering wheel, her eyes focused on the car ahead of her. She wondered if they would talk at all. The looks they shared over dinner suggested they would not. Kay's eyes were smoldering, and it was all Jacqueline could do to keep breathing at a normal pace. In fact, it was all she could do to remain seated. Kay's eyes promised . . . *so* much. They had made love last night, yes. But it had been tentative, hesitant at first. It was new for them as they learned what pleased the other. Tonight, oh tonight, there would be no hesitation. She could see it in each look Kay gave her. Her eyes blurred as she imagined Kay moving down her body, Kay's hot mouth finding all her secret places, Kay's mouth moving between her thighs to make her come.

"Sweet Jesus," she murmured.

By the time she pulled into Kay's driveway, she was nearly shaking with nervousness, with anticipation. She took a deep breath, the night air cool after the earlier rain. Closing her eyes, she tried to regain some control over her body. But when she opened them, Kay was there, waiting.

"Come inside, Jackie."

The words, spoken so quietly, promised so much. Nodding, she followed Kay through the garage and into the kitchen. Kay didn't bother with lights. She grasped Jacqueline's hand and led her through the house. Jacqueline offered no protest. But when they walked into Kay's bedroom, Jacqueline was nearly gasping for breath. Her heart was pounding so hard in her chest, it was nearly painful.

But she had no time to think. Kay turned, facing her, her hands sliding up Jacqueline's arms as she took the one step necessary for their bodies to touch. Jacqueline moaned as she pulled Kay close, her lips seeking, finding Kay's mouth. Kay's mouth was as hungry as her own, and Jacqueline felt weak when warm hands found their way under her shirt.

Kay pulled away for only an instant, her blue eyes locking on Jackie's. "I want to make love to you until you're begging me to stop," she whispered. Her hands moved, covering Jackie's breasts. She knew there would be no bra to hinder her.

"*Kay*—"

"And I'm going to make love to you like you made love to me." She moaned as Jackie's nipples hardened even more. "I'm going to . . ." She closed her eyes as one hand traveled down Jackie's body, slipping intimately between her thighs. Jackie moved against her hand, and Kay could nearly feel her wetness through her jeans. "I want my mouth right there, Jackie."

Jacqueline groaned, holding Kay's hand to her, pressing it hard against her throbbing clit. Her knees literally buckled, and Kay was there, holding her. She found Kay's mouth again, but it was Kay's tongue that came out to do battle, leaving little doubt as to who was in control.

Before she could think, Kay had her naked, and Jacqueline watched as Kay removed the last of her own clothing. The bed was soft under her, and she licked her lips, waiting, watching, as Kay came to her.

"Tonight, you're mine," Kay murmured as her lips closed over an aching nipple.

"I've always been yours," Jacqueline whispered. She closed her eyes, giving herself to Kay as Kay's wet mouth traced a path lower across Jacqueline's body. Expert hands spread her thighs, and Jacqueline quivered as Kay's mouth covered her.

She knew, in that instant, she would never be the same.

CHAPTER THIRTY-THREE

The early morning chill woke her, and she reached out, trying to find Jackie's warm body. But the bed was empty.

Kay sat up, listening to the silence. She closed her eyes. *Please be here.*

She walked barefoot through the empty house, her hand trembling as she turned the doorknob to Jackie's room.

"No, no, no," she murmured. She ran into the kitchen, impatiently shoving the curtains away from the window. *Oh, Jackie.*

The black Lexus was gone. Kay let the curtains fall back into place as she sunk down to the floor, not trying to stop the tears that poured from her eyes.

Jackie was gone.

CHAPTER THIRTY-FOUR

Jacqueline stood on her balcony, cursing the fog. It was nearly June. Where was the sunshine?

But she knew where it was. Her sunshine was in a tiny town in East Texas. She brought her hand to her chest, trying to chase away the hurt. Six weeks had done nothing to ease the ache in her heart.

She went back inside, her eyes moving around the familiar room, her desk and computer mocking her. She'd not been able to write since she'd been back. She made a couple of half-hearted attempts, but she had no flow, no rhythm. Her only saving grace was that she had no deadline looming. She had finished the last of her edits before she left Pine Springs.

Before she left Kay.

It seemed like the right thing to do at the time—leaving. The longer she stayed there, the deeper she would get. Kay, too, for that matter. She closed her eyes, still able to recall with exact clarity, how it felt to have Kay's mouth on her. And if she'd stayed, they would have continued their *affair*, their secret affair. And Jacqueline knew, for awhile at least, she would have been content to hide what they had. But not indefinitely. That's not who she was. She'd been run out of town once because she refused to hide. She wasn't about to start now. But Kay, oh Kay, couldn't be open about it. Her family, her business came first.

It was ironic, really. Kay was worried about losing her business, and here Jacqueline was, with more money than she knew what to do with. To say she had been astounded by her father's wealth would be an understatement. Obviously, Madeline had been surprised as well. The portion that he left her would allow her to live as exorbitantly as she wished for the rest of her days. But still, that evidently was not enough to convince her to drop the suit she filed, even though two judges had ruled against her. John Lawrence said Madeline's other option was to contest the will and the bequest of Pine Springs Lumber to Jacqueline. And apparently she had fond memories of the beach house on Padre Island. She wanted that as well. Jacqueline shook her head. She couldn't understand her mother's obsession with Keys Industries, the lumber mill, with Jacqueline herself. Why would she want the headache of owning Keys Industries when she now had *millions* and nothing but time to spend it?

But really, it hadn't been a headache. She and Greg communicated almost daily by e-mail and spoke on the phone a couple of times each week. No, Greg had things running smoothly. Jacqueline had no worries there.

No, her only worries were personal. Like how was she ever going to recover from Kay? When was she going to be able to get on with her life? And would she ever let another woman touch her?

She glanced at the phone lying next to her computer. Every day she had to fight the urge to call Kay, to see how she was doing. Obviously, she was making out okay. It wasn't like Kay had been calling either. After her initial inquiry as to how Kay was, she and

Greg avoided the subject. And Greg wasn't stupid. Surely he knew the reason she left so abruptly. Surely *everyone* knew. But his words still troubled her. Kay had been very quiet, he said. Kay had pulled away from them again, just like she did after her divorce. The thought that Kay had withdrawn from her family—the thought that Kay was alone—bothered Jacqueline more than she wanted to admit. Yes, it was her fault. Part of it. But it was also Kay's fault. She would never have moved their relationship to such an intimate level if Kay hadn't initiated it. Because she knew that Kay couldn't handle it, and she knew that she would be leaving again.

But she couldn't resist Kay, couldn't turn away from her touch, if only for a few nights. It was the hardest thing she ever had to do—pulling out of Kay's arms that night, leaving her sleeping peacefully, unaware that when she woke, she'd be alone again. Jacqueline would be out of her life. Again.

CHAPTER THIRTY-FIVE

Kay looked up from the book she'd been reading, startled by the knocking on her front door.

"It's me."

Kay sighed, then marked her book and tossed it on the table beside her recliner. What in the world could Rose possibly want at this hour.

She held the door open. "It's nine thirty."

Rose pointed at her wrist. "Got a watch, but thanks."

"What are you doing here? Don't you have kids to look after?"

"The twins have been asleep for an hour, and I just now got Lee Ann to bed. She thinks she's all grown up and can stay up with us now."

"And your husband?"

"Greg's got his nose in his computer, what else is new?"

Kay followed Rose into her kitchen, watching as Rose helped herself to a glass of tea.

"So, here I am, because I can't stand it a second longer," Rose announced.

"What are you talking about? *Greg*? Are you guys having problems?"

"*Greg*? No. We're fine," she said with a wave of her hand. "He's *always* loved his computer more than me, nothing's changed there. I'm talking about you."

"Me?"

"Yes you, and don't tell me nothing is wrong, that's not gonna fly anymore."

Kay turned away, going back into the living room. "I don't know what you're talking about."

"The hell you don't! You're driving me crazy with this silence, Kay. Mama's worried sick about you, Lee Ann thinks you're fixin' to die or something, and Eric, of all people, thinks you have man issues."

"Man issues?"

"Yes, he thinks he's a psychologist or something. He's planning on bringing Josh back again in two weeks."

Kay wrapped her arms around herself, facing Rose. "Tell Eric to leave me alone about Josh," she said quietly. "I mean it, Rosie."

Rose walked closer. "Tell me what's wrong, Kay. Please?"

"Nothing."

"Dammit, Kay. You've been like this since Jackie left. I know you miss her being around, but it's not like you won't see her again. Knowing you two, you probably talk on the phone every day."

Kay shook her head. "We don't talk."

"You don't talk? Why not?"

Kay shrugged. God, she did *not* want to have this conversation with Rose. But she just couldn't shake the depression that had swallowed her up since Jackie walked out of her life. Even now, the smile she tried to fake wouldn't form. She just felt empty inside.

"Kay? Why won't you talk to me?"

"Oh, Rose, because you wouldn't understand."

"Are you sick? I mean, is something wrong with you?"

At this, Kay did smile. "No, Rose, I'm not sick."

"Then what? Is it just Jackie being gone?"

Kay stared at her sister, the words wanting to come out, almost *needing* to come out. She nodded finally, unable to stop the tears that blurred her vision. "Yes, it's just Jackie," she whispered.

Rose spread her hands. "What? I don't understand."

Kay closed her eyes. "I love her."

"Well, Jesus, Kay, is that supposed to shock me?"

Kay shook her head. "No, I *love* her, Rose. I'm . . . *in* love with her. I've . . . I've made love with her. I . . . *love* her," she managed before tears closed her throat completely. She stood there, arms still wrapped around herself, and sobbed.

"Oh my God," Rose whispered. "Oh . . . my *God! Made love?*"

Kay felt Rose walk closer, felt the tentative arms that attempted to comfort her. Through their whole life, Kay had never broken down in front of Rose, not even when Billy Ray put her in the hospital. But she couldn't stop the flood of tears now over her loss of Jackie. She didn't care if her declaration shocked Rose. It was too much of a relief to have said the words out loud.

"Kay, please," Rose said as she patted her back. "Please, don't cry. You don't *ever* cry."

"I'm sorry." Kay pulled out of her arms, reaching for a tissue from beside her recliner. She blew her nose and wiped her eyes, waiting for Rose's inquisition.

"Kay, I don't know what to say. I mean . . . what *happened?*"

"Jackie happened, Rose, that's all. Jackie happened."

"But, are you serious? You *slept* with her?" Rose whispered, looking around the room as if they might be overheard.

"I told you that you wouldn't understand."

"But Kay, you're straight! You were married, for God's sake!"

"Oh, Rose, I only married Billy Ray because Jackie was gone. Don't you see? I didn't know what I felt then, I couldn't put a name to it." Kay paced across her living room, trying to put words to her jumbled thoughts. "Not even when I found out Jackie was a lesbian. I never thought that label applied to me. I just loved her. She was my best friend. I thought that was all. So, yes, I married Billy Ray." She stopped pacing and stared at Rose. "And it was so awful, Rose. He was so very . . . very *rough* with me. I could hardly stand his touch, Rose." She felt tears form again. "He . . . he raped me on more than one occasion. That last night included."

"Oh my God," Rose murmured. "Kay, why didn't you tell us?"

"Tell you what? That I didn't want to have sex with my husband, so he resorted to rape?"

Rose pulled her into another hug. "Oh, Kay, I'm so sorry. I had no idea."

"You always assumed he just beat me?" It was one subject they had never discussed—Billy Ray's abuse.

"Mama and I suspected he hit you, yes. But before we could work up the courage to talk to you, he put you in the hospital. He was gone, we didn't see the need to bring it up to you."

"I appreciate that. And you're right, I didn't want to talk about it."

"You told Jackie what really happened that night, didn't you?"

"Yes."

Rose cleared her throat. "When did you two . . . become . . . you know."

"Lovers?"

Rose nodded, her face colored slightly with a blush.

"The Sunday before she left, actually."

"But then why did she leave, Kay?"

"She left because I told her I couldn't be *open* about it. I told her I could never tell you or Mama. I was worried about my business." Kay sighed. "All stupid, meaningless stuff that I was so worried about."

"Surely she understood your concerns. I mean, this is Pine Springs, not California. Can you imagine the talk around town if you two were a *couple* for God's sake?"

"Obviously I can or else I wouldn't have been so concerned about it."

"But, you're like, really *in love* with her?"

262

"Yes. Very."

"And she loves you too?"

Jackie had never said the words, no. But Kay knew. She knew it by the look in her eyes, by the way she touched her . . . the way she screamed Kay's name when she came.

"Yes, she loves me."

Rose shook her head. "I just don't get the whole gay thing, Kay, I'm sorry. I just can't even imagine what it's like in bed. I mean, what do you *do*?"

"Jesus Christ, Rose! I'm confessing that I'm in love with another woman—that I have been living in *hell* for the past two months without her—and you want to know about *sex*?"

"I'm sorry, but Kay, I just don't understand that whole thing."

"I know you don't, and I told you that you wouldn't. It doesn't matter anyway, Rose. She's gone." Kay paced again. "And I'm sure you didn't want to know about all this, but I feel better having told you. It felt good to say it out loud."

"So now what?"

"Now what?" Kay shook her head. "Nothing."

"Nothing? But you said you loved her."

"I do, Rose. But the fact remains that I'm here in Pine Springs—with my business, with my family—and she's in California. And the two don't mix."

"I can't believe she would just leave you like that."

"Rose, she didn't just leave." Kay again wrapped her arms around herself. "I chose my business and my family over her."

"But Kay—"

"And not a word of this to Mama. Promise me, Rose. I can't deal with Mama knowing."

"Of course I won't tell her. God, can you imagine *her* reaction?"

Kay didn't have long to wait. At exactly nine o'clock the next morning, Mama walked into her shop. *I'll kill Rose.*

"We need to talk, Kay."

"I don't know why. Obviously, Rose has already done all the talking," she said quietly, glancing once at Mrs. Cartwright. "And you can tell her for me that she's dead meat!" she hissed.

"Let's go into your office." Mama nodded at Mrs. Cartwright. "How are you this morning, Gladys?"

"Just fine. What are you doing away from the café?"

"Oh, Rose has worked there long enough to finish with the breakfast crowd. You need to come by for lunch tomorrow. I'm making up a big mess of chicken and dumplings."

Mrs. Cartwright smiled. "I might just do that. Seeing as how you won't give out your recipe!"

Kay cleared her throat, waiting patiently.

"Sorry. Talk to you later, Gladys."

Kay closed the door of her tiny office, waiting only a second before turning to face her mother.

"Rose has a big fat mouth."

"She loves you, and she's worried about you. We all are."

Kay shrugged. "So, now you know." Kay turned away. "I'm so sorry, Mama. I never wanted you to find out."

"Oh, my sweet Kay, I'm not shocked, if that's what you're thinking. I'm not even surprised. It's always been Jackie for you."

"Mama? What do you mean?"

"From the beginning, the two of you were inseparable. And as teens, you didn't care one bit for Danny or Billy Ray. It was only each other you had eyes for. I saw it then, Kay. But Jackie left, and you got married and I didn't give it another thought."

Kay paced in front of her desk, her mother's words shocking her, to say the least.

"Mama, yes, it was always Jackie. But we were friends. I didn't know it was something more. Not until she came back." She paused. "And I can't believe we're having this conversation."

"Rose tells me you're in love with her."

Kay's face turned scarlet. "Oh, Jesus, Mama. I can't talk to you about this."

"If a daughter can't talk to her mama about being in love, who can she talk to?"

Kay covered her face. "I can't believe I was so worried about you finding out. I was so worried about what you would think of me."

Her mother wrapped her arms around Kay and pulled her to her ample bosom, rocking her gently.

"Kay, you're my daughter, and I love you. And as long as I can remember, Jackie has been included in our family, and I've tried to treat her as one of my own. We all love her as if she's family, Kay." She pushed Kay away, holding her at arm's length. "The light went right out of your eyes when Jackie left, just like it did all those years ago. She makes you happy. I don't care about the physical part of your relationship, Kay. Mothers don't need to know everything. But she's the one that makes you happy. Don't forsake that for your family."

Kay cried. There was nothing else she could do.

CHAPTER THIRTY-SIX

Jacqueline sat at her desk, unconsciously drumming the keyboard with her fingers as she read the last few paragraphs she'd written. She shook her head. It still wasn't flowing. For one frightening moment, she wondered if it would ever flow again.

She glanced at her cell as it rang, then went back to the monitor.

It would be Ingrid. She'd been calling nonstop for the last month. In the last few voice mails, she threatened to show up at her door if Jacqueline didn't "come back to the living," as she put it. But she wasn't in the mood. Wasn't in the mood to talk, wasn't in the mood for company, wasn't in the mood—for life.

So, she let it go to voice mail, like always. Perhaps that's why the knocking on her door didn't startle her. She let out a heavy sigh, silently cursing Ingrid for making the trip.

She opened the door, her admonishment of Ingrid dying on her lips as she stared face-to-face at Kay. She was aware that she'd stopped breathing.

"What are you . . . what are you doing here?"

Kay's blue eyes locked on her own, causing her heart to jump painfully in her chest.

"I'm in love with you. And I won't live another day without you."

Jacqueline steadied herself on the door, her eyes never leaving Kay's.

"What about . . . what about your family?"

Kay smiled gently. "Mama told me if I didn't come after you, she was going to come get you herself."

Jacqueline closed her eyes. "You told them?"

"Yes."

She opened them again, and Kay was there. "And you're in love with me?" she whispered.

"Totally."

Jacqueline took a step backward. "I think I may cry," she murmured, a hundred different emotions warring inside of her as she tried to grasp the fact that Kay was actually here, and that Kay was in love with her. *Oh my God.* She slowly rubbed her chest, feeling the heavy, constant ache of the last few months begin to subside.

"Jackie?" When their eyes met, Kay asked the one question that had been haunting her. "Are you . . . I mean, do you . . ."

"Oh God, Kay, I've loved you forever."

Kay finally let her relief show as her eyes gentled. "Good. And Jackie, just so we're clear here—don't you *ever* leave me again."

Jacqueline gave in to the tears, letting them flow freely, not caring that Kay saw her vulnerability. The only weakness she had was Kay.

"I *promise*. I will never leave," Jacqueline whispered.

It was Kay who closed the door, Kay who found the courage to move into Jackie's arms.

"I love you so much, Jackie," Kay breathed, her mouth moving against Jackie's. "Don't cry. I'm sorry it took me so long to get here."

Jacqueline couldn't speak. She simply held Kay to her, squeezing her tight, letting their bodies reacquaint. They had plenty of time for talking. Now, now all she wanted was to *absorb* Kay.

She took a deep breath, aware of her contented smile as Kay's lips moved gently across her face.

Oh, yeah. *Now* she was in the mood for life.

Publications from
BELLA BOOKS, INC.
The best in contemporary lesbian fiction

P.O. Box 10543, Tallahassee, FL 32302
Phone: 800-729-4992
www.bellabooks.com

THE KILLING ROOM by Gerri Hill. 392 pp. How can two women forget and go their separate ways?   1-59493-050-3 $12.95

PASSIONATE KISSES by Megan Carter. 240 pp. Will two old friends run from love?
1-59493-051-1 $12.95

ALWAYS AND FOREVER by Lyn Denison. 224 pp. The girl next door turns Shannon's world upside down.   1-59493-049-X $12.95

BACK TALK by Saxon Bennett. 200 pp. Can a talk show host find love after heartbreak?
1-59493-028-7 $12.95

THE PERFECT VALENTINE: EROTIC LESBIAN VALENTINE STORIES edited by Barbara Johnson and Therese Szymanski—from Bella After Dark. 328 pp. Stories from the hottest writers around.   1-59493-061-9 $14.95

MURDER AT RANDOM by Claire McNab. 200 pp. The Sixth Denise Cleever Thriller. Denise realizes the fate of thousands is in her hands.   1-59493-047-3 $12.95

THE TIDES OF PASSION by Diana Tremain Braund. 240 pp. Will Susan be able to hold it all together and find the one woman who touches her soul?   1-59493-048-1 $12.95

JUST LIKE THAT by Karin Kallmaker. 240 pp. Disliking each other—and everything they stand for—even before they meet, Toni and Syrah find feelings can change, just like that.
1-59493-025-2 $12.95

WHEN FIRST WE PRACTICE by Therese Szymanski. 200 pp. Brett and Allie are once again caught in the middle of murder and intrigue.   1-59493-045-7 $12.95

REUNION by Jane Frances. 240 pp. Cathy Braithwaite seems to have it all: good looks, money and a thriving accounting practice . . .   1-59493-046-5 $12.95

BELL, BOOK & DYKE: NEW EXPLOITS OF MAGICAL LESBIANS by Kallmaker, Watts, Johnson and Szymanski. 360 pp. Reluctant witches, tempting spells and skyclad beauties—delve into the mysteries of love, lust and power in this quartet of novellas.
1-59493-023-6 $14.95

ARTIST'S DREAM by Gerri Hill. 320 pp. When Cassie meets Luke Winston, she can no longer deny her attraction to women . . .   1-59493-042-2 $12.95

NO EVIDENCE by Nancy Sanra. 240 pp. Private Investigator Tally McGinnis once again returns to the horror-filled world of a serial killer.   1-59493-043-04 $12.95

WHEN LOVE FINDS A HOME by Megan Carter. 280 pp. What will it take for Anna and Rona to find their way back to each other again? 1-59493-041-4 $12.95

MEMORIES TO DIE FOR by Adrian Gold. 240 pp. Rachel attempts to avoid her attraction to the charms of Anna Sigurdson . . . 1-59493-038-4 $12.95

SILENT HEART by Claire McNab. 280 pp. Exotic lesbian romance.

1-59493-044-9 $12.95

MIDNIGHT RAIN by Peggy J. Herring. 240 pp. Bridget McBee is determined to find the woman who saved her life. 1-59493-021-X $12.95

THE MISSING PAGE A Brenda Strange Mystery by Patty G. Henderson. 240 pp. Brenda investigates her client's murder . . . 1-59493-004-X $12.95

WHISPERS ON THE WIND by Frankie J. Jones. 240 pp. Dixon thinks she and her best friend, Elizabeth Colter, would make the perfect couple . . . 1-59493-037-6 $12.95

CALL OF THE DARK: EROTIC LESBIAN TALES OF THE SUPERNATURAL edited by Therese Szymanski—from Bella After Dark. 320 pp. 1-59493-040-6 $14.95

A TIME TO CAST AWAY A Helen Black Mystery by Pat Welch. 240 pp. Helen stops by Alice's apartment—only to find the woman dead . . . 1-59493-036-8 $12.95

DESERT OF THE HEART by Jane Rule. 224 pp. The book that launched the most popular lesbian movie of all time is back. 1-1-59493-035-X $12.95

THE NEXT WORLD by Ursula Steck. 240 pp. Anna's friend Mido is threatened and eventually disappears . . . 1-59493-024-4 $12.95

CALL SHOTGUN by Jaime Clevenger. 240 pp. Kelly gets pulled back into the world of private investigation . . . 1-59493-016-3 $12.95

52 PICKUP by Bonnie J. Morris and E.B. Casey. 240 pp. 52 hot, romantic tales—one for every Saturday night of the year. 1-59493-026-0 $12.95

GOLD FEVER by Lyn Denison. 240 pp. Kate's first love, Ashley, returns to their home town, where Kate now lives . . . 1-1-59493-039-2 $12.95

RISKY INVESTMENT by Beth Moore. 240 pp. Lynn's best friend and roommate needs her to pretend Chris is his fiancé. But nothing is ever easy. 1-59493-019-8 $12.95

HUNTER'S WAY by Gerri Hill. 240 pp. Homicide detective Tori Hunter is forced to team up with the hot-tempered Samantha Kennedy. 1-59493-018-X $12.95

CAR POOL by Karin Kallmaker. 240 pp. Soft shoulders, merging traffic and slippery when wet . . . Anthea and Shay find love in the car pool. 1-59493-013-9 $12.95

NO SISTER OF MINE by Jeanne G'Fellers. 240 pp. Telepathic women fight to coexist with a patriarchal society that wishes their eradication. ISBN 1-59493-017-1 $12.95

ON THE WINGS OF LOVE by Megan Carter. 240 pp. Stacie's reporting career is on the rocks. She has to interview bestselling author Cheryl, or else! ISBN 1-59493-027-9 $12.95

WICKED GOOD TIME by Diana Tremain Braund. 224 pp. Does Christina need Miki as a protector . . . or want her as a lover? ISBN 1-59493-031-7 $12.95

THOSE WHO WAIT by Peggy J. Herring. 240 pp. Two brilliant sisters—in love with the same woman! ISBN 1-59493-032-5 $12.95

ABBY'S PASSION by Jackie Calhoun. 240 pp. Abby's bipolar sister helps turn her world upside down, so she must decide what's most important. ISBN 1-59493-014-7 $12.95